THE NEW SAM TILSON ESPIONAGE THRILLER

HEAVEN'S FIRST LAW

TOM QUILLER

BOOK 1 IN THE
COLD SECRETS
SERIES

THE PAST IS A DIFFERENT COUNTRY AND ITS AGENTS ARE HOSTILE

Copyright © 2024 by Tom Quiller
All rights reserved.

This is a work of fiction. The story, all names, characters, and incidents portrayed are fictitious. No identification with actual persons (living or deceased), places, buildings, and products is intended or should be inferred. Any such resemblance is purely coincidental.

No part of this publication may be reproduced, distributed, or transmitted in any form or by any means, including photocopying, recording, or other electronic or mechanical methods, without the prior written permission of the publisher, except in express incidences in which the use of brief quotations are used for a review of the publication.

Published by Dream Paladin Publishing

First Edition: August 2024

DREAM PALADIN
BOOKS

THE COLD SECERTS SERIES

Captain Sam Tilson Books
A MOCKERY OF HONOUR
(a short story prequel – free with the newsletter)
HEAVEN'S FIRST LAW
THE VILEST CONCEITS
ANGER OF THE WISE
NO GOOD BY STEALTH
ANCESTOR OF SORROW
(Coming November 2024)
IN SHADE OF MOONLIGHT
(Coming May 2025)

THE NORSE KRIMOLOGY STRAND

Detective Frida Skardet Books

BAPTISM OF ICE
(Coming March 2025)

"Order is Heaven's first law."

– Alexander Pope

For Clare. For Fin. For Emily.

Forever.

contents

PROLOGUE		1
1.	CHAPTER 1	7
2.	CHAPTER 2	19
3.	CHAPTER 3	29
4.	CHAPTER 4	41
5.	CHAPTER 5	51
6.	CHAPTER 6	63
7.	CHAPTER 7	75
8.	CHAPTER 8	83
9.	CHAPTER 9	91
10.	CHAPTER 10	101
11.	CHAPTER 11	109
12.	CHAPTER 12	119
13.	CHAPTER 13	129
14.	CHAPTER 14	137
15.	CHAPTER 15	145
16.	CHAPTER 16	153
17.	CHAPTER 17	165
18.	CHAPTER 18	173
19.	CHAPTER 19	183
20.	CHAPTER 20	193
21.	CHAPTER 21	203
22.	CHAPTER 22	213
23.	CHAPTER 23	221
24.	CHAPTER 24	229
25.	CHAPTER 25	237
26.	CHAPTER 26	247
27.	CHAPTER 27	257
28.	CHAPTER 28	267
29.	CHAPTER 29	275
30.	CHAPTER 30	283
EPILOGUE		289

PROLOGUE

Two men hung in mid-air. They reached the end of their repel and darkness enveloped them. Suspended from the end of their lines, they waited patiently for the next step in their mission.

Stuart Ritchie, a wiry Scot with flaming red hair, and Arun Bhatta, short, compact and the hairiest man this side of the Himalayas both originated from 40 Commando.

They were well-trained and experienced soldiers, and so far this training mission had not proved too testing. As they dangled from their ropes, the two men took a moment to assess their surroundings.

The only sounds were the slight rustling of their gear and the gentle summer breeze making the ropes sway. The sun had set several hours earlier, and they had timed their approach to the disused train viaduct so they would arrive at 3am.

Admittedly, hanging 100 feet off a bridge was not everyone's cup of tea and it was a precarious position to be in. But they were used to danger, it was what they were trained for.

The mixture of standard British Army gear, along with their own personal preferences coupled with the strong mental faculties and physical strength provided them with the necessary tools to deal with almost any situation.

After a few minutes, the order came through for them to proceed. With practiced ease, they released the locks on the carabiners on the ropes and began to make their way down towards the target. The darkness and silence were allies as they moved swiftly and silently towards their objective.

The rope was of kernmantel construction, with a multi-strand core protected by an abrasion-resistant woven sheath. The low-stretch rope reduced bouncing, which meant a lot when you're handling explosives. For that is what the men were now doing. Their goal was to simulate the destruction of enemy lines of communication, achieved by planting and detonating explosives on the bridge's superstructure.

A third man was squatting on the railway line that ran across the viaduct, defending the others from any attack that might come from above. Corporal Ben "Ernie" Wise, of 42 Commando. Sandy hair, a sunny disposition, and a sarcastic wit.

Like the rest of his team, he was armed with the newly-arrived The Knight's Stoner KS-1 assault rifle, designated in the UK as the L403A1 equipped with advanced optical and thermal sights as well as muzzle suppressors. Usually, they'd have been wielding the Heckler & Koch 53A3s, but this was the headline addition to the Royal Marines Commando lead strike teams' arsenal.

They were all also sporting new helmets from the same manufacturer as the rifle: US arms company, Gentex. These were themselves endowed with the new, fused Binocular Night Vision Device produced by L3Harris.

Despite their origins in separate Commando Units, all of them were members of the Special Boat Service – the UK's SBS elite soldiers drawn almost uniquely from the Royal Marines Commandos. For that reason, they had been given the job of field-testing the new kit ahead of its wider rollout the following year.

Wise was crouched at the top of the middle line slowly rotating his body through 180 degrees using the light-weight image-intensifying passive night vision goggles to pierce the darkness.

The fourth man in the squad was Captain Sam Tilson, also of 42 Commando. Tall and dark with a face that was way too young for his 29 years of age, blue eyes hidden behind his own L3 Harris goggles. He was the squad's commanding officer. It was his job to make sure the mission was carried out successfully and his men returned to the pickup zone safely and with all their limbs intact. Or as near as damn it

He secured his line, nodded to Wise and repelled off the side of the bridge to join his men 100 feet below him. He was about to find out that no amount of cutting-edge kit can save you when life decides to throw you not so much as a curve ball, but more of a live grenade.

"Explosives," he said into his throat mike, his voice sounding hoarse.

This one word set all three of them opening the pouches on their uniforms to find the small packages of PE-4 explosives they contained. This was a British plastic explosive, similar to C-4 and also based on RDX but with a plasticizer different from that used in its better-known stablemate.

Old Meldon Quarry, located in Devon, was the setting for these events. Nowadays, it welcomes a multitude of visitors - some hiking or biking, others for a refreshing swim in nearby Meldon Pool. A select few adrenalin junkies come for daring adventures like bungee jumping. And, of course, there are the trainspotters who come to explore the remnants of the abandoned railway.

The landscape today is typically serene, although it holds traces of its industrial past. Not so long ago - back in the 1970s - this place would have been bustling with the extraction of the local limestone. But these days it is closed. However, it remains one of those places that – to those excited by the great outdoors – always elicits enthusiasm.

It is also a favourite of the British Military due to the proximity of the 50 square mile area of Dartmoor, known as the Dartmoor Training Area. This has a rich history of military use by the Armed Forces of the United Kingdom. The Royal Navy, the Royal Marines, the British Army, and the Royal Air Force all utilize the ranges for training exercises. The area is supported by two training camps, one at Okehampton and the other at Willsworthy, with the former being used as a base for that day's Special Boat Service exercise.

While the special forces unit drawn from the British Army – the Special Air Service, or SAS – is far better known, the SBS remains less popularised. It is a unit within the Royal Navy that specializes in maritime counter-terrorism and special reconnaissance operations. Their members are trained to operate in all environments, including deserts, mountains, and urban areas.

This particular exercise was taking place in the Dartmoor Training Area to simulate real-life scenarios on challenging terrain. The quarry, now overgrown with grass and gorse bushes, adds an extra level of difficulty to the training.

The SBS team had navigated their way cross country and through the old tunnel to access the high viaduct and reach their objective unseen.

All was going well, and the squad had reached its goal earlier than expected. They had caught an "enemy" platoon of Grenadier Guardsmen by surprise in their patrol base on the other side of the hill through which the tunnel ran. To the "Swimmer Canoeists" – as the SBS were colloquially known – this was par for the course.

The four-man troop would have time to plant the explosives on the frame of the viaduct and leave before the rest of the "enemy" forces even knew they were there.

For some reason Tilson had been feeling angry all day. Every now and then as he and his men approached the target, his breathing had been uneven and once or twice he'd snapped at them unnecessarily. He'd thought he was just "hangry".

Certainly, after the assault on the Grenadiers, he had needed to rest and neck some scran. But his headache and the feeling of lead in his limbs persisted and he'd had to hand over leading the troop to "Ernie" Wise.

Tilson put his performance down to his being slightly rusty. He'd taken extended compassionate leave recently for the death of his father and his physical training had slipped a little during the hiatus.

As he hung there, he felt his heart beating far faster than it should have been. Tilson wondered if it was just the thrill of the mission but as he attached the plastic explosives to the metal framework of the bridge, he realised he was also feeling very heavy headed again. As if he had been drinking red wine on a four-day bender and was now waking to the results. Indeed, his mouth felt so dry, he couldn't even summon any saliva.

This was most definitely not normal. Momentarily dismissing this, the officer reached into another one of the pouches at his waist for a detonator. As he withdrew it, he fumbled, and the detonator fell from his grasp. Only a lightning quick response with his other hand prevented it falling into darkness. Tilson shook his head. What the hell was going on?

He quickly placed the detonator into the PE-4 explosive and prepared to abseil the remaining 200 feet to the ground below. As he released the mechanism on his harness that would allow him to descend, his hands shook and suddenly, he felt as if he could not keep his eyes open. Everything ached and he was sweating, too. He could feel the dampness in his Norwegian army shirt and beading at his temples.

With his heartbeat racing 60 to the dozen and his head pounding, his hands loosened on the rope, and he slipped. Slowly at first and then with increasingly alarming speed, he plummeted down through the air and the rush of wind to his face gave him a moment of clarity.

He realised he had been feeling odd since they deployed from the Merlin helicopter the day before. Special Forces soldiers were trained to ignore such things but perhaps Tilson had made an error of judgement. As this second of clear headedness passed, a thin smile crossed his lips, and his last thought was that this was the perfect example of 20/20 hindsight.

The other guys in his troop heard his body hit the ground and there followed a disconcerting silence. There was an unspoken anxiety that the worst had happened; that for Captain Sam Tilson this was his last mission for the SBS or indeed any other military unit.

CHAPTER 1

To the uninitiated, the grey-white building on the north bank of the Thames looks much like any of the other governmental edifices. This grand – if somewhat nondescript – block houses the UK's Defence Security Services, otherwise known as MI5. It appears large and imposing because it is meant to. The structure, however, is very far removed from the Babylonian architecture of its foreign counterparts at the Secret Intelligence Service – or MI6 – that resides a mile upstream on the opposite bank of the river.

The main entrance to MI5 is found on Millbank opposite some trees that in summer give off an air of boulevard or avenue but that today seemed stark in their bareness. Most employees enter the secret world of Thames House via the three doors with their airport style security and watchful private contract staff. To the side there is even an entrance for visitors which is very similar to those found in any police station up and down the land.

There are also several other entrances dotted about the ground floor of Thames House, the main secondary one being round the back on the junction of Thorney Street and Page Street. This is primarily used for vehicles and is a bit more discrete. That said, it does have security staff in navy pullovers and high-viz jackets outside its yellow grilled gates along with a row of red-tipped security bollards that can be raised or lowered at their discretion.

As he approached the building walking down Page Street, Sam Tilson ignored the men who eyed him with a flirting suspicion. Instead, he turned right and walked towards the 60s monolith of Millbank Tower. He was the only person on the street and as he paused to inspect the instructions he had been sent, one of the security guards folded his arms and openly stared at him.

Tilson nodded at the guard and continued walking, the chill wind funnelled down the narrow street straight into his face. Almost at the turning point where Thorney Street bends round to the river he found another door. Smaller. Looking like it was unused. Nevertheless, this was the entrance he'd been told to report to.

Darkened brown glass – the same colour as old bottles of ale that used to line the shelves of the pub where he grew up – cast his reflection in more drab tones. It made his sun-browned skin seem almost chocolate and his crisp blue suit the colour of fresh cowpat. Tilson smiled. His former Commanding Officer, Colonel Ben Faulkner, had a peculiar verbal tick that meant he didn't appear able to say the word "shit". Other expletives were fine, however.

As he stood before the ale bottle door, Tilson was transported back to Faulkner's office at Hamworthy Barracks, Poole shortly after his stint in hospital. Outside the plain square window, a wind was buffeting the familiar line of chestnut trees, sending leaves tumbling and spiralling to the ground. Tilson didn't like to think about this too much; too painful.

"Well, this is a fucking cowpat of a mess, Sam," Faulkner said. Tilson was standing to attention in front of the senior officer's desk.

"Yes, Sir."

"How do you get Type 1 diabetes anyway?" Faulkner looked up from the paperwork he'd been shuffling.

"Not sure, Sir," Tilson grimaced. He genuinely had no idea. "Usually, it's a childhood diagnosis. But it can, rarely, occur during adulthood."

"So, you're a bloody rarity now!" Faulkner was attempting an understanding smile.

"You could say that, Sir."

"But you know what this means? Medical discharge. No 'ifs' or 'buts'."

"Seems so, Colonel."

Faulkner stood up now, coming round the desk in an effort to sympathise with Tilson's plight.

"At ease, Sam," he said, placing his hand on the younger man's shoulder. "Take a seat."

Faulkner indicated two upholstered red armchairs that looked very out of place in the almost portacabin style office. They weren't the most luxurious or antique of armchairs, but they certainly beat the orange plastic one that was positioned right in front of the desk.

Tilson lowered himself into the chair – his left leg still a little stiff from the fracture he'd suffered on impact with the Devon turf – and waited. Faulkner circled the other one, paused, and then finally sat opposite him. He took a deep breath and leant forward; hands clasped into a steeple pointing directly at Tilson.

"Got a proposition for you."

Tilson raised an eyebrow. Anything right now would be a godsend. As far as he was concerned, he had mere weeks remaining in the Royal

Marines Commandos and then he'd be out on his ear. No matter how honourable that discharge was he would no longer be a "Royal", no longer be a serving member of His Majesty's armed forces.

He'd be a civvy. He knew it was stupid, but the superiority he felt to anyone outside the military had been drilled into him since his very first days at Lympstone. Before, even. It was something he knew he'd had to deal with, but was Faulkner dangling a lifeline?

"I'm all ears."

"Good, good," Faulkner sat back now, smiling. He seemed pleased with himself. "I've been speaking to the people at Box 500 about you..."

Box 500 was one of the many nicknames for MI5, Britain's internal security service. Tilson smiled at this.

"I see you approve," Faulkner continued. "And they think they can give you a spot in Thames House."

"That'd be amazing, Sir. Thank y-"

Faulkner held up a hand to silence him. "Don't thank me yet, Sam. I've no idea what they'll have you doing. Could be counting paperclips, for all I know, some cowpat like that. Although they'd be foolish not to make use of your special skills."

Tilson found this memory– only a matter of months earlier – amusing and moved towards the brown door with a grin.

As he did, it opened. At first, he wondered if it was automatic but a small, man with a short Afro and a dark blue security guard uniform appeared from behind the door. Tilson could see he was holding one of the metal handles.

"Morning," the guard said.

"Hello," Tilson ventured, and he stepped inside.

"My name's Aston," the guard said, closing the door. He had a nice, soft West Indian accent. "I'm the day door at entrance four."

Tilson was uncertain if this information required a response so just nodded.

Aston walked over to a high wooden desk and climbed onto his seat, his legs slightly dangling from above the stone floor. He licked a finger and flicked a page in what looked like an old ledger of some sort.

"Captain Tilson, is it now?"

Tilson nodded again, smiling. "'Sam', please."

"OK, Sam. Ya up on the fourth floor. No lift 'ere." He looked up now and smiled broadly as if he took pleasure in this.

"Stairs will do fine," Tilson replied. He pointed at an obvious stairwell off to the right behind Aston. "That way?"

"It is, Capp'n, but breathe easy. You'll have to wait for yuh escort. First day 'n' all."

Tilson bobbed his head. Made sense. "Have you been here long?" he asked.

Aston regarded him carefully. "Long enough, Capp'n."

"Sam," Tilson said again.

"I *could* tell you," Aston said, leaning over the desk conspiratorially. He then looked left and right before gazing straight at Tilson's face. "But then I'd have to kill you!"

He roared with laughter at this and rocked in his chair. The laugh receded into a chuckle and finally a cough. "Aston, leave di man alone, yuh a hear wah mi a seh?"

Tilson turned to see a young woman wearing a powder blue jumper and dark trousers. Her naturally curly hair was straightened and pulled back in a loose bun.

"Just a likkle joke mi a mek, yuh know?" Aston grinned at the new arrival.

The young woman tutted at the security guard in mock annoyance and turned to Tilson holding out her hand.

"Ebony Fadipe."

"Sam Tilson," he replied, accepting the handshake. It was firm and dry, her hand elegant and well-manicured.

"Let's go up, yeah?" Ebony indicated the stairs.

"Thanks, Aston," Sam said as he passed the guard.

Aston smiled and performed a mock salute. "Good luck, Capp'n!"

Ebony led the way and started to climb the stairs.

"I want to see how fit you really are, Mister Marine."

"Royal," Tilson said.

Ebony paused in her climb and turned, an amused frown toying with her eyebrows. "You what?" "Royal. Marine. We're quite proud of that bit."

"Gotcha," she said. "*Royal*." The stressed word was accompanied by a perfunctory smile, Then Ebony Fadipe turned back and continued up the stairs, Tilson now trailing in her wake like an admonished Labrador.

***

Elsewhere in the building – the posher end of things altogether – a meeting was underway in one of the Faraday cage meeting rooms. A number of these existed at MI5 for discussions that in no way could be recorded, intercepted, or eavesdropped upon. Failing to make the most of the large table and its 20 chairs, two men sat at one end, away from the door.

One was wearing a blue, pin-stripe suit belying his old-school approach to things. That, and his slightly oiled and thinning salt and pepper hair, told everyone that he was both important and senior.

The two were not necessarily exclusive but in the case of Douglas Marchbanks, they were inextricably entwined.

For Marchbanks was the Assistant Director of Operations – styled AD/OS – in the Secret Intelligence Service, MI6. He was the very powerful iron fist behind the velvet-cushioned throne. What he didn't know wasn't worth knowing, and what he did could topple governments.

Dubbed the butcher of Vauxhall Cross, Marchbanks suffered no fools and indeed gained his nickname by "redistributing" anyone who didn't measure up to his exacting expectations. If you messed about with the butcher, you ended up cut.

While his demeanour was that of a stockbroker from the days of brick-like mobile phones and Black Monday crashes, his character was anything but. He sat, very straight, large hands clasped before him on the boardroom table. He was eyeing the man opposite him with a mix of dispassionate fascination.

For the man across the table from him was his opposite number – or thereabouts – in MI5, Anthony Gray. He was, in fact, the Deputy Director of D Branch and had a far more relaxed air about him; charcoal suit and dark desert boots. Marchbanks would have quietly sneered at them if he saw someone in the street wearing this get up. But they were not on the street and Gray was equal to the butcher in his sanguine efficiency.

For his part, Gray was also far more louche in his posture, almost slouching. He genuinely did not give a fuck about the old school cloaks or Russell Group University daggers that Marchbanks – and to a greater degree, the whole of MI6 – represented. He was a product of the State School System and Marchbanks was a Harrovian.

But while their backgrounds differed widely, they both shared a passionate vision of, and for, their country. They weren't exactly friends; they were more like two different weapons systems aimed at the same target. More sword and pistol than chalk and cheese.

"So," Marchbanks said.

"Malcolm Fox," Gray replied.

Marchbanks nodded. "It's... thorny."

"That's a fucking understatement!" the MI6 man flinched at Gray's cavalier swearing. "Sorry, Douglas. But it is."

"You said you had a solution."

"I said I had a 'plan'. Solution? Mmm. Let's hope so, eh?" Gray opened a briefcase at his feet and took out a very thin personnel file. "I prayed and god was very good indeed and dropped this in my lap."

He slid the file across the table and Marchbanks reached out a hand to run his sausage fingers down the spine of the manilla cover.

"Bit meagre, Tony?"

"Yeah. And that's the beauty. Take a look." His eyes flashed with pride momentarily.

Marchbanks opened the file and quickly read its contents.

"Special forces. I'm impressed. Don't get many of them this side of the river." He smiled like a snake.

"And just arrived off the boat," Gray leant forward and tapped the top of the file. "See the date? First day today."

"Serendipity indeed." Marchbanks moistened his lips with a deliberate tongue. "And this 'plan' of yours?"

"Simple. We send him. *I* send him. He retrieves the wallflowers and returns."

"And he'll fly under the radar very nicely."

"He won't need to," Gray said enthusiastically. "He'll be fucking invisible! No one knows he's here. I stuck him in the shittiest of shitholes."

"Shithole?"

"ICE."

"Oh. Oh, poor him."

"Yeah, well, give him a day or two to die of fucking boredom. Then poof! I appear like his fairy godmother and give him a special secret mission. Special forces can't resist that shit. He'll cream himself."

There was a moment's silence while Marchbanks took in the tirade of swearing.

"Delightfully put." Then he stood. "Well, that's that then."

"Need a taxi, Douglas?"

"It's a lovely morning. I'll walk." Marchbanks headed for the inner door of the meeting room. Then he stopped and turned slowly. "His name was redacted on the file. I'd prefer if I knew who it was. Cross the 'i' and dot the 't', you know."

He scrunched up his nose as if he was apologetic for the demand and they both smiled humourlessly at the weak joke.

"For your ears only then, Douglas. His name is Tilson. Sam Tilson."

***

"Well! Welcome, Sam."

Ebony had ushered Tilson through a large office containing six desks, three other people and a mountain of paper files. In the far lefthand corner a door was propped open with a multicoloured stuffed cat. And through that was another desk, also with piles of paper on it.

The woman behind the desk was almost as wide as she was tall. Not overweight, just square in shape. She had a blunt bob of greying mouse-brown hair, a stub of a nose and possibly the most piercing eyes

Tilson had ever come across. She stood up as she saw him, and Ebony introduced Anne Barnard.

"This is your new home," Anne said, and she shook his hand. A perfunctory action that was over before he'd registered it happening. "We're naturally very excited to have a Royal Marines Commando join us."

Tilson cast an askance look at Ebony when Anne used the word 'Royal', and she returned his side-eye with a slight smirk.

Playful or sarcastic, he couldn't decide. Maybe both.

Anne was already bustling through the door. Tilson got the impression she bustled everywhere.

"This way, Sam. That's it!"

She was standing in the middle of the room now, all eyes trained on her. She raised a hand and wafted it in the direction of a sandy-haired man in his 40s with a long face and nose.

"Gareth Hazel – the only boy in the village," she said. "Until your arrival, of course."

Hazel nodded. "Hello."

"He's our maths whizz. And part of the furniture. No offence, Gary, dear."

Hazel shook his head with eyebrows raised. "No, no..."

Anne turned to Ebony. "Then there's Ebony who you've met. She joined us not that long ago from GCHQ. So, you're kind of the fresh meat."

"What the hell does that make me?"

At the end of the office, her desk behind the door was a third woman. She'd kicked the door shut so she could now be seen. She was almost impossible to age. Forty, fifty? Platinum blonde with large blue eyes, huge eyelashes, and a beauty spot under her right eye. She was smiling broadly – cheekily – at Tilson in a way that women of a certain age tended to.

It makes you indispensable," Anne said, grinning. "Camille DeSouza, our service mobile. That means she's worked in every department and knows everything and everyone in the building. One of the best documents people in the Service."

Tilson moved forward to take her hand and found himself returning her inane grin; it was extremely infectious, and he knew instinctively they were going to be friends.

"So, that's us. The very small – but perfectly formed – Inconclusive Covert Enquiries unit."

"ICE," Ebony said gliding forward and taking a seat at one of the desks. She bobbed her head at the desk opposite hers. "That's you."

"Yeah," Camille said. "ICE. You can guess what we get called. Or did until we got a bloke in here."

Anne gave a single snort of laughter. "The Ice Maidens!"

"I was thinking of the frigid three," Camille frowned. "Ice Maidens is way too polite. When was that, Anne? The Sixties?" They both laughed.

"Hadn't we better tell him what we do?" This from Hazel. Timidly, quietly.

"Of course!" Anne turned back to Tilson. "We check over old missions and operations. We look for things that may have been missed either by mistake or on purpose. We see if there isn't connective tissue that may link to the modern day or suggest why other things went wrong. What was bad luck and what was bad spy craft. Or even treason."

She let that sink in for a second and then continued. "Of course, more often than not, it isn't as serious as that. Just human error. But we look under every rock, revisit every dead letter drop, review every file." She lifted her arms in an expansive gesture to indicate all the paperwork lying about.

"Some might think it slow or unnecessary or even boring. In the same way people think Shakespeare is too complex or inaccessible and everything needs to be dumbed down."

Tilson had a nasty suspicion she was talking about him. He'd never been a Shakespeare fan. He hadn't seen a play since his primary school nativity and what little he knew about The Bard was used as clichéd quotes on inspirational t-shirts or mugs. He smiled weakly.

"Like observation posts," he heard himself saying. "They're seen as boring by people who maybe aren't as strategic as a soldier."

Shit. It had sounded like a dig, and he'd been trying for rapport.

"Of course," Anne said. It seemed to Tilson she used this phrase a lot. It was a verbal tic. Perhaps it gave her time to think.

"It's important work, Captain Tilson," Anne said stiffly. Then she bustled back to her office. "Ebony will look after you," she said over her shoulder.

Tilson looked across his new desk at Ebony. She cocked her head at him as if he were a naughty puppy. Then she leaned forward and whispered: "Real smooth. Never got round to those diplomacy studies, eh Royal!"

CHAPTER 2

Tilson spent that first morning doing mostly dull admin things – pass, computer log in, staff handbook and then some computer training. By the time lunchtime swung around, Ebony was showing him some of the electronic file work she was doing on MI5's bespoke computer interface and operating system known as NEXUS. Tilson was sure this would have been just as boring, but Ebony made it far more diverting than he'd imagined it would be.

She was going through all the files, starting with the latest ones. These were the closed files, the "complete" ones that had been added to the charmingly named "discretionary archive unit" database. Ebony explained that a physical DAU facility existed under some mountain in Wales: a repository of the more sensitive paper files from the days before word processing, local area networks and floppy discs.

The more modern, electronic files had to be keyworded so that they could be searched with greater ease. Any name, place, date, reference to other files and a long list of other criteria all had to be added to the records ALT text. It seemed to Tilson that this was extremely laborious and lugubrious work. But Ebony had a passion for it. Apparently, her efforts were already yielding results.

"See," she said, pointing at her computer screen. Two files were displayed on a search results page. "That name? 'Michael De Havilland'?"

Tilson nodded, leaning forward on the office stool he was perched on.

"That name appears in relation to an assassination attempt made on Edward the Eighth."

"The one that abdicated?" Tilson clarified. "That's him." She shot him an encouraging smile. "Well, he also cropped up in a file that was closed the other week."

"And that's down to you?"

"Yep!" Ebony shut the data window and turned her chair to face Tilson. "Listen, we don't usually head for the pub on a Monday, but I thought we could make an exception, seeing as it's ya first day."

She smiled that infectious smile.

"Sure," Tilson said.

"Introductory pint?" She faltered. "Or are you a hard spirits man?"

"I can be, but let's not rush things," he joked archly.

They stared at each other for a moment, and Tilson noticed Hazel watching him from between a crack in two piles of paperwork.

"Anyone else coming," Tilson said loudly. "Gareth?"

Hazel realised he'd been spotted but lacked any guile in disguising this fact, especially for a spook. His cheeks flushed a light shade of beetroot, and he mumbled about just having a quick one.

"Boozer on a Monday?" Camille asked, then snorted as if her reply was a foregone conclusion – which it probably was. "Try and keep me away!"

"What about Anne?"

"Nah," Ebony lowered her voice. "Think she's teetotal."

"She seemed quite dry." Tilson smirked.

Ebony shook her head. "Great. *Royal* dad jokes. S'all I need. Dinner?"

For a moment, Tilson thought she was asking him out on a date but then realised she was talking about lunch. He nodded.

"I've just gotta shoot up!"

Ebony frowned. Tilson smiled at her distaste.

"Insulin," he reassured her. "I'm diabetic."

The statement still felt alien to hear himself say. To him it might as well have been *I'm disabled*. It was something he was sure he'd never get used to. But he was trying to take it all in his stride, despite the fact the diagnosis scared him far more than any tour of Afghanistan.

It was genuinely life changing. And he was trying to be a good boy; he wasn't eating chocolate or taking sugar in his coffee. He was pricking his finger before and after every meal and adding the blood sugar levels to an app he kept on his phone.

After lunch in the stark surroundings of the basement café, Tilson returned to his new desk and watched as the time clunked by on an old analogue clock on the far wall. He'd been given access to a host of files on which Ebony had already worked her magic. He was supposed to be cross referencing them for any links. Trouble was, these were all contemporaneous, and the likelihood of a match was slim.

As Tilson ploughed through them, a brace of dawning realisations crept up on him. One, that this exercise was indeed just that: an exercise – designed with the sole purpose of keeping him busy. And two. Two was the killer. What the fuck was he going to do here? There was paper pushing. A lot of it. And digital versions of the same. But not a lot of action. Why had they stuck him there? It wasn't exactly the double-O section.

Standing at the bar of The Marquis of Granby pub several hours later, Tilson put this question to Ebony while the other two were still sitting at their corner table.

"Ya wanna leave us already?" Ebony seemed genuinely pissed off.

"No. It's not that," Tilson cursed his lack of ability with words. "I just... wonder if there's an active service element to this unit?"

Ebony laughed and Camille looked up from her Aperol Spritz. "An 'active service element'? Fuck me, Royal!" She picked up her white wine spritzer and headed back to the table. Tilson plucked his pint of Doom Bar pale ale from the bar and headed after her.

As he arrived, Ebony was finishing her first sip.

"Jack Reacher here doesn't think we're worth his time," she said, staring coldly at him from behind her wine glass. There was an awkward silence.

"Oh," Gareth managed, before looking down at his own pint, as if the meaning of life were to be found in its amber depths.

"Whadya mean?" Camille asked. She was looking at Ebony for an explanation not Tilson, which was a good sign.

"He wants to go out all gung-ho, guns blazing apparently. Asking about active service duties." Camille regarded Tilson with disappointment. "Not here, sweetheart. None of us are exactly field operatives."

Tilson nodded. "Look, I didn't mean any disrespect. I can see the work you do is –"

"We do," Ebony corrected him. "The work *we* do. We're supposed to be a team. Even if ya new." "Anne has final say so, but what we find is passed onto other agents in the National Security Advice Centre," Camille explained.

"Maybe," Gareth looked up with a smile of unconvincing encouragement. "Maybe that's why you're here, Sam?"

Everyone turned to stare at him.

"Maybe Anne wants to keep things in-house, as it were. Maybe Sam is a field operative for us, for our investigations."

"Good point, Gary!" Camille said enthusiastically. "Maybe he is just that."

"And maybe he isn't," Ebony added quietly. Then without a glance in Tilson's direction, she downed her drink, stood up and walked from the pub, leaving the door open.

Tilson's first works outing didn't last much longer after that and when he left, he headed straight for the Tube ignoring his hunger pangs.

***

It was about half an hour by Tube from Pimlico Station back to Tilson's minuscule studio flat in Stratford, but it was good thinking time. On the train he mentally listed off his successes from day one: he'd managed to piss off his boss, alienate his colleagues, annoy the only one he liked – Ebony - and even become a joke to the bloody doorman. He did grin at this, but then sighed loudly enough for a middle-aged woman sitting further down the carriage to turn and glance at him.

Not exactly a litany of success.

He was just concluding that Inconclusive Covert Enquiries may not be for him after all when the train pulled into Mile End. The doors hissed open and a group of white teenagers in hoodies came rampaging onto the train. Two of the youths swung in opposite directions around a red plastic pole, like some weird performance at a strip club, while the other three engaged in some form of leapfrog game on the seats.

The woman who Tilson had disturbed earlier looked over her shoulder again, but her expression was much more worried than before. And, of course, looking in the first place was a mistake. These hyenas immediately picked up on what they thought might be prey.

"Easy, fam," the tallest teenager said. He had a slate grey hoodie with some pirate-like design on the back. "We're not meaning no harm, yeah?"

He swaggered up and sat down in front of the woman, leering and grinning.

"Specially to a milf like you, innit?" his red-clad comrade said and bumped fists with the third in their motley crew, the broadest – fattest – of the five. They all took up position in seats opposite their victim.

For her part the woman held the leader's gaze.

"Think she likes you, bro!" said the fat one. "Pretty soon you two be lipsing!" The hyena brayed at this.

"Yeah. Bare jokes!" the leader replied before standing up and sitting back down, right next to the woman.

Now she smiled, trying to appease him. "I'm, married." She held up her wedding finger. "see?"

"Cuz! She flippin' you the bird, fam! Nah. What is this joke?" the one in red said. "Reckon she got beef wid you!"

Whether he was being funny or whether he really believed the finger the woman had shown them was her middle one, wasn't clear. What was clear was that this was escalating.

The Tube train's engine pitch changed as it started to pull into the next station. This was where Tilson was getting off and he fully intended it to be where the gang of hyenas was getting off too.

Tilson stood and steadied his legs against the swaying of the carriage and made his way towards the door. He could feel the youths all watching him now. He didn't look at them, but instead smiled at the woman and raised his eyebrows.

"Vicky? Is that *you*?" he moved away from the door and towards the woman. She looked at him with confusion.

"I…"

God! How long has it been?" Tilson was now standing above the woman. "Is this your son?"

He nodded towards the leader of the gang. The woman was even more confused now, but the leader was outraged by this.

"She ain't my mum, fuckin' twat." He pulled down the waistband on his trousers to show the handle of what Tilson guessed was a large kitchen cleaver. "Why don't you run, boy!"

Tilson held his hands up as the others crowded around him in a mock gesture of surrender. "Sorry, lads. No offence meant!"

The Tube started to judder to a halt. He was running out of time. Tilson held his hand out to the woman. "This still your stop, Vicky?" His eyes silently implored her to go along with the charade and it seemed that she finally twigged.

"Oh, yes. Thanks. Er…"

"Mark. I'm a friend of your husband." The woman was now on her feet, her hand clasping tightly at Tilson's. He propelled her away from the youths, gently towards the doors. "We met at… was it the Christmas –"

"Let *that* go." The leader had drawn the cleaver and was waving it at the woman and then at Tilson. "Or I'll wet ya."

The doors hissed open and Tilson turned to smile at the leader. He stood his ground, putting one arm up to bar anyone from leaving the carriage and guided the woman off the train.

The gang just stared at him. They must have thought he was crazy, but they also could see that he had just taken on a whole different demeanour. Tilson stood tall now whereas before he'd been almost stooping. His voice now took on a harsh, humourless tone.

"You know, to me, a 'wet' is a drink, a beverage," he said. "But I'm guessing you don't mean you're putting the kettle on."

The door closed behind Tilson, and he removed his arm from the rail, standing loosely. The teenagers all stood still not really knowing what to do. He could see the woman running up the platform outside, her arms flailing at a member of London Transport staff standing by the address system.

"Which is ironic because you're about to be in very hot water."

"Slice him, Micky!" this from the red-clad gang member. He was trying to egg his leader on.

"Mate. Micky couldn't fucking slice bread."

In a lightning move, Tilson darted forward and slapped the cleaver from Micky's hand.

He could feel the adrenalin pumping, but noticed the train was not moving.

Micky jumped back but red produced a smaller knife from his pocket – some kind of lock knife – and tried to attack from the side. Tilson side-stepped this and using red's momentum slammed him into the doors.

Tilson turned back to the group as the teenager dropped the knife and grabbed at his head, whining in pain.

"Anyone else?" Tilson eyed the remaining trio evenly. They simply stared back, like disturbed deer on the meadow before fleeing.

The train doors opened with a hydraulic whisper, and they did flee, leaving their two friends to whatever fate awaited them. No honour among idiots, Tilson thought, his heart still racing.

Micky-the-leader was rising from his seat and looking at Tilson as if he had grown another head. Tilson went to move forward and stumbled as if drunk. Shit. He knew what this was. His breath came quickly now, raggedly drawing air from the carriage like a museum piece vacuum cleaner.

Micky had retrieved his cleaver and was approaching Tilson uncertain at first but then gaining in confidence as he saw his quarry falter.

"You're a joke, fam. Acting all hard 'n' that. I'm on a Big Man Ting, innit?" he raised the weapon but then he flicked his gaze over Tilson's shoulder.

"Leave him alone!" It was deep, male voice.

"Alright, you little shit, we've called the British Transport Police." The woman and the London Underground staff member had boarded the train at the doors through which Tilson had pushed her moments before.

Micky didn't seem to like the odds anymore. "You a wasteman!" He spat on the floor of the carriage right in front of Tilson and then followed his friends onto the platform and away.

"You Ok?" the woman was squatting down looking with concern at Tilson's white face.

Tilson nodded. "Will be... Have you got any chocolate?"

The woman opened her handbag and began trawling through its copious contents for something. As she did this, Tilson dragged himself up and sat in one of the trains seats. She handed him a crumpled Twix and he gratefully ripped into the wrapper, breathing hard as he stuffed the chocolate bar into his mouth.

"Make sure he doesn't get away," he said with his mouth full, pointing a shaky hand at the youth in red.

"Don't worry about that," said the uniformed man. "I got 'im!"

"Thank you," the woman said. "You might have saved my life there."

"No…" Tilson gave an ironic smile as he swallowed the last bite of Twix; it would take a few minutes for the sugar to take effect, but he'd be fine. "Thank *you*! You *definitely* saved mine!"

CHAPTER 3

The next day, Tilson arrived at Thames House early with a cardboard box of pastries bought at a high-end patisserie on the road simply called Victoria. He knew he'd messed up. He felt guilty and he wanted to at least try to make amends. He greeted Aston with a cheery wave. At least he didn't seem pissed off with the newest agent in MI5.

The security guard doffed his cap in a mock salute and once more referred to Tilson as "cap'n" before letting him make the ascent to the ICE office. Halfway up. Tilson realised he hadn't offered the man a cake and ran back down, taking the stairs two at a time.

He was just proffering the open white box to Aston when Ebony arrived.

"What's this then?" she asked. "Bribery?"

Tilson smiled at her but although she smiled back, when she whispered in his ear her words were as laced with vitriol as the pastries were with sugar. "It'll take more than a chocolate eclair, Royal."

She did take one, though, and popped it in her mouth as she headed to the staircase.

Aston chuckled. "She's a wild one, for sure. But 'er bark is worse than 'er bite!"

Tilson nodded. Sage words. He hoped they proved correct. At least the box was lighter as he climbed the steps behind Ebony. She studiously avoided eye contact with him – even when they turned the corners at each landing. He slowed his ascent to let her get well ahead of him. He didn't want any awkward moments of her holding the door open or forcing a confrontation before she was ready.

He managed to enter the office about 30 seconds after Ebony only to find the gang was all there already. Gareth Hazel looked like he'd slept there. He certainly seemed to be wearing the same crumpled, beige clothes he had been wearing the day before. Camille was sipping at a small cup of Starbucks coffee. She was immaculately turned out. Cream blouse and a fuchsia skirt, her makeup and hair perfect. She looked up and attempted a tight-lipped smile.

"He's brought cake," Ebony said, sitting at her desk.

Camille was on her feet. "Ooh. Nice." Her smile was considerably broader now. She came over and took the box from Tilson. He gave it up willingly and was about to sit down when Anne came out of her office.

"Don't make yourself comfortable, Sam," she said and then noticed the cakes. She moved over to the box that was now on Camille's desk and peered at them over her reading glasses. Tilson froze. Was he being fired? Had Ebony dobbed him in? Or Camille for that matter?

"The AD wants to see you," Anne said selecting a millefeuille and placing it on a piece of A4 she was holding.

Ebony whistled in mock admiration. "Assistant Director on your second day, eh? Impressive!"

Camille was still finishing her mouthful of custard tart. "Don't be mean, Ebs. He's trying."

Anne frowned. Whether the grimace was because of what Camille had said or the fact that when she said it, she'd managed to pebble dash her keyboard with yellow crumbs, wasn't clear.

"He says he might have some use for your unique talents, Sam."

"Oooh, did you wish *very* hard?" Ebony quipped.

***

As he had no idea where the Assistant Director's office was, Anne had taken him by the elbow and guided him through the building.

"I see you've made a friend when it comes to Ms Fadipe."

Before Tilson could answer she held up a hand. "I don't want to know. Just... be professional. I'll have a word with her to ensure she does likewise, and we can move on."

Tilson nodded. He was quite sure Anne could be very scary.

When they arrived outside a thick wooden door, Anne paused. "Be aware that Anthony Gray can be ruthless and slippery as hell," she said, and beamed at him as if she was telling him he'd won the lottery.

She knocked on the door and went in without wating for a reply.

They had entered a large, well-lit room with a desk in the far corner and a small boardroom table with six chairs around it closer to the door. Gray himself was standing at the large, lead-lined windows as if he'd been posing there, waiting for the door to open. He tuned slowly and smiled.

"Ah, Anne! Great to see you." He came forward and held out an elbow. Tilson wondered what on earth he was doing, and then recalled that the elbow touch had been very fashionable during the Covid Pandemic.

"Just dropping him off," Anne said. "I'll leave you to it, Tony."

"No." The word was a definite command. "It's perfect that you've come. You need to hear this, too." He indicated the boardroom table. "Take a seat."

Then he walked up to Tilson and cocked his head. "So, *this* is our SBS Captain!" This time, he stuck out his hand and Tilson took it. The palm was a little moist and the grip not overly exerted.

"Sir," he said.

Gray laughed. A quick, nasal noise that seemed to lack conviction. "That's not how we do things over here," he said. "Maybe at Vauxhall Cross. But not here. Please, sit."

Once the three of them were seated at the table, Gray leant forward, his hands clasped before him.

"I need a favour, Anne. I need to borrow this young man from you." He sat back watching Anne's reaction. She looked at Gray evenly.

"Of course," she said.

"Well, it's not so much 'borrow' as 're-assign'," Gray added. "Temporarily, of course. The job I have would have fallen under your remit anyway."

Anne frowned. "Field work?"

"Yes. Even old stuff sometimes requires an agent outside of your quiet corner of the spy world."

He turned to Tilson. "Not that it's very exciting. No jumping off cliffs and fucking Russian honeytraps!"

Gray's eyes darted to Anne who seemed unruffled by his swearing. Perhaps she was used to it, Tilson thought.

"Right," Tilson said with a smile.

"More of a holiday, really," Gray said. "Very easy. It's an all-expenses paid trip to Norway." "Norway." Anne echoed. She was thinking hard. "Malcolm Fox?"

Gray seemed annoyed for a moment and then recovered. "Very good, Anne! I'm impressed."

"He's my era. Reading obituaries is how I keep up with old friends."

"And he is...?" Tilson interrupted.

Gray waved a hand for Anne to explain.

"Latterly he was a diplomat, deputy ambassador to Oslo for a quite a while. Retired about six years ago?"

Gray nodded. "Seven. Been living in a small house he bought in the middle of nowhere, writing his memoires from the diaries he always kept."

Anne looked at Gray with narrowed eyes. "You're very well informed."

Gray shrugged. "Have you seen where we are, Anne? It's our job to be informed."

"So, you want me to go to this guy's house and do what?"

"Retrieve the diaries and any sign of a manuscript."

"You think Malcolm would break the Official Secrets Act?" Anne asked with a tinge of disbelief.

"I have no idea. But I like to cover my arse in case things go tits up."

Anne nodded. "You see," she explained to Tilson. "Before the FCO, Fox was at both MI6 and then MI5. Even served on the JIC."

Tilson was impressed. Not many got to operate at both the Secret Intelligence Service and the British Security Servies. And working for the Joint Intelligence Committee was a serious honour.

"So, he's been about a bit." Tilson said. "Knows a thing or two..."

"Precisely," Gray said. "And we'd rather he didn't share any of that knowledge." He paused. "It's a precaution."

Tilson nodded.

"And like I say, it seems to fall well within ICE's remit. Old secrets. That kind of shit." He smiled. "Not to denigrate your work, Anne."

"Of course not." Her voice and look were acidic.

Gray clapped his hands together. "Good. I'll get the necessary admin done and you can be on a plane tomorrow. There's a small file to read. The address of course and contacts. The woman you'll find most useful will be his housekeeper. Ingeborg Olsen."

He stood up signalling the meeting to be over.

"Right," Tilson said. Anything seemed better than sitting in the fustiest, dustiest corner of Thames House.

He and Anne rose from their seats.

"Bit of a homecoming for you, Sam." Gray said. Tilson cocked his head. "You served in Norway, right? Arctic Warfare."

Tilson nodded. "Mountain Leader Training Cadre, yes."

"Excellent. A busman's holiday!"

"If you say 'holiday' *too* much, I'll have to mark this time away as annual leave, Tony!" Anne smiled thinly at Gray and bustled from the room, with Tilson trailing in her wake.

***

Anne swept into the ICE office like an unexpected landslide. She was pointing at people and issuing orders.

"Gareth, I want everything we have on one Malcolm Fox, late of this parish and the FCO."

Hazel went to speak but Anne shook her head. "Before it became the FCDO in 2020." He nodded mutely and set about his task.

"Ebony, see if there's anything in the recent files about him. Dig deep. He'd be little more than a footnote these days.

"Camille, did you ever meet him? Does anyone else still working here know him? I did, so there must be others. Make subtle enquiries around the building. In person preferably."

Camille stood. "I'm on it."

"Everyone ready for team briefing in one hour." She turned to Tilson who stood helpless. "You're part of this team whether you like it or not. We're not going to send one of our own into a bear trap uninformed."

Tilson couldn't help smiling. This loyalty was unexpected but very welcome. "You think it's a trap?" Anne beckoned him into her office.

"It's very suspicious," she said, moving to the rear wall where an antique kettle and a jar of tea bags resided on a small, incongruous Formica surface. "Malcolm Fox had fingers in every pie there was. He was very well connected. There were rumours that he had several people fired for the things he discovered about them. These days that wouldn't happen, HR would step in. But back then the word of a senior agent was all that was needed to receive your marching orders."

As she spoke, Anne put the kettle on to boil and added a Yorkshire Gold tea bag each to a couple of flower-patterned bone China cups. She bobbed down to open a small fridge under the countertop and stood up holding a two-pint carton of semi-skimmed milk.

She completed the tea making process and continued her personal briefing. "Why would Gray send you? That's my concern. We have a myriad of other agents, some probably a lot closer to Norway. If it really is a simple retrieval mission." She paused, stirring the second cup. "Unless."

"What?" Tilson accepted the cup from her and sat on the 90s faux leather seat opposite the desk.

"He could just be lording it over us. Over me. He's never really seen the point of this department. The DG disagrees so we remain.

But DGs come and go, while *others* get promoted. Perhaps he's even hoping you'll mess up."

"No offence taken," Tilson said evenly.

Anne smiled. "Oh, I'm sure you're very capable. The Metropolitan Police report that crossed my desk first thing testifies to that."

She raised an amused eyebrow.

"Right." Tilson acknowledged that she now knew about his altercation on the Tube.

"But nonetheless you are inexperienced in the field."

"I've done the training."

"Yes. But a classroom is very different to the real McCoy. You should know that Sam."

Tilson bobbed his head in agreement. She was right. "So, we have three possibilities," he said. "One. It's a trap of some kind. Two. It's simply a power move. Three. It's a test I'm expected to fail."

Anne smiled over the rim of her floral cup. "Of course, there's always the fourth possibility."

"Which is?"

"That this is exactly what it appears to be. A simple retrieval operation." There was a twinkle in her eye now. "I often think Freud would have made a good a spook when he said 'sometimes a cigar is just a cigar'."

***

Half an hour later, the whole team was gathered back in the outer office. Anne held sway in the middle of the room, everyone else seated at their desks, paperwork and detritus tidied away so everyone could be clearly seen, the strip lighting bathing them all in a harsh white light. The drab grey November light from the windows being almost negated.

"Gareth, let's hear from you first," Anne said.

Hazel cleared his throat and began to read from a notebook that housed his scribbled notes alongside quite a few shapeless doodles and patterns.

"Malcolm Fox. Born 1950, Berkshire, to a British father and naturalised Norwegian mother. Short Service Commission in the Coldstream Guards between 1968 and 1974 before joining the Foreign Office." He looked up at Anne to confirm that this was the correct nomenclature for the time. She nodded and he continued. "From there, transferred to MI6 in 1965, working on the periphery of the Oleg Gordievsky intel before playing an active part in his exfiltration from the USSR across the Finnish border in 1985."

There was sage nodding from all round. Even Tilson knew that Gordievsky had been perhaps the greatest double agent of the Cold War, supplying invaluable information to the West for over a decade.

"During the Soviet–Afghan War, Fox served as part of the annual mission to the Mujahideen resistance," Hazel continued. "At the end of that conflict in 1989, he moved on from MI6 to MI5, taking up a position in the counter-terrorist directorate under Sir Patrick Walker."

"Walker went on to become the DG here in 1987," Anne said. "Retired in 1992. Good man."

Gareth cleared his throat again, obviously wanting to finish his part of the briefing. "OK, Gareth, go on."

"Thank you. Fox then became involved in the negotiations with the IRA and Sinn Fein as well as the growing threat from the Middle East and Islamic fundamentalism."

"He genuinely did get about, didn't he?" Tilson ventured.

"Fingers in many pies," Anne echoed her earlier comment.

"Finally, he rejoined the FCO in 2000 and went on to become a liaison between them and the Joint intelligence Committee before retiring in 2015 and joining a Norwegian arms company as a non-exec director. He died last week of a stroke in his house nearby. According to the local police, no signs of foul play."

Gareth glanced down at his notebook as if he might find more information there, but then looked up once more, his cheeks slightly flushed with the embarrassment of public speaking.

"Well done," Anne said. She sounded sincere. "As you can see, we've got a man with more experience in the secret world than most, but who generally flew under the radar. He probably knew a hell of a lot of what was going on, and so his dairies – if full and frank – could pose a security risk. Ditto any manuscript for his memoirs.

"Gray has informed us that the diaries have the codename 'wallflowers' and the manuscript – if it exists – has been designated as 'honeysuckle'. Your codeword for contact is 'gardener'."

Tilson committed all three names to memory.

Anne turned to nod her head at another of her team. "Camille?"

Camille puffed her cheeks out. "Not much to say, really. There are a few people who remember him – mostly on the older side. But they've not got the best of memories. I mean they don't really recall him. He was nondescript. Flew under the radar. A spook's spook I suppose."

She looked round the team. "Sorry. Not much help. I didn't speak with the high ups. I didn't want to make them suspicious or anything."

"I thought as much," Anne said. "The fact he 'flew under the radar' as you put it tells us a lot. Fox was careful. Prudent. Knew the game. That may be why he managed to get so far. That's why his treasured memories are causing concern to Gray." She paused.

"Ebony?"

"Nothing much to say here, either. There was a bit of an increase in Russian Signals Intelligence traffic around the Northern Schengen area about the time of his death, but nothing concrete. Nothing mentioning him by name."

"Could there be any other reason for increased SIGINT?"

"As Sam will know, the Royal Marines are over there right now, but that's regular," Ebony looked at her screen. "Sweden took delivery of its new Patria armoured vehicles. The..." she faltered. "The Pansy... *Pansarterrängbil* 300?"

She grimaced.

"It's a new six-wheel troop carrier," Tilson interjected. "All part of the current expansion programme in the Swedish Armed Forces. They want to join NATO and are concerned about Russia."

"Aren't we all," Anne said. "Well, I can see why that might have the Scandinavian airwaves lit up like a Christmas tree. But not proof it wasn't about Fox. Anything else?"

Camille waved. "I've got Sam's tickets, she said. "BA0766 tomorrow morning. Departing Heathrow at 10.55am; arriving Oslo at 2.10pm. World Traveller."

No first class for him, Tilson thought. He grinned. "OK."

"And then it's on by train from Oslo to Myrdal at 4.25pm. It's almost five hours, so make sure you pack a good book!"

"I've done some checking about your destination," Gareth piped up. "Myrdal is in Norway's mountainous 'rooftop', 866 metres above sea level. It's a remote mountain station serving as the junction between the Oslo-Bergen main line and the famous Flåm Railway."

"What's the 'florm' railway?" Ebony asked.

"Flåm is his ultimate destination," Camille said. "It's where Fox had his house."

"Never been, but it sounds very off the beaten track," Anne said. "Not a great place to be ambushed by anyone."

Tilson agreed. "And I presume I won't be armed?"

"You presume correctly, Captain," Anne replied, amused by the idea. "You're not part of the diplomatic service in Norway, so no unlicensed firearms."

"OK," Tilson said again. But he didn't think it was OK at all. He was going in on his own passport, unarmed and totally unprepared for anything untoward that might happen. If it did happen, of course. Which it might not. But if it did, he'd be isolated and probably out of contact with the room he now stood in. He glanced at each member of his new team in turn all looking at him with a mix of eagerness and pride. Even Ebony. He smiled. "Thank you," he said. "I'll do my best."

CHAPTER 4

Tilson was at Heathrow Terminal Three by 8am. He'd managed an early night and preferred to have a little time to spare at the airport. One reason this time, was that he was genuinely going to take Camille's advice and pick up a good book from W H Smith. He'd checked in online and had a small cabin bag with him. No baggage in the hold to slow him down once he got to Oslo at the other end of the flight.

While he was browsing the bestsellers, he noticed an older woman dressed in a business suit and carrying a briefcase. The reason he'd noticed her was that as he'd manoeuvred the aisles of giant packs of wine gums and inflatable neck pillows, she'd been looking at the same display of books on a little table. She was still doing it now.

The reason this was odd was that the table had a maximum of 12 titles on it. So far, as he could figure, she had picked up three or four of the books and examined them for a while, turning them over to read the blurb and then opening them to read – or at least look at – some random page halfway through the narrative.

Tilson wandered away from the books and over to the magazines. He picked one up and pretended to read its contents page, all the while surreptitiously eyeing the woman. Perhaps he was jumping at shadows, but his training had included this exact scenario. So much so that he wondered if Tony Gray or Anne Barnard were testing him. Was he meant to go up to her and say "busted!" or something?

As he watched, she put down the book she had been perusing for a few minutes and cast her eyes over the remaining tomes. Tilson was dying to go over there and see what could possibly be so interesting about the whole table that it was taking her this long to make a decision. Then she flicked her glance at him. Just for a second. He was still reading the contents but saw this in the periphery of his vision.

He put the magazine down and picked up another – *Time* – one that he actually intended to buy. Then he moved very deliberately towards the woman. She didn't flinch at his approach but instead picked up yet another bestseller and turned it over to read the back.

Tilson came to a halt on the opposite side of the table to her and cast his eye over the twelve piles of books – all differing in height like a 3D representation of a graphic equalizer. If she was tailing him, she was cool as ice; she looked up at him and acknowledged his presence with a slight smile. He returned the polite, yet peculiar face people always pull in these situations. A tight-lipped movement with a slight raising of the eyebrows.

She was old enough to be his mother – somewhere in her 50s, he reckoned – but still attractive. Blonde hair cut in an authoritative bob that still managed to be feminine. He nails well-manicured and painted a soft pink colour. Her lipstick matching with makeup equally muted, applied strategically and expertly, not trowelled on. Now he was staring, he realised. Shit. She looked up and smiled more warmly.

"Anything good," he said, trying to make his question the reason he'd been looking at her.

"I'm not the best person to ask," she said, putting down the book she'd been holding. "I always take an age to make up my mind."

Her accent was somewhere in the middle ground of so-called received pronunciation with slightly modern, softer tones. There might even have been a bit of a northern lilt in there. Yorkshire maybe?

"My husband's always complaining about my reading," she said.

Tilson nodded. She was warning him she wasn't interested. If she were following him, she might have been more open to his advances.

"Yes, my partner's the same," he said. "Thanks."

With a repeat of the same tight-lipped expression, he retreated to the back wall and selected the book he'd been meaning to pick up in the first place: Rory Stewart's *Politics on the Edge*.

He turned and walked over to the self-checkout. As he did so, a bald man in a grey overcoat came weaving through the crowd towards the woman at the table and gently squeezed her arm. She smiled at him as he smiled back and then she waved at the table with an exasperated expression.

Tilson assumed his instincts had been right. Just an indecisive woman choosing a book. He paid for his book and magazine, added a pack of Extra peppermint chewing gum and stuffed them into his Mountain Hard Ware Powabunga 32 backpack. A swift trip to the departure board told him his gate had been announced and he should make his way there.

He turned to see what had happened to the woman and her husband, but they had disappeared. No doubt swallowed up by the sheer number of thronging holidaymakers and businesspeople rushing to and fro with their drag-along suitcases.

***

Boarding for the British Airways flight to Oslo started at 1.45pm, approximately 25 minutes before they were supposed to be taking off. The Airbus A320 airliner comprised a front cabin of 48 Club Europe seats – identical to those behind them in the cattle class of Euro Traveller except that the middle position in each row is turned into a kind of table between the aisle and window seats. Passengers in these seats boarded first and then they started letting the hoi polloi on from the back row – number 28.

Tilson watched as the Club Europe passengers – mostly business-people alongside one or two influencer types in $500 trainers and second tier watches – were called forward. Some travelling with him in the Euro Traveller cabin were already queueing up at the barrier policed by two British Airways staff – a thin Asian man and a larger redheaded woman.

Tilson could never understand this behaviour. Boarding takes place by seat or row number, not how far forward in the line you were. He always booked towards the back so he could get on and get settled. And he had done this the night before, claiming the aisle seat in row 26.

When that area of the aircraft was called, he made his way on board, checking out his fellow passengers as he went. As he passed through the first cabin Tilson noted that there were quite a few rows that were empty. Either those seats would be available for upgrades, or their occupants were still at the champagne bar or perhaps the Wetherspoons pub in the terminal.

It wasn't a full flight by any means in Euro Traveller either. Not many holidaymakers going to Oslo in November. Tilson was however dressed as if going on a walking holiday: dark brown canvas trousers with a pair of Columbia Expeditionist Shield boots and a grey fleece shirt over a white tee. He was also carrying a black North Face Coldworks Insulated Parka in the Hard Ware backpack.

His row was unoccupied – proximity to the toilet almost always ensured that and Tilson could sit immediately without risk of being disturbed. This allowed him to stare down the aisle to see what was happening. He could also clock any latecomers and stragglers.

When everyone had been seated for several minutes, the captain came on the address system and informed everyone they were just waiting for a couple of passengers and that if they didn't turn up in the next five minutes, their luggage would have to be removed from the aircraft's hold, which would delay them by half an hour or so. This always slightly unnerved Tilson. The reason for the precaution of removing errant passengers' bags was in case they held explosives. This had been a tried and tested method of smuggling a bomb on board long before the terrorist attacks in New York and Washington DC of September 11th, 2001, had tightened all security measures.

Three minutes later, a smattering of muted, sarcastic applause came from the Club Europe cabin. Presumably the couple had finally arrived, and they could get going.

Tilson smiled to himself and was about to relax and read the copy of *Time* he'd bought, when a painfully thin man who was part of the cabin crew dashed past, leaving little to the imagination as to his mood. The irritated movement of the steward had clipped Tilson's shoulder and now he looked up to see what was happening.

The two late arrivals were still standing, trying quickly to stow their hand luggage in an overhead compartment. They looked angry. Tilson's heart skipped a beat and his feeling of relaxation disappeared like breath on a mirror. It was just too much of a coincidence for his liking.

The latecomers were the blonde bob book lady and her grey-coated, bald husband.

***

The flight from London Heathrow to Oslo Gardermoen airport only takes two hours and fifteen minutes but to Tilson this was an eternity. His mind was racing the whole time. It was frustrating to have two potential foreign hostile agents in such close proximity with no way of shaking them.

Tilson had constructed a scenario in his head for what might have happened at Heathrow. Blonde bob and grey coat had "made" him as he checked in, no doubt spying from a distance. Then they had purchased tickets for that flight, booking the class at the front of the aircraft. In that way, if they arrived after all the others had boarded and because they would be disembarked first, no one in Euro Traveller would see them.

Whether they knew they'd been blown, Tilson didn't know and that might be his only advantage. He knew they had checked bags, too, and that meant they would be waylaid in baggage reclaim while he could slip out of the airport straightaway with his small backpack.

The only hurdle to clear was immigration. He didn't want them to see him or put himself in a position where they might think he'd seen them. Fortunately, the fact that they would be off the plane first played to this. But he couldn't leave it too long otherwise the advantage of the time it might take the baggage handlers to unload their suitcases onto the carousel would be lost.

When the Airbus had touched down and taxied to its stand, Tilson made sure he was reading his English Norwegian phrase book – a hangover from his deployments to the country and his inability to gel with Duolingo or any other language app. In this way he avoided eye contact with the couple and also didn't find himself standing there like a lemon for ten minutes while he waited for the rest of the passengers to disembark. When his time came, he moved calmly down the aisle of the aircraft, and thanked the thin male member of the cabin crew now standing at the door. He had, albeit unknowingly, really helped him out.

Striding up the slope of the corridor that attached to the A320's door, Tilson looked for someone to play their part in the next stage of his plan. He hit upon a couple in their 40s, both fit and similarly dressed to him. He skirted around a few other passengers to fall in line behind them. He couldn't see where his tail had got to. It didn't matter for the time being.

When they got to immigration, they were filtered into differing lines, although most were EU and UK – still, ironically coupled for foreign arrivals' purposes. The forward progress of the passengers was halted as they waited patiently for a border guard to beckon them.

If you're a visitor to Norway, your passport must be stamped when you enter or leave the country. If you are stopped by the police or indeed other border guards, they will use the date in your passport to check you have not overstayed the 90-day visa-free limit for stays in the Schengen area. If it isn't marked correctly, they'll assume you have overstayed the visa-free limit and you'll be on the next flight home.

It was now that Tilson caught sight of the couple, about twenty metres away in another line. The way the queue snaked back and forth meant that they had their backs to him. But soon they would round the bend and be able to see him. Hence his selection of the outdoorsy pair right in front of him.

"Never enough immigration officers," he said, catching the man's eye. He was wearing a cream fair isle jumper and had thinning blonde hair.

They got into a conversation about hiking and skiing and Tilson did reveal he was heading for *Flåmsbana* railway. This elicited huge smiles from them both and set them off on a rambling reminiscence about how magical it was and such a highlight. It was gorgeous, the woman said, her bright blue eyes twinkling at the memory.

By the time Tilson's turn came to be checked through into Norway proper, the pair he suspected of following him had gone through only a few minutes earlier. It had not been long since they landed and Tilson hoped the baggage handlers in Norway were as slow as they seemed everywhere else.

The border guard – a man about his age in a crisp blue shirt with dark epaulettes and tie – did not take long to examine the travel documents. Then he brought his stamp down hard twice, once in the spongy ink pad and then again on a random page in Tilson's passport.

"Welcome to Norway," he said in almost perfect English. He added a well-practiced, humourless smile. "Enjoy your stay."

Tilson doubted 'enjoy' was going to be the watchword of this mission, but he smiled back equally devoid of mirth and started walking briskly through the airport.

Surprisingly he was greeted by a huge duty-free area of the sort one usually found in departure lounges. Tilson mused that this was really quite a sound idea and thought about looking for a bottle of Lagavulin whisky – his favourite single malt. Then he caught sight of the woman and the man he suspected of following him lurking at the number five baggage carousel, which was still devoid of luggage. He quickened his pace going through the green channel at customs and finally exiting the airport limbo of between worlds and onto Norwegian soil proper.

Tilson followed signs for the trains, walking as fast as he could without drawing undue attention to him. He wanted to make sure he left the airport station before his tail even retrieved their suitcases. He was in luck. The next *Flytoget* Airport Express train left at 15:00 in under four minutes.

The futuristic silver train stood at platform one of Oslo Lufthavn station. Tilson thought it looked remarkably like the early Japanese bullet train and guessed it must be a very swift method of transport to Oslo Central. Indeed, an announcement in Norwegian and then in English assured passengers they would be at their destination in only nineteen minutes.

Tilson took up position in the first carriage near the entrance so he would see if his friends arrived before departure. He only had to wait two minutes, but it seemed like an eternity. Then, with a soft pinging sound the doors closed, and the silver train moved smoothly away from the station. At the last second, he saw the woman with the blonde bob appear on the platform, looking around for something. Presumably him. But she didn't spot him and then she was out of sight.

Tison allowed himself a smile. He'd managed to ditch them. Properly this time. Then the smile faded. How had they known to be at Heathrow to tail him in the first place? How had they known he'd be travelling? They must have known who to look for at Terminal Three as well. That begged the most crucial question. How had they known it would be *him*?

CHAPTER 5

It had just started snowing over the Norwegian Capital as the silver train pulled into Oslo Central. Its sloped nose approached the buffers one minute later than scheduled. Very quickly after the first crystal started to fall, the snow turned to large flakes floating down from the darkening sky above. They were lit from the below by the station's lights, giving the atmosphere a truly festive feeling, albeit an early November day.

Tilson waited for the other passengers – already jostling by the doors – to disembark first. Only when his carriage was empty did he finally grab his rucksack and make his way to the now open doors. He could feel the cold blast of air from outside, already minus two, mid-afternoon.

As Tilson stepped off the train, he gazed up between the crack in the ceiling between the train and the platform surface. He loved the snow. Not only for misty and probably inaccurate memories of Christmases in Suffolk where he grew up building snowmen in the field and tobogganing down the surprisingly steep hill nearby.

Later came his Mountain and Arctic Warfare training: being plunged into ice holes and the burning of the cold, the snow holes they dug to survive in, the beauty of the mountains and the entire wintry landscape, best taken in while cross-country skiing. He'd only been at the unironically named Camp Viking the winter before.

The newly established facility in northern Norway was built to serve as the hub for Royal Marines Commandos. The MOD had and the Norwegian government had ploughed money into a new base of operations when it became clear that the High North was once more becoming a key theatre.

Purpose-built in the village of Øverbygd, forty miles south of Tromsø the base had been busy when Tilson was there. It accommodated a vast force of personnel from the UK's Littoral Response Group (LRG), the commando-led Royal Marines force which reacts to emerging crises in Europe. The thousand-strong force was there ostensibly for Exercise Joint Viking.

Tilson reflected that it had been his last major deployment in the SBS. However, that was in his past. He had to remain focussed on the job at hand. This was his future now. Whether he liked it or not. And so far, the jury was out.

He checked the Norwegian Trains app on his iPhone 13 for the departure of the train to Bergen. He had time – as long as he moved quickly – to achieve the several objectives he wanted to accomplish.

Tilson moved swiftly up the sleek, modern travelator into the main station concourse before heading through the shopping arcade with its mix of the unfamiliar and the ubiquitous; branches of Accessorize and 7-Eleven opposite a Norwegian newsagent cum supermarket branded *Narvessen*.

A nearby cashpoint of the DNB bank had an elderly gent in a suit and tie just completing his transaction. Tilson stepped up to the machine and turned to check that there were no idiots lurking, trying to spy his PIN.

He then withdrew the largest amount of Krone he could: ten thousand, equivalent to just under £750. If he was being tracked across Norway, which he guessed he was, then cash would help him disappear. Anyone paying by card leaves a breadcrumb trail of electronic purchases that makes it supremely easy for those with the right tech to follow every move.

Tilson folded and pocketed the notes before moving on, avoiding the escalators up to the mezzanine. He kept up his brisk pace past an incongruous branch of Boots *Apotek* – apothecary, or chemist – and down another escalator and out into a large, open square. The snow was not settling. Yet. But the grey flagstones of the city were glistening in the streetlights as passers-by donned hats or pulled hoods over their heads against the inclement weather.

Ahead of him was the Jernbanetorget stop on the Oslo Tramway, part of the largest transport hub in Norway. He followed the tram tracks north and then turned left onto Biskop Gunnerus Gate. A Blue Tram honked its horn at a pair of teenage girls and Tilson saw the driver shake his head as the girls moved off, giggling at something on their phones.

The sound of the horn drew most people's attention and Tilson used this to stop at the raised pavement of another Tram stop and look around. Was there anyone he recognised from the train or even the blur of faces at the station? No one caught his eye, so he turned on his heel and continued down the broad road before forking right onto Kirkeristen, a road that curved around the 17th Century Oslo Domkirke, actually the third Cathedral in Oslo's history; this version having been completed in 1697 after the city had been affected by a great fire 73 years before that.

In the shadow of the elegant but slightly stunted spire of the Domkirke, Tilson completed his self-imposed side quest. He crossed the threshold from Storgata in between a dual aspect Domino's Pizza into the heated interior of a shop with a vast and luminous lime green sign above the door that read simply "XXL". He was quickly accosted by an enthusiastic young shop assistant and asked – in perfect English – if he needed help.

Minutes later, Tilson was facing an older man with a grizzled beard and unkempt salt-and-pepper hair. He thought this look suited the atmosphere of a rugged camping and hunting store very well. To begin with, this wildsman sales rep was suspicious of the foreigner wanting a knife.

So, Tilson switched to Norwegian, persuading the guardian of the knives that he loved the country, its people, and its terrain. All true. He'd had to make up some story about going hunting with his cousin in Telemark to really persuade the older man that he was legit. Once that lie had been spun, the shop assistant had been almost eager to help Tilson select the best tool for the job.

In the end, Tilson had chosen the *Øyo* Nordic Hunting Knife. It was robust and slim, accompanied – in its box – by a black leather sheath. The blade itself was 12.5 cm long, 0.39 cm thick and made from stainless steel. The handle was a little short for his liking but was made of a roughly textured composite material. It was grooved and punctured by two tubular rivets with an additional hole at the tip of the hilt for different lanyard and other paracord applications. Although the leather sheath wasn't a premium one, it'd get the job done nicely Tilson reckoned, with its secure fit and drainage hole.

Paying with the notes from the cash point and placing his purchase in his backpack, Tilson left, receiving a cheery wave and a call of *god jakt!* – good hunting. Tilson grinned at the irony. He hoped he wouldn't be hunting anything other than the diaries and manuscript, but he wasn't going to continue with his mission unarmed. Not after the couple on the plane had spooked him a little.

The last matter he had to attend to was that of his diabetes. He'd have to eat something before the five-hour trip on the train. And the red and orange insignia of Burger King beckoned Tilson in, promising an identi-kit experience to that in the UK. With a few added regional varieties, he noted as he perused the menu displayed above the uniformed servers' heads.

Alongside the mainstays of the Whopper and the Chicken Royale were alien burgers like the Double Cheesy Cheese and the Halloumi King. Chilli Cheese fries nestled in glaring technicolour yellow next to their regular cousins.

He played it safe with a Whopper meal with a Coke *uten sucker*, which turned out to be Coke Zero, rather than Diet Coke, which he was happy about. Eating in afforded Tilson the opportunity to sit in the window and people watch. More accurately, he was watching for people watching him. He picked out several suspects either in the restaurant or outside that might fit the bill.

On a line of five metallic seats for waiting passengers, just outside Burger King sat a woman sipping a hot chocolate. Tilson placed her somewhere in her thirties. Or later twenties? Could even be forties? She was wearing a blue woolly bobble hat pulled low over her face and somehow that made it difficult to age her. Which might have been the point.

A well-groomed man in a mid-length lined leather coat and a baseball cap was examining the departures board right ahead of him. He just stared and stared as if willing his train to appear. That or he was trying to search for his train. And that might have played were it not for the fact that – in a display of true Scandinavian organisation - all the two dozen or so trains leaving in the next one and a half hours had already been assigned platform numbers. So, what was he looking for?

Across the concourse was a clothing shop called *Passasjen*. Just within its arched open entrance were a trio of large, round plastic daisies acting as a seating arrangement. On one of these a little girl in a pink baseball cap was crawling around while her bored mother sat on the second, guarding two white, wheel-along suitcases.

They didn't interest Tilson. It was the mixed-race man on the third dais that caught his interest. Passing between that shop and the fast-food outlet was a steady stream of people coming and going. So, it had taken him a while to spot him. Tilson tried not to let it be known he'd seen the man in the grey shell suit, but he seemed to be watching the British agent intensely. Perhaps he was just in a daydream or maybe he was a thief sizing Tilson up as a mark.

He wasn't sure. Why would any trained agent be so obvious? But maybe it was a double bluff. He shook his head at the clichéd idea.

The one Tilson really didn't buy was the well-built man standing at one of the back-to-back phone booths, talking animatedly into the receiver. Who in this day and age didn't have a mobile cell phone? Was he a technophobe? Had he lost his phone? Had it stolen? It seemed implausible. But then the man re-cradled the receiver and stood looking at the handset as if dumbfounded.

He was wearing a brown cloth cap and a black, hooded coat over dark blue jeans and a solid pair of black boots. Then he turned as if he felt Tillson's gaze upon the back of his neck.

The two of them locked eyes for a brief millisecond, Tilson chewing on his burger, the man with the black hair staring back angrily. It was Tilson who broke eye contact, pretending to search for a chip. Last thing he needed was trouble. Especially if it was unnecessary.

As Tilson dumped his refuse in the bin beside the counter, and walked to the platform, the Bergen train was already boarding. He moved down the travelator once more and found not a silver bullet train this time but a much more snub-nosed affair with a bright red livery surrounding the dark glass of the windows and the bright orange doors. Tilson guessed that if the train ever needed digging out of a snow drift at least it wouldn't get lost.

***

One platform over, with a pair of unoccupied train tracks between them, sat a man on a blue plastic bench. He was about the same size as the MI5 man he was watching, but thicker set. More like a rugby player compared to the frame of a runner or rower belonging to his target. A powerful leopard to Tilson's wiry cheetah.

This watcher had a comma of dirty blond hair and deep, brown eyes. He looked like a native but could have been from anywhere in Europe. His clothes were nondescript, neither business-like nor overly casual. A neutral figure against a neutral background, blending in. Hiding in plain sight.

He gazed up from his phone at Tilson as he boarded the Bergen train a few carriages back from the engine. Then he stood very casually, performed a little stretch, and started up the slope towards the end of his platform. Once at the top he casually moved across to the platform for the Bergen train and strolled down the slope.

Knowing Tilson was sitting somewhere on the train ahead of him, the watcher pressed the button to open the first set of doors on the first carriage. The orange slabs parted and allowed the watcher on board.

He swept the carriage quickly with his penetrating gaze and then sat with his back to the wall of the rearmost bulkhead of the train.

Once settled, he pulled out his phone and typed in five enigmatic words: "Gardener coming to prune wallflowers". Then, on the next line he added what seemed like an odd football score: "Alpha 2 Echo 5". This last was actually his call sign. His codename. A meaty index finger hovered over the send button for a moment and then he pressed it. The watcher sat back and pulled out a charger, unravelling it with an easy, looping motion.

His movements were being watched by a skinny, plain-looking young woman with the pinched features of a Slavic country. Her bleached blonde hair had cut into an elfin look and was stuffed haphazardly under a baby blue woolly hat. Her face was further disguised by a pair of horn-rimmed glasses. The woman was already seated at the other end of the carriage. She'd watched as Tilson strode past her window five minutes earlier and had seen the watcher move from his bench on the opposite platform and then reappear on this one and board the train.

Leaving at 4.25pm the Bergen bound service was one of only six regular trains a day between Norway's two most important cities. As such, it was already half full when she came aboard five minutes after the man she had been partnered with on this mission.

He was a thirty-two-year-old man with a barrel chest and early male pattern baldness in tar black hair. His nose was long; a pointed hook jutting out between dull, tree-bark brown eyes. There was a glimmer of dark intent deep within them but not a huge amount of intelligence. This specimen of Russian brute force was sitting by the door to the next carriage, facing her. She managed to catch his eye and glanced surreptitiously over her shoulder. Hook-nose gave a discreet nod as he set up a pair of wired earphones. *Yes, he'd seen him.*

At exactly twenty-five minutes past the hour, an overweight train guard in an orange high-vis jacket and grey peaked cap ambled onto the platform carrying a small, rounded paddle. With a flourish, he removed the whistle he was carrying in the breast pocket of a jacket he was wearing underneath.

He placed the metal instrument to his lips and then – with the over-exaggerated movements of a person who knows they are being watched – took one last look at the time displayed on his Fitbit and checked it against the clock hanging by the platform number board. Satisfied that both were in agreement, he then waved the paddle to signal the driver to set off into the cold, wintry evening. He added a long blast on his whistle causing the air to bloom momentarily in condensation.

As the train pulled away from the station a few sparks flew as the wheels and the ice that had formed on the rails interacted. The lights aboard flickered momentarily but no one gave the slightest sign that they were concerned.

Now that they were moving, Tilson took the opportunity to call the office at Thames House. As he dialled the number, he took the chance to covertly scan the carriage. He was looking for minutiae, the merest detail. Anyone who might have the slightest suspicious piece of clothing or who was too nervous or too calm for that matter. Just someone who looked out of place. Sometimes, his instructors at the MI5 instruction establishment had told him, it would be pure instinct.

He saw nothing out of the ordinary, but something told him there was probably another tail on the train. The Number he'd dialled buzzed twice before it was answered.

"Hello. Reception. How can I direct your call?" The voice was flat and female.

The cover was that of a nameless hotel. This was not only in case someone randomly dialled the number but also for the benefit of those who would undoubtedly be listening in from hostile security and intelligence services.

"Room 35. Ninth floor," Tilson said.

"Your name?"

"Gardener."

There was a slight pause as the call handler checked the database for active codewords.

"Please hold, Mister Gardner. I'll try to connect you to 935 now." Radio 4 started playing down the line. An interview with a correspondent in Gaza. Then it cut off as Anne took the call.

"Mister Gardener. How *are* you? I must say I wasn't expecting to hear from you *quite* so soon."

Tilson winced at her thinly veiled criticism that he was calling in too early. But he hoped what he had to say would change her tune.

"I just wanted to thank you for the gifts when I left." Gifts referred to a tail. A brief silence. "Oh, well!" Much cheerier now. Playing the part. "You're very welcome. I hope you got the right one?"

"A matching pair," Tilson said. "I'm sure they'll make a great start to my collection."

I had no idea the gifts had already arrived if I'm honest," Anne said. She was questioning his belief that he was being tailed.

"Very prompt delivery," he replied, trying to sound pleased. "Did you have any… *care* instructions for them? Or the others?" This was skating on dangerously meagre ice. A pause from Anne.

"Actually, I'm sure you can handle it if they *really* need your attention."

"Right. Just wanted to make sure."

"No problem. Do call me when you've settled in."

There was a click and then the number keypad displayed on the screen of his phone vanished. She didn't believe him. But why not? Maybe she thought he was overreacting? Jumping at shadows? Or perhaps she thought the mission was compromised and didn't want to give the game away? Whichever it was, the message was clear. Wait before calling in again.

CHAPTER 6

The idea that travelling long distances by train is either romantic or luxurious is one peddled by Hollywood seemingly for some misplaced, rose-tinted yearning for a bygone age that possibly never existed.

After sitting in the same seat for a few hours, Tilson reckoned he could do with a table of white linen and silver cutlery awaiting a *Cordon Bleu* menu of exquisite delights. Not to mention the company of a slinkily-clad woman with which to spar verbally and then tumble into a sumptuously comfortable bed in a massive sleeping cabin.

Instead, all he'd had was a trip to the twin vending machines - one for snacks and the other for coffee – located two coaches up from his. He'd selected the Norwegian equivalent of a Kit-Kat called a *Kvikk Lunsj*, washed down with a vintage cappuccino. For company he had the scowling figure of an old woman sitting in the seat opposite him. She was the size of a large teddy bear and wearing an unflattering grey jumper which matched her equally grey hair, pulled back in an austere bun.

She was leaning her head on the windowpane, cushioned with a Nordic winter hat. Also, grey. She seemed to be trying to sleep. Tilson couldn't truly be sure because her eyes were so deep-set and wrinkled as to make them almost invisible.

He shifted his weight and half turned in the lightly padded chair for the hundredth time since his return with his feast. This elicited an eyebrow raise from the grey woman and a slight sigh. She hunched up in annoyance and folded her arms.

Cutting his losses, Tilson decided it was time to take a stroll – get the blood circulating in his legs and alleviate some of the boredom. He had tried reading, but he just couldn't concentrate. He was aware that he suspected the train to have a tail on board but that he hadn't really checked the other passengers.

He moved down the aisle between the seats in his carriage, swinging – almost ape-like – from one handhold to another on the back of the seats to offset the jolting motion of the train. Just over half the seats had been occupied when he boarded, and some twenty percent of the passengers had left the train at the stations that served much larger towns, especially Drammen, Hønefoss, Geilo and Finse. So, people were now pretty spread out, making it difficult to hide.

Tilson noted those that looked up at him, curious as to why this strange man was moving around – especially as the vending machines were in the opposite direction. They probably weren't the people he was looking for. Again, why make yourself known; why stand out?

By the time Tilson reached the penultimate carriage to the rear of the train he was almost convinced that it was, in fact, clear. As soon as he could see into the last coach, however, this assumption vanished with the same sensation as a wasp sting. Immediately painful and increasing in severity as time went on.

He could see one of the people he'd picked out at Oslo Central as a possible enemy watcher. It was the woman who'd been difficult to age, now devoid of her blue hat. At least this let Tilson make a more accurate guess at early 30s.

She hadn't seen him yet and, with a sweep of the rest of the carriage, Tilson could be gone, secure in the knowledge she hadn't noticed him. But then he realised that he couldn't see the faces of the people seated against the bulkhead containing the doorway in which he was currently lurking.

Tilson edged forward, moving with the sway of the train. His back pressed against the righthand frame of the door, one that contained a luggage rack. He was relieved to see both seats empty. Slowly, he moved back a few paces and then advanced again, this time with his back snug with the wall to the left.

He felt winded by what he saw. It was the balding black-haired man who had been so agitated on the phone at Oslo Central station. This potential enemy watcher was seemingly dozing with a brown woollen cap over his face.

As Tilson withdrew, his heart beating at double speed, the woman looked up. He couldn't have looked more suspicious if he'd tried. Her eyes widened in recognition, giving her away immediately. But it didn't really matter. They both knew who – or at least what – they were to each other.

The ex-Royal Marine moved swiftly out of her field of vision and began his looping, striding return to his seat. Before he reached its relative sanctuary, he felt the train slowing. The digital clock on the wall of the carriage ahead read: "21.10". They were approaching Myrdal. His stop. And, he assumed, hers.

Outside, it was dark as the sun had set a long time ago now, but at least it had stopped snowing. A sporadic cluster of lights from the tiny village they were approaching started to show through the windows of the carriages.

Tilson grabbed his North Face parka and put it on hurriedly before snatching the Hard Ware rucksack and moving to the doors. The train was now coasting to a halt, and he could see a collection of long railway sheds passing in front of him. Some were white and some that peculiar orange red that decorates so many Norwegian buildings.

Since the time of the Viking raids on Northumberland and East Anglia, Myrdal had been nothing more than a pasture used by the farmers of the Flåm valley. The area was not on any main road and almost no one had ever heard of the place with its beautiful and serene surroundings. But then came the railway.

Myrdal went from being an anonymous mountain pass to the centre of the biggest building project in the country at the time. Akin to the gold rush town of a similar period in the USA, the town sprung from nothing and had a thriving community of over one hundred permanent residents. A simple church and the school were built to tend to the community's needs. There was even a restaurant and shops.

Today, Myrdal is really more a collection of small houses in a remote mountain pass than an actual conurbation and supports almost no permanent residents. The only way to reach Myrdal still is via the railway – and some hiking trails, but these are seldom used in the winter and certainly not by tourists.

At 867 metres above mean sea level the station is nestled between two long tunnels on the Bergen Line: the Gravahals Tunnel to the west and the Vatnahalsen Tunnel to the east. Apart from giving the smattering of locals access to some form of public transport, Myrdal station is chiefly used as a junction between the mainline and the little *Flåmsbana* railway.

Almost all passengers using the station are changing trains between the two lines, and Tilson was no exception. However, he was only one of a handful of people who got off. That was because there was no connecting train to Flåm that night. He'd booked into one of the local hostels while he was travelling. It was the only one open at that time of year – the *Snøfelt Hotell*.

One of the people who had disembarked was the man with the black hair now standing 20 meters away, his cap under the black hood of his coat, stamping his booted feet in the sudden cold of the minus three-degree air temperature. To give him his due, he didn't seem interested in Tilson at all. There was no sign of the woman in the blue hat. She wasn't three. Had he been wrong about her?

With time to spare Tilson himself took a moment to examine the small station. There were three platforms, all with an icing of snow, all shrouded in a wind-swept mist of condensation and dry snow giving it an ethereal, otherworldly air. Platform 1, where he was standing, was the principal platform on the mainline, and across from him was platform 2. This served as an alternative for trains on a passing loop of track. As the mainline is single track, the passing loop allowed regional trains to cross with freight services, and occasionally with other passenger trains.

Behind him, the train emitted a soft two-tone alarm to let everyone know the doors were closing. Tilson turned to see the man in the cap climb back onto the train and a moment later the doors slid closed.

As he watched the carriages move at increasing speed past his position, Tilson caught a glimpse of that woman in the blue hat. Again, their eyes met but her expression was neutral; she wasn't giving anything away. She didn't need to. Sitting next to her now was the man in the cap. He was talking to her as she gazed at Tilson. Then the moment was stolen away by the acceleration of the train. So, they were working together. A two-person tag team.

Now the only person on the remote and silent platform, he started moving up the platform to the large cafeteria and gift shop that had replaced the restaurant some decades previously. His boots crunched on the layer of snow that covered the ground. Indeed, it was everywhere, on every sloped or horizontal surface.

Alone now, the light and warmth of the Café Rallaren were extremely welcome. Tilson had seldom felt more isolated. Even those tasked with his surveillance had abandoned him. And why not? There was nowhere for him to go until morning. And no way of getting there.

He pushed open the door to the café and it was immediately clear this had ceased to be a restaurant a long time ago. It did at least serve some hot food as well as snacks, though. To one side were a few cramped shelves of souvenirs, and ahead an unmanned luggage storage counter. Tilson noted from a battered sign that there was also another facility they offered – a bicycle rental facility albeit only available from June to September. He didn't think he'd be needing that service anyway.

Across the room from a strange collection of travel paraphernalia consisting of an old suitcase, a walking stick, a couple of hats and some shoes that hung on the wall was a wooden countertop crowded with plates and metal baskets of crisps. Behind it was a middle-aged woman with a mop of mouse blonde hair under a white paper hat, a couple of small moles on her chin and a slash of pink lipstick around her mouth. She smiled as he approached.

Tilson engaged her in Norwegian.

"Good evening. Do you have any hot food left?"

The woman, who had a name badge over her right breast that read *Tuva*, shook her head. "I am sorry," she said and swept an arm towards the glass cabinet that ran along one half of the counter length. "Just what we have here. You are the last train tonight, so we will close after this."

Tilson nodded and told Tuva that was fine. What they had there was not very much: a rather sad piece of cake that seemed to share some DNA with an apple tart, and one tired cheese roll wrapped in cellophane with salad drooping from every side. He bought both and added several packs of different flavoured crisps and a handful of strange chocolate bars.

"We have some coffee left, if you are cold," Tuva volunteered.

Tilson said he'd take whatever she had. Smiling, she turned to pour the dregs of a glass bowl coffee jug sitting under a percolator into a jolly orange cup. As she gave him the beverage, he asked her if she knew the *Snøfelt Hotell*.

She did. "Oh yes. Trygve's place. Such a nice old gentleman." Tuva gave him directions and Tilson thanked her, passing over a few kroner to pay for his makeshift meal.

With the rucksack slung over his shoulder and a plastic carrier from the café in one hand, he started walking through the snow away from the station into the cold night air. He left the glow of the station lights behind him and passed down a deserted track to the second building on the right – a bright yellow house; the only one with a warm glow showing in the windows.

***

Trygve turned out to be a skinny older man with pewter hair and a broad smile that made his already wrinkled eyes crease into mere slits. He welcomed Tilson into the small guesthouse and quickly shut the door behind him to prevent the heat escaping. From the hall, the MI5 man could see three rooms.

Beyond the steep wooden staircase that led to the first floor, was a simple kitchen with a range and a cylindrical water heater above it. Beside him to the right was a small sitting room or snug with a cast iron wood burner, a fierce fire burning behind its glass doors. And to his left a tiny dining room set up with three two-seater tables and a sideboard with several dry condiments.

"Come in, come in," Trygve said. "Sit down."

Tilson just wanted to retire to his room, but he didn't want to be rude, and the man seemed lonely. Which made two of them. So Tilson took up position on one of the very small sofas that sat across the room from one another before the fire.

"Aquavit?" Tryggve asked with a twinkle in his eye.

Tilson knew aquavit of old. It was a common drink in the mess in Northern Norway; a strong spirit originating in the Nordic region, with each of the Scandinavian countries claiming ownership of at least a regional variation of the drink. Most shop-bought varieties started at 37.5% proof, but the homemade or augmented kind could be much stronger.

In the cool North of Europe, a proud aquavit bottle is the maypole around which celebrations swing. Aquavit is also something of a symbol for Scandinavian cuisine. Some have a taste of fruit or certain herbs like dill, but in Norway it's caraway seed. Most are matured for months in casks – generally of the cherry wood variety.

"Mmm. Yes please," Tilson replied.

Tryggve bent down and retrieved two small tulip shaped glasses and a bottle from the cupboard below and placed them on the surface above the sideboard. With a widening grin, he turned and showed the bottle to Tilson. It was *Linie* – the most famous and oldest brand of aquavit in the world. The ship on its blue label is there to represent that fact that the particular cherry casks – the *Oloroso* – are stored on board ships and cross the equator twice – supposedly on their way to Australia and back – before returning to port for bottling.

This makes Linie a real delicacy and not cheap. It's a proper ocean themed drink and one that Tilson had always enjoyed. He smiled and nodded appreciatively at the old man.

Tryggve held up one bony index finger, indicating there was one more thing to complete the party. Again, he vanished from the room and reappeared with a plate of curled, grey and white pickled herring also from the refrigerator.

His host poured out two generous glasses of the lightly golden liquid and passed one to Tilson. Now they could tuck in. Tryggve made solid eye contact with his British guest and raised his glass.

"*Skål!*" he said in a strong voice and downed his glass.

"*Skål!*" Tilson echoed and did likewise.

They chatted and drank for a couple of hours, the older man regaling Tilson with the story of the heroes of Telemark. This was a daring commando raid on a Nazi heavy water plant in a region not far from Myrdal and where Trygve said his family originated. The former Royal Marine knew the tale well but to hear it told with such gusto over a glass or five of the local tipple in the flickering of the firelight on such a cold Norwegian night was a rare treat.

When Tryggve had finished his tale and they had both been sitting in quiet contemplation for a few minutes, Tilson asked if he knew the local area well. Tryggve nodded. He was a hunter, too, although knee trouble stopped him in his tracks – literally – a couple of years ago. He would don his white jacket and trousers to head out on the hills taking refuge in the cabins if he needed, hunting moose or deer.

At this, Tilson sobered up a bit.

"Do you still have them?" he asked.

"My winter hunting gear? Yes, I think. Somewhere. Why?" Tryggve frowned.

"If they're no use to you anymore, I'd like to buy them," Tilson said.

Tryggve laughed, thinking he was joking, but when he realised the younger man was serious, he stood up and left the room, returning after several minutes with a neatly folded jacket made of a lightweight material in slightly off-white colour.

"No trousers," he said apologetically. "No idea where they've gone."

They sat down once more and agreed on a price. Trygve said he could add it to the total of his bill and pay in the morning. The wily old man could tell that Tilson was up to something, but he had the good sense not to ask any questions. He also seemed to have taken a shine to him.

Seeing this was the case, Tilson risked one last question. If it was an emergency, would he be able to get from Myrdal to Flåm on foot?

The Norwegian steepled his hands and squinted at Tilson. "Not on foot," he said. "Maybe skis. But don't ask for them. We have none here!

"If you became lost or had to spend the night in that wilderness, there is not much to help you except those huntsman's cabins. But they are remote and dispersed widely. Only a true local would know their whereabouts and how to get to them. I wouldn't advise it."

There was a pause while Tilson considered this. So, his only real option was the train. No matter if his surveillance returned or not.

"Thank you."

"Well, if you've no more peculiar questions, young man, I must go to bed," Tryggve said. "That is the last of the wood and I'll be buggered if I'm going out there again tonight!"

Tilson laughed and glanced at his blue-dialled Omega Seamaster GMT 300 Co-Axial. It was just past midnight.

"Now let me show you to your room. The first train leaves at 10.15, so you need not rise with the dawn." They stood. "I will be up before that, however. With your departure, I will be shutting up the house for the winter. Come."

Tryggve turned and led the way upstairs – pointing out a narrow bathroom – into a small bedroom with a low ceiling and a bed so covered in blankets and quilts as to make it look somehow overweight. He bid his guest good night and left, closing the door behind him.

After a trip to the bathroom to alleviate himself of the aquavit and to brush his teeth, Tilson climbed under the layers of the bed and soon fell into a deep sleep, his breath making small clouds in the air as the warmth in the room gently faded away.

CHAPTER 7

The sky was a startling blue over Myrdal the next morning. The temperature was hovering around minus two by the time Tilson returned to the station at 9.45am. The train for Flåm was already standing ready to depart. For no obvious reason the third platform used only by these local trains is numbered non-consecutively as platform 11.

It was deathly quiet and once more he was the only person standing in the frigid air. He tried to board the train, but the doors were locked shut. Of course, the driver would be in the café keeping warm and probably having a cup of coffee. His or her deserted train – number 1881 – was a dark green colour and consisted of four carriages. Tilson wondered if it wasn't overkill, to have so many. Especially given he was the only passenger. So far.

He knew that the train from Bergen would arrive soon, but he had no idea how many would be making the connecting journey. He assumed a small percentage. But not for the first time on this mission he was mistaken. When the larger, scarlet express train came to a halt and the doors opened with their sing-song chime, a crowd of people disembarked.

Tilson scanned the faces of each person that got off, but saw neither the woman in the blue hat nor the man with the cap. His attempt at locating his tail was hindered by the fact that almost half of the 50 or so people were carrying skis and ski poles, most wearing helmets, and some even had goggles already covering their eyes. It made it impossible to tell what any of these winter sports enthusiasts looked like.

The Oslo train departed after a few minutes, leaving the crowd on the platform milling around like so many multi-coloured flamingos, chattering away excitedly. Tilson did his best to blend in, making a show of examining his iPhone, while really trying to get a better look at his fellow passengers.

The driver of the train – an overweight man in his forties with lank, shoulder-length hair crammed under a black and silver uniform cap – emerged from the café and walked slowly to his engine. The grunt he let out as he made the effort to climb up into the cab was audible over the excited babble of the tourists. Moments later, the doors opened, and everyone poured into the carriages, almost filling them.

As soon as the doors closed once more, and the little train set off down its single-track line to wind down the 20 km to the coast of Sognefjord, a recorded information guide started playing in Norwegian first and then in English.

The soothing female voice informed everyone that, with a gradient that varies between 2.8 percent and 5.5 percent, it is the steepest railway in Europe. Tilson guessed he might find it precipitous for altogether different reasons.

He had to admit, however, that the views were spectacular and the railway itself a masterpiece of Norwegian engineering. One thing, the guide announced, that the line is renowned for is its spectacular turning tunnels that twist in and out of the mountains – twenty in total, eighteen of them built by hand.

This made the journey a strange one of bright sunshine reflecting off the snow-laden peaks and utter darkness of the underground realm. When the train did have sight of daylight, he could see rivers cutting through deep ravines with tiny farm buildings clinging to their steep slopes. Below the treeline was a sporadic forest of coniferous pines.

The train made what Tilson thought was an unscheduled stop at Vatnahalsen *stasjon*, where all those with skis crowded the doors to leave the train. Clearly there was some resort based there and they were day-trippers after some downhill or cross-country skiing action. Above, the sky was turning grey and low wisps of cloud and snow-blown eddies were forming.

With the train now less than half full, Tilson tried once more to spot anyone he recognised, but he couldn't. At least none of those in his carriage looked like anyone he'd spotted in Oslo.

Then the evergreen train made its layover at the wild and beautiful Kjosfossen waterfall. The driver came over the loudspeaker to inform passengers they had a few minutes to get some air, enjoy the view and take photographs.

The platform at Kjosfossen station is little more than a triangular platform jutting away from the railway line, sandwiched between two tunnels. There was scarcely room for the carriages of the train to fit along its length and the engine at the front had to take position in the foremost tunnel to fit into the tiny station.

What the small stop lacked in size it more than made up for in spectacle. Immediately across from the train was the waterfall. Usually it was a fast-flowing torrent of water tumbling down a 93-metre cliff via several rock shelves, that day it was now a blue-white ice sculpture. Even with its peak now hidden in cloud, Tilson was distracted for a moment by its majesty.

As he stepped from the train with the remaining tourists he paused to gape at the frozen abstract snapshot of nature's power and beauty. His gaze wandered from the waterfall to its surroundings: snow covering the stone and lichen of the cliff itself and halfway up the slope to the right stood a ruined farmhouse.

Its roof had long since collapsed, and the chimney breast stuck out from the snow cover like the hand of a drowning man desperate for attention. A wooden frame was still in place around one of the two windows that were visible from his position, holding out against time and the elements.

At the base of the waterfall, a well-maintained metal post-and-rail fence prevented people from falling or climbing down for a closer look. This was a wise precaution as the course of the river flowed under the platform itself and continued downhill behind the train. Nonetheless the barrier was lined with people leaning on it as they took their photographs, eager to secure the scene for posterity hurrying because the low cloud threatened to envelop it at any moment.

It was then that Tilson spotted him.

The black-haired man who had been wearing a black hoodie and cap the day before was now dressed in a drab olive, knee-length coat with a light brown, fur-lined hood. It was his pinched features and hook nose that gave him away. Tilson had given him the nickname "Vulture" overnight and it suited him well.

Vulture seemed not to have noticed Tilson, although the MI5 man knew this would not be the case. Instead, he was standing just behind the fence, his smartphone pointing up to supposedly photograph the tourist spot. But the angle he was holding it was too much and had he been really taking a picture all he would have captured was the bank of slowly shifting grey-white clouds.

Somehow, Tilson had to shake his tail. Pretending to be searching for the perfect angle for a holiday snap, he moved down the platform passing behind Vulture. He reached the end of the platform where a wooden slatted waste bin stood alongside a box for grit or sand. He pretended to take a photo, but instead checked the Norwegian train times instead. There was no signal there, but he had taken screen grabs from the app the previous day.

With all eyes still on the waterfall and the train driver nowhere in sight, Tilson slipped away down the side of the train and into the tunnel that hid the rear end of the final carriage. The train depended on overhead cabling for its electricity supply so there were no live tracks for him to worry about. It was a short distance for him to inch down the side of the train to the back and stay there in the darkness, his black North Face Coldworks letting him blend in with the shadows.

His intention was to let the train depart without him. He hoped that Vulture would naturally assume his quarry had boarded the train once more and then follow suit, eager not to lose him. This would take the enemy to Flåm, yes, but what option would Vulture have once he discovered Tilson was not there?

He could either get the next train back which departed forty minutes later and didn't reach Kjosfossen again until 12.15pm. Or he could wait at Flåm for the next train to arrive from Myrdal at 2.05pm, hoping Tilson was on that. Either way it was a dilemma and a long period during which Tilson would be out of scope and there was no guarantee he would find him again.

For his part, Tilson's plan then was to climb the barrier and wait in the ruined building up the slope. This would afford him a reasonably clear view of the station and any train that pulled in. He would wait to see what Vulture did and then react accordingly. If push came to shove, he could get the train to Bergen and pick up a car hire there to drive to Flåm. Whoever it was following him would then be totally lost.

Pleased with himself for assembling this plan in about five minutes, Tilson waited as the train guard – almost identical looking man to the driver except for the addition of rounded glasses that made him look like Geppetto – started herding the tourists back onto the train. This took a while but then Tilson heard the doors chiming and the guard blowing his whistle.

The train began to move steadily away from him, but Tilson remained hidden in the tunnel. He was worried that he might be spotted by an eagle-eyed tourist or employee and have the train judder to a halt only for him to be escorted sheepishly back on board. Fortunately, this fear never materialised, and train number 1881 disappeared into the gloom of the curving tunnel ahead of it.

Only now did Tilson move, his feet crunching on the frozen stones between the rails. Perhaps it was this that gave him away.

"You can come out, *tovarich*," a deep voice called in accented English. Russian. Obviously, Tilson thought, cursing his hubris. Not such a great plan after all.

As he emerged from the darkness, he could see Vulture was standing where the bin and the grit box were. In his right hand was an SR-1M Vektor semi-automatic pistol. It is dubbed the *Gyurza* meaning "blunt-nosed Viper". Tilson wondered if this would have been a better designation for his enemy than "Vulture". This one was fitted with the optional Picatinny rail adapter and quick-detach tactical suppressor.

The Vektor is the preferred sidearm of several Russian and Kyrgyzstan forces, but Tilson guessed this one belonged to an officer of the Main Directorate of the General Staff of the Armed Forces of the Russian Federation. Or, more commonly, the GRU – Russian's military intelligence agency of the Army. Not to be confused with the FSB, the modern-day continuation of the Soviet KGB.

Tilson began by playing dumb. "I'm sorry. I didn't realise the train was leaving," he said in Norwegian.

The Russian shook his head. "You're Norwegian is pretty good, *pravda*," he said with no trace of a smile. "But we can end the games. We know who you are."

Tilson came forward, feigning concern. "Are you transport police?" he asked, maintaining his Norwegian.

"Stop there, Sam." The GRU operative brought this weapon up to eye level, now aiming very specifically at Tilson, who stopped immediately. "Good. Now, all we want to know is, why are you here?"

"Have you seen the view?" Tilson smiled. The Russian shifted his aim and loosed one shot from his weapon. It made a popping sound similar to a bubble of gum bursting after over-inflation. A chip of stone was blasted off the tunnel wall behind Tilson's right shoulder.

"Please. This is the perfect place for hiding a body, *da*? You will not be found until spring. Now, place your hands on your head. I am sure you know how."

Tilson was calm but scared. Although the Russan had a gun, he didn't seem intent on killing him. Indeed, he appeared almost reasonable in that he just wanted information. Or at least confirmation. Perhaps another tack would prove more useful.

Placing his hands on his head, sightly forward of his crown, Tilson interlaced his fingers. "I'm here for a funeral," he said.

"A funeral," the Russian echoed. "A joke of yours, yes? And whose funeral would that be, *tovarich*?" His use of the word "darling" or "dear" was a bit laboured and it almost made Tilson smile.

"An old friend of my father's."

"You are speaking of Mister Malcolm Fox, *verno*?"

So, he did know why Tilson was there. Or he'd suspected and wanted confirmation. Whatever it was, the Russian had shown his hand. That was certainly why he was there.

"Who?" Tilson tried his best acting.

The Russian smiled and narrowed his eyes. "You are MI5. This man died a few days ago. He was one of yours. You are here for his... possessions." He moved closer, twisting the SR-1M slightly, making sure his next shot would not miss. "But now you have seen us, forced us to reveal ourselves."

Tilson had to do something. Fast. "Please," he said. "I am British, but I don't know what you're talking about!" It didn't take much to portray the fear he was projecting. "I think there's been a mistake. I'm not who you think I am! Honestly."

"Honestly? We had hoped you would gather this man's possessions for us and then we could collect them." He shrugged. "Now, we cannot."

"So, what happens now?" Tilson asked.

The Russian edged forward, his teeth gritted, his eyes now a hard, pale steel. It was very clear what happened now.

"As I told you, your body will be found next Spring."

CHAPTER 8

Tilson moved with lightning speed, dropping down suddenly, sweeping his right leg across the ground and taking the Russian off his feet. Another pop sounded as the Vektor discharged, this time up into the air. Then he leapt up and across the ground, bringing his knee down on the man's groin as his hands grabbed at the weapon still held in the Russian's right hand.

Despite the incredible pain the GRU agent must have been feeling, he managed to keep a tight grip on the gun. He was trying to manoeuvre it into a firing position that would hit Tilson. Fortunately, he was younger and fitter, had his Royal Marines and SBS – not to mention brief MI5 – training to fall back on. He had also learnt his lesson about his blood sugar levels.

Most members of the public are unaware of the training the armed forces and the police receive due to how fights of this nature are portrayed on TV.

After a minute of struggling, Tilson managed to force the Russian's gun hand away from his body and over the icy wooden deck of the platform. Immediately, he began smashing his enemy's wrist into the ground again and again. Finally, the man grunted in pain and resignation, releasing the weapon so it slid across the ice away from the pair of them.

Jumping to his feet, Tilson gave a sharp jab with his fist to the man's throat and told him to stay down. For his part, the Viper's blue eyes bulged as he grabbed at his neck almost totally prevented from breathing. As he flailed on the ground, Tilson ran over to the SR-1M auto and picked it up.

What now?

He couldn't just kill a GRU agent. Not without serious repercussions and probably a diplomatic incident – not necessarily with the Russians themselves but certainly with the Norwegians. His plan of waiting for the next train was not going to fly. He had to get away from the station. And the only way to do that was to climb the frozen waterfall.

Taking a running jump at it, Tilson vaulted the fence that ran around the wooden platform. He felt something drop from his pocket and heard a clatter as it hit the concrete walkway below. But he had no time to stop. Behind him he could sense the Russian already on his feet, struggling to walk but coming after his quarry, nonetheless. In front of Tilson was a four-foot-tall wall that he climbed onto quickly and began pulling himself onto the surface of the frozen water.

There is more than one way in which waterfalls freeze, and how they do so is key to how they are climbed. The way they are frozen can tell you how secure a climbing structure they will provide. If one is formed over a solid base – be it rock or more permanent ice – it will be far safer and more stable. However, this one had not been constructed in that way. Only a month before it had been a completely free-flowing waterfall. So, scaling it was not an advisable course of action. Unfortunately, Tilson had no choice.

To make matters worse, he had no ropes or crampons; he possessed neither helmet nor other basic kit. What he did have on his side was that the Kjosfossen waterfall consisted of several gentle rock shelves and not a sheer drop.

Tilson was already fishing out the hunting knife he'd purchased in Oslo to act as a makeshift icepick, allowing him to get a handhold on any of the more precipitous surfaces, using the butt of the Vektor he'd taken from the Russian agent to act as a hammer.

As he made his way across the first relatively flat plateau of the falls, Tilson turned back quickly to see what was happening with his stricken foe. He was unsurprised to see the man at the fence, clutching his throat and hunched over patently still in pain but watching his adversary intently.

What he hadn't bargained for was the sight of the green *Flåmsbana* train reappearing from the tunnel it had departed into only a few minutes before. The conductor must have done a headcount, found two passengers missing and ordered the train to reverse to retrieve the errant tourists.

Tilson had to act fast before he was spotted. He half ran, half skidded along the first shelf to the right of the waterfall and onto the snow-covered stone outcropping. Shinning up the icy rock face, he quickly made his way into the ruined farm building and once inside, leant his back against the wall, trying to control his breathing so the clouds of condensation streaming from his mouth didn't give away his position.

He listened as the brakes on the train screeched and the hydraulic hiss of release indicated the train had stopped. This was followed by the sing-song tones of the doors opening and then shouts from the guard as he saw and made his way over to the fallen Russian. Another Norwegian voice joined that of the first – presumably the driver joining his colleague to help get the incapacitated passenger back on board.

In the still quietness of the little railway halt, Tilson thought he could hear the Russian growling to the train staff. A moment later he heard the guard calling up the waterfall.

"We are calling the police! If you hide up there, you will die of cold."

Tilson cocked his head. Not true. He wouldn't die at all. He was trained for this and had adequate kit that would see him survive for at least three days. He remained silent.

"Last chance. We will take the train now."

Another couple of minutes passed. With a heavy sigh, the guard let out an expletive and then the doors chimed once more accompanied by the hiss of hydraulic brakes, and the train began to pull away again. Tilson was left in the quiet with only a light wind whispering through the open door and windows of the old structure in which he stood.

Contemplating his next move, he stood still, his breathing now gentle and even. He could stay in this shelter and wait for the next train – or the one after that. However, he imagined that the police would be waiting at Flåm station with a description of his appearance and clothing courtesy of the GRU man who – no doubt – claimed Tilson attacked him and was armed with a gun.

The other alternative was to complete his journey to the small town by travelling cross county. It can't have been more than a dozen miles, but he knew of old that in this terrain even small distances could be telescoped to become protracted and dangerous. And the fact the police imagined he was armed and homicidal might even mean them sending out a search party or a helicopter, perhaps.

Then a third possibility occurred to him. He didn't have to wait for a train to travel along the tracks, he could simply walk along them. It would be downhill all the way and mostly protected from the elements by the tunnels and so-called avalanche galleries. His only problem would be meeting the train coming back on its return journey. However, by then he could be off the line and using the road that runs alongside the track nearer to Flåm itself.

With this seeming the most sensible way forward, Tilson clambered down from his refuge in the ruined farmhouse and down to the concrete walkway below the fence. Here he found what had fallen from his pocket. The iPhone. Its screen was smashed and when he tried to turn it on, nothing happened. Had the GRU agent stamped on it?

He pocketed the phone and hauled himself over the guardrail back onto the platform. Before he set off, he took the lightweight jacket he'd bought from Tryggve from his backpack. The white covering would help him stand out in the tunnel if a train did come ploughing down the track and also it gave him a different look the police didn't know about and thus wouldn't be looking for.

***

The call made to the Norwegian police at Flåm by the stationmaster had been picked up by an administrative constable seven and a half miles to the north in the town of Aurland. This tiny police station is not actually open to the public except by appointment and is only staffed by one person, in this case constable Lars Lindberg. He relayed the call to Lærdal *politistasjon* – a much larger facility up the coast, a further 20 miles north of Aurland.

Here, the report was examined, and the decision was taken that a patrol car should be dispatched to investigate. So, Julie Solberg and Øyvind Iden duly climbed into their four-wheel drive Volvo V90CC patrol car marked with diagonal high vis yellow and black stripes and began the 35-minute drive to Flåm.

Policing is scarce in Norway – especially in outlying areas. The common constabulary is the National Police and Sheriff's Office, which also comprises six agencies that can lend a hand when things get busy or start to go beyond the normal day-to-day criminal jurisdiction.

One of the agencies is the Norwegian Police Security Service, reporting directly to the Ministry of Justice and the Police. This organisation is in essence a similar body to the UK's MI5, dealing in counterterror, counter espionage and offences against the security and independence of the Norwegian State. But there were no officers of this agency within 100 miles of Flåm.

The mission of the National Police is to ensure a steady, efficient, and flexible service for the benefit of the public. There are 27 local Police districts, each under the command of a *Politimester* – Chief of Police – who has full responsibility for all criminal regulation in his district. Each police district is headed up by its own headquarters with the other police stations – some of which are unmanned – serving as outlying points of public contact and reassurance.

There are only some 12,000 officers in the Norwegian Police Security Service, and that morning one of them in particular was running late.

Inspector Frida Skardet needed to persuade her teenage son that getting up and going to college was a good idea. She had even made him a light breakfast of a cup of black coffee and a pair of crisp breads, topped by thin slices of *Brunost*, the famous Norwegian brown cheese, which tastes more like caramel than actual cheese.

"Breakfast is on the counter," she called up the stairs to Tomas' room. All that came back in response was the sound of some dark heavy metal band thrashing the hell out of their guitars and drums. Frida paused at the bottom, holding the handrail, and gazing up expecting the miracle of a genuine reply. It did not come.

She shook her head at this and then had to smooth her short brown mop of hair back down to its more usual state. Resigned to no verbal communication from her son but taking comfort from the fact that at least he was awake, Frida grabbed her keys and swept through the front door. She had covered her standard Police Service uniform with a thick, padded blue coat. It was only a few minutes' walk from the modern two-bed house to her first port of call.

She was investigating a road traffic accident a couple of days before. Although, she mused, "investigating" may have been too strong a word. The first party was a local fisherman. She even knew him. A friend of her ex-husband. But she wouldn't hold that against him.

Most people knew everyone else round there; it was such a small, isolated community. She also knew the other party in the accident. A former teacher who was getting on a bit. Her car was a truck that was almost as old as she was. Frida suspected she was just nearing the time to give up her license, but she wasn't going to be the one took it away from the old lady.

After she'd completed taking statements from both – with neither really knowing who to blame – she headed for the concrete frontage of the Lærdal police station.

When she arrived, she found Ivar Kielland was leaning on the frame of his office door, eating a pastry. He was a large man – tall and wide – with a kindly face offset by a greying, slightly patchy moustache and a furrowed, bald pate that could make him appear stern when he needed to.

"*Hei hei*, Frida," he said cheerfully. "Tomas causing you some trouble?"

"No trouble, Chief," she replied, taking her coat off and hanging it on the modernist hatstand that sat in one corner of the outer office. "But apologies for being late."

Kielland waved her apology away. "Processing traffic reports?"

"My exciting life." Frida smiled and went over to get a coffee from the machine.

"It's funny you should say that." Kielland moved away from his door and followed his junior officer over to the percolator. "We have had a report of a man with a gun on the *Flåmsbana* just now."

Frida paused in her coffee making and turned, one quizzical eyebrow raised. "You're kidding."

"Apparently another man was assaulted. Finnish tourist." Kielland indicated two unoccupied desks nearby. "I sent Julie and Øyvind down there to take a statement.

"A gun?" Frida was still taken aback. "A rifle?"

"No. This wasn't a hunting incident. He had a pistol! Attacked this guy at Kjosfossen." Kielland was smiling so broadly he looked like an excited child on Christmas day.

Frida frowned. "That *is* unusual," she said, almost to herself.

"That's an understatement," Kielland said. He had taken the coffee pot from the machine and was pouring two cups. He handed one to Frida. "Perhaps the traffic reports can wait, eh?"

"Julie and Øyvind will have to get on the train back to the waterfall. I should go down there myself. I'll take Peder."

"No rush," Kielland said, slurping his coffee. "They're holding the train and have cancelled the others from Myrdal for the time being." Frida bobbed her head. Whoever was stranded at Kjosfossen wouldn't be going anywhere.

CHAPTER 9

Tilson was lying in the snow. He had exited the last tunnel above the town some time earlier and had climbed the nearest slope to scan the terrain with the Steiner 10x50 Military Marine Binoculars that he'd brought with him in his backpack. They weren't standard Royal Marines or SBS issue by any means, but they were his personal preference and had seen some action over the years.

Now they were surveying the quiet, quaint port of Flåm. Really more of a fishing village with incongruous additions the small town was surrounded on three sides by steep mountains and one the far side, opposite Tilson's position, by the innermost shore of the Aurlandsfjord, one of the arms of mighty Sognefjord – the country's longest inlet – that leads, eventually, to the North Sea.

Snaking away beneath him to the north were both the railway line and the road, following the course of the river Flåmselvi. In fact, the river has two names, despite being only some 25 miles long. Where it rises as runoff water from the Omnsbreen glacier near Finse, the river is known as the Moldåni. It then flows through a number of inland lakes before entering the Aurland Municipality. Here it becomes the Flåmselvi and its mouth flows into Aurlandsfjord.

The Flåm watercourse is one of the few major remaining watercourses in the region that has not been purloined for the production of hydroelectricity. That said, there are two smaller power plants in the river. Tilson's earlier stop off – the Kjosfossen waterfall has a generator at its peak that provides electricity for the Railway. There is also an old power plant in the lower part of the river at Leinafoss which has been rebuilt. But both these are small affairs. Nothing like the bigger, dammed power stations one imagines.

Nestling in the middle of the river valley was the unmistakable silhouette of the *Kyrkje*. Norway is famous for its stave churches but although Flåm Church is not one of them and was only built in 1670 it is built on the site of a stave church and using materials from the old building that dated back to early Fourteenth Century.

This little structure with its pointy wooden steeple and surrounding graveyard was Tilson's interim destination. He wanted to use it as a staging post for his approach to the house that belonged to the British diplomat whose papers he was there to retrieve.

Tilson smiled. Such a seemingly easy task. And yet it had become almost murderous and certainly fraught in the last 24 hours. He hoped that by showing his hand, the GRU agent had taken himself out of the game because he was probably still being interviewed by the police. It helped level the playing field a tiny bit and Tilson knew he would need every advantage he could get to successfully complete his mission.

He'd already lost the ability to use his phone. The last thing he needed now was to be identified by the authorities. Usually, he would have waited for darkness to gain entry to the house, but Tilson had decided that time was now against him. He had to get in as soon as he could, find the papers, and then get as far away as possible from the area – preferably back to the UK – before any of this blew up further.

He stood and checked his watch. According to the Omega it was already fast approaching 12pm. He estimated it would take him about half an hour to reach the church and then a further 15 minutes to get to the house. He should be there by 1pm. If he could find what he was after quickly. He'd be out of there by early afternoon.

The tricky part would be getting away from Flåm afterwards. There's no way he could take the train and he imagined that there would be police looking for him or at least have APBs out for him at car hire offices and the like. One option was to steal a car. Perhaps Malcolm Fox had an old Saab or similar in his garage and the keys would be nestled beside his personal papers. Then again, perhaps not.

Half smiling at this flight of fancy, Tilson began to trudge down the hillside towards the road. Without his phone to check in, he just hoped someone was watching over him.

***

On the fourth floor of Thames House, the ICE team had been trying to raise Tilson on his mobile for some time. They hadn't been calling the iPhone but sending slightly cryptic text messages that had become increasingly worried in tone over time. Anne was brooding at the back of the room as Ebony's fingers flew across the keyboard of her computer, a few feet away.

Something told Anne she may have been a bit harsh with her rookie recruit. She had not reminded herself that he may be new, but in fact Sam Tilson was no rookie. His Royal Marine Commando training and experience in the battlefield spoke to that. Able to take the silence no longer, she stepped forward.

"Any luck, Ebony?"

"Just coming," she replied.

She collected herself and looked at some notes hastily scrobbled on an A4 pad. "We knew he was meant to be on the first train from Myrdal this morning, but we also know that he didn't make it to the end of the one at Flåm. Or at least his phone didn't. The last GPS location we have for its signal is in Myrdal, but I know that the train makes a tourist stop in the mountains to take pictures of the scenery and especially a waterfall up there."

Ebony hit the return button with a flourish and sat back. Images began to pop up on her screen. They all showed a snowy railway platform taken from different angles alongside photos of the waterfalls, and even the tunnels and the train.

"I pulled these from social media – all uploaded in the last twelve hours," Ebony said.

"There 'e is!" Camille spoke up, pointing over Ebony's shoulder.

Sure enough, they could all see Tilson in the background of someone's holiday snap. He was peering up at something; perhaps he was gazing at the waterfall. They then spotted him or his coat or boots in other shots.

"Who's the man in the green coat? He's kept close to Sam, hasn't he?" It was Hazel. They all turned to look at him except Anne who was already scanning the digital images. She could see the same man with the black hair several times over.

"You're right!" she said. "Well done. Yes, he's always watching Sam and never looking at the view."

"Nice one, Gary!" Camille added.

This must have been the tail that she had dismissed as Sam being skittish. Everyone knew it but no one said a thing.

"I'll have to apologise when he gets back," Anne said quietly. "Until then, we need to find him. He's clearly in danger just as I suspected."

"I can do a similar search for images at Flåm station," Ebony suggested.

"Please do so. And save all those images that have this man – or Sam – in them. Cross reference with our database, Let's see if this tail is known to us."

Once more Ebony went to work, filling in search parameters and drawing on the dredging software GCHQ utilised when they needed to trawl social media.

"Should someone go out there?" Hazel again. "Or perhaps we should let the high-ups know we need help?"

Anne looked at him. "I appreciate your concern, Gareth. But you know this department hangs by a thread. If we let the high ups know we can't handle what's supposed to be a simple retrieval mission, we'll be shut down before you can say 'knife'. I presume you don't want that?"

"No," Hazel replied suitably crestfallen.

"No," Anne repeated. "But I'll consider your proposal to send a second asset. Thank you."

Hazel looked up. She'd saved his blushes.

"Here we go," Ebony had finished her search and once more images were appearing on her screen. But these were not of peaceful, fun-seeking travellers.

"Oh dear," Camille said. "That doesn't look good."

The screen was showing picture after picture of a police car, two officers and a general hubbub around the train. The man with the black hair was clearly visible talking with the police. But of Sam, there was absolutely no sign.

"Right," said Anne. "I'm sending one of you out there. We haven't got time to put together a legend or any kind of cover, so you'll have to travel as yourself. First flight to Bergen, then hire a car. Get to Flåm as soon as possible. Break the speed limit. I don't care."

Hazel looked hopefully at Anne.

"Who are you sending?" he asked.

***

A red house once meant you were from Scandinavia's upper classes, because they built their homes with red bricks. So, red paint made a wooden house seem wealthy, even if the owners weren't. For this reason, red became popular, and then became merely a tradition that people followed with no real inkling as to why.

Only one of the five houses Tilson was looking at from the church across the river was red. The other four were white, almost camouflaged against the snowy backdrop of the forest which climbed the valley sides behind them.

His target – the house belonging to the diplomat Malcolm Fox – was right in the middle of the five, its side facing the river and the frontage being to the right. In the drive stood a small, pale blue car. Tilson doubted that it was the sort of vehicle Fox would have driven, but he could have been making assumptions.

As the coast seemed clear enough, Tilson left the sanctuary of the church and made his way calmly to the bridge just upstream of the houses and crossed it. As she did so, he felt the familiar sting of the iced East winds of a Norwegian winter. Even through several layers, they were cold, and on his bare face positively freezing. His breath fogged the air as he walked.

There was no one around as he strode the last few feet to the drive. The car turned out to be a Nissan Leaf, a small electric saloon in two-tone metallic blue with a pearl black roof and door mirrors. It looked quite new. Tilson frowned when he saw it was plugged into a charging point on the wall of the house.

Beyond where the car was parked stood a double garage. Surely that was where any car would have been left by the deceased man? On closer inspection of the ground, Tilson could see that despite a fresh covering of snow in the past hour, the tyre tracks leading from the vehicle were fresh.

Tilson looked up and around at his surroundings. Someone was here.

He grasped the Vektor handgun in his pocket and pressed on up to the front door. Now he could see that it was very slightly ajar. With one final check behind him, Tilson pulled the gun out and gently eased the door open.

Moving swiftly but silently, he entered the house and swept the hall, checking behind the door first. Content that there seemed to be no one in his immediate vicinity, he stopped dead still and listened, cocking his head this way and that to pick up the slightest sound.

Then he heard it. A ragged breath. Muffled but accompanied by a strange squeak. Like an asthmatic mouse. He moved forward, staying light on his feet, ready to react, his weapon held ahead of him in a double grip. No stupid sideways gangster movie posturing for him.

He moved slowly into the living room situated to the right, trying to pinpoint the origin of the weird sound. He checked the room, behind the furniture and curtains, and then proceeded quietly into the kitchen. Immediately, he froze.

On the floor were several drops of blood, and on the side by the sink was a kitchen knife – clearly removed from the wooden stand to one side where a tell-tale slit was missing its incumbent. The blood from the knife was slowly pooling around it and had started pouring into the sink from the draining board.

A small thump came from an upright cupboard in the far left-hand corner, almost making Tilson jump. Instead, he tightened his right-hand grip of the gun, and moved his finger from the trigger guard onto the trigger itself, now poised to fire. Avoiding the red drips on the floor Tilson reached out to the cupboard handle with his left hand, almost at full stretch.

He yanked the door open fast, hoping to take anyone within by surprise. He need not have bothered. Inside was a woman. Fifty, maybe sixty. She had been gagged and was bleeding from a nasty stomach wound no doubt inflicted by the kitchen knife.

She stumbled forward, her breathing rasping and catching in the back of her throat with the squeaking sound Tilson had heard as he entered the house. He caught her and set her softly down beside the cupboard that now only contained a bucket and mop and other cleaning products. Her eyes flickered open and Tilson removed the gag with the slow, gentle movements of a lover.

"Who did this?" he asked in Norwegian.

The woman's eyes began to close. But then she rallied. There was blood everywhere now, including on Tilson's white coverall jacket. She did not have long. There was little point wasting time calling an ambulance when she would have vital information for him. It felt wrong not to, but time was critical.

"A woman," she said and coughed, wincing at the pain. Then she managed to grip Tilson arm. It was very weak, but the gesture was in desperate earnest.

"Tell my *Lille Bjørn* – Helena – I love her."

Tilson nodded. "Of course." He tried a small smile of understanding.

She reciprocated. "Thank you."

"Your attacker," Tilson pressed. "Did he take anything?"

The woman shook her head. "She," she corrected him. "She asked me about the diaries."

"Are they here?"

The woman looked at him with suddenly fully alert eyes.

"You can trust me," Tilson said. "I worked with Malcolm."

"She searched," the cough came again, and they both knew she was close to the end. "But they're not here," she wheezed. "Malcolm asked me to hide –"

With one final convulsion, blood spewed from her mouth and across Tilson's face. He ignored it and slowly eased her to the floor and after a brief pause out of respect, searched her pockets.

He found her driving permit in a small purse along with a set of Nissan car keys and a good old *Kwik Lunsj*. Tilson realised he hadn't eaten for a while and knew he had to keep his blood sugar levels up, so he cleaned his face with a cloth run quickly under the tap, and then devoured the chocolate in three bites.

The licence stated that she was Ingeborg Olsen, confirming that she was indeed the housekeeper that Anthony Gray had mentioned at his briefing. She lived in Flåm. Tilson guessed she cleaned for a few houses around there. Helena he assumed, must be her daughter. He committed her address to memory.

The diaries were not there. Ingeborg had hidden them. But where? The only thing he could possibly do was find Helena and give her Ingeborg's last message. If she didn't know where the diaries were then this was over.

Before he could make a move though, his heart froze once again. The wail of police sirens cut through the eerie silence of the blood-smeared kitchen. And they were getting closer. Of course. Whoever had stabbed Ingeborg knew Tilson was going to the same place. He was about to be framed for murder.

CHAPTER 10

Frida Skardet regarded the man sitting in the stationmaster's office. He looked like a thug. Slightly oily, thinning black hair, a hook nose, and tiny, close-set eyes. He also had a large frame – a barrel chest – making him look dangerous and powerful.

When she'd worked in Bergen, she'd seen his sort a hundred times or more. Eastern European, short black hair, inched features, huge head. She wondered if this was racial profiling. She decided it probably was. She dismissed the thought and was quietly angry with herself. Her strong moral code and passion for the truth were joint drivers of her life and career. If there was a difference, she joked to herself.

The alleged victim, sitting nursing a cup of coffee from the restaurant, was – apparently – a Finnish citizen by the name of Antti Isotalo. He had already given a statement to Constable Øyvind Iden and she'd read it.

According to the report, he had been accosted by the man – English, he thought – at Kjosfossen and taken into the tunnel behind the train. There the man held him at gunpoint with some form of automatic handgun – Antti was no expert, he said.

When the train pulled away the man had demanded money, jewellery, and any other valuables. He had handed everything to him, and he was sure the Englishman was about to shoot him when the train returned, and the assailant ran away up the hill towards the waterfall.

Part of being a police officer – especially a detective – was an instinct for things. Frida was known for her no-nonsense attitude and her eye for detail. She liked to question suspects and witnesses alike, always trying to get to the bottom of every case but treating everyone equally. That fact of the matter was that until proven otherwise, she didn't trust anyone. And this story reeked of utter bullshit. Of course she couldn't prove that was the case, but she wanted to keep Herr Isotalo in her sights for a while yet. It all seemed so improbable.

The Norwegian Police University College is the central educational institution for the police service in Norway. Basic training for police officers is a three-year university college education aimed at providing a broad practical and theoretical foundation.

The College has a comprehensive education programme. The key areas are policing tasks, crime investigation and prevention, along with prosecution and administrative responsibilities, in addition to leadership. Research at the Norwegian Police University College comprises both short and long-term projects and is concentrated on police duties, the effects of policing, the role of the police, and other aspects of police operations.

While the first and third years of the study programme are taken at the College, the second is a year of on-the-ground training with one of the four wings of the Norwegian Police Service. Students are divided into groups at training units in police districts around the country.

For Frida this year on the streets had been with the Norwegian Police Security Service in Bergen. The *Politiets Sikkerhetstjeneste* (PST), is further subdivided into various units dealing with counter-intelligence, counter-terrorism, counter-proliferation and organized crime.

There is also a counter-extremism unit, investigation unit, surveillance unit, technology unit, security analysis unit and foreign citizens unit. In addition, the PST is in charge of all VIP protection domestically and abroad. The body reports directly to the Ministry of Justice and is – in essence – very similar to the UK's MI5.

Part of Frida's time was spent in the counterintelligence unit and part in the organized crime unit. That's why she had seen men like the one sitting before her many times. And that was why she was certain he was an illegal. The Finnish passport was perfect, and maybe it was genuine, but she suspected that the black-haired bear of a man was in actuality a Russian. Either part of the Mafia or a member of their security services. Or both. The lines were easily blurred.

She moved across the room and delicately pulled the chair away from the desk before arranging herself deliberately on its cushioned seat. The thug looked up at her dispassionately. Then he tried a wan smile and Frida returned the gesture.

"Herr... Isotalo," she began, letting him know she was either having difficulty with the name or the veracity of it. "I am Inspector Skardet. I just want to check a few details of your statement."

He nodded. "Of course," he said. His expression had not changed, Still the dumb half smile, trying to project innocence and a lack of experience in all this criminality. She'd seen that hundreds of times, too.

"You say that your alleged assailant was English. A UK national. Is that right?"

"Yes."

"How do you know?"

"His accent was not good," The Russian said. His own Norwegian accent wasn't that good either, but it certainly wasn't English.

"I see. Anything else?"

"He swore in English when the train returned," the man said.

"And you can speak English?"

"Yes. I watch all the history romance shows. *Downtown Abbey*. *Bridgington*." Frida smiled. This was the most implausible thing she had ever heard and getting the names slightly wrong was a bit of a giveaway, but she had to commend him for it. If he hadn't had a face that spoke of punch-ups and knife fighting it would certainly have made him seem genuine. However, she didn't recall much swearing in *Downton Abbey*.

"Me, too," she lied.

"And you say this British attacker was going to shoot you before the train came back?"

"Yes."

"Why would he do that?"

"I do not know. I am not a mugger."

She nodded.

"Thank you, she said. "I'd like to keep you here in case the man returns. He sounds like a dangerous type."

The man shook his head. "No. I must be going on with my holiday. I am meeting friends. I will be safe."

"Are your friends here?"

"Nearby – up the coast."

Frida was about to terminate the interview when the door to the office burst open. It was constable Solberg. She was wild-eyed.

"Inspector, there has been another incident," she said breathlessly. "A murder!"

***

In the Kitchen of Malcom Fox's house, Tilson returned to the cupboard where Ingeborg had been hidden and retrieved a bottle of *Jif* surface cleaner and a cloth. His nose was filled with the sickly-sweet smell of fake "pine forest" as he hurriedly wiped down the surfaces he had touched. The smell of death was also beginning to permeate the air and he knew he had to get out of the house as quickly as possible.

The sirens were now so close it sounded like the car was in the next room. Tilson replaced the cleaning fluid and pocketed the slightly blood-stained cloth. That done, he darted to the back door, the furthest from the sound, and fumbled with the keys to open it.

Then, taking the keys in case he needed to return he dashed through the door and locked it from the outside. Taking huge – almost comical – strides so as not to disturb the snow on the ground too much, he made for the treeline of pines that stretched up the hillside behind the house.

His heart raced as he ducked into the shadows of the trees and leant up against a trunk in the secondary row of trees, breathing hard. The police car was approaching fast, its flashing lights illuminating the forest in blue and red. He breathed a sigh of relief that he'd made it out ahead of their arrival.

After a few seconds, he heard the car come to a halt and the siren was suddenly silenced. He risked looking over his shoulder, around the tree. He saw the Norwegian Police Volvo and three people jumping out. Two were women, one blonde and one older, darker with a bobbed cut. She reminded Tilson of the actress Tamsin Greig. The third person was a man with reddish hair.

The older woman started pointing and the younger officers followed her instructions, one moving around the building to the back door while the other moved up the steps to the open front door. Both had their sidearms drawn.

The female constable was now only about forty feet away from Tilson, but she was focused on the house. He tried to steady his breathing as it was causing small short-lived clouds of condensation to form in the air – something the police officer might well spot. In the end, he brought a gloved hand up to his mouth and breathed into the material to dissipate his exhalations.

Then there came a shout from inside the house. The male officer had obviously found Ingeborg's body. The female constable near him ran to the back door now but found it locked and so sprinted round the front to help her colleague.

When all three police officers were out of sight, Tilson knew he had to move quickly. He had to get out of the area before they discovered him. The only leads he had were still Helena Olsen and her mother's address from the driving license. He'd have to find both before the day was over but to do so he would need the cover of night.

With no further hesitation, Tilson took off, running through the trees, his feet pounding the snow, and the branches whipping at his face and clothes. Once he stumbled and nearly fell on a hidden tree root, but he was able to keep his balance and continue moving. He could see the lights of the cars in the distance, and he hastened his pace. The trees seemed to stretch on endlessly, and he felt as if he'd never escape the shadows, but he reached the proper outskirts of Flåm within an hour. Then, he cautiously came down the valley and emerged behind a row of shops, their bins neatly lined up and cardboard stacked beside with a light dusting of snow on them.

The sky was beginning to darken, and he checked his Omega. Just gone half three. He reckoned sunset should be less than 15 minutes away. He took the Hard Ware rucksack from his back and then removed the white coverall jacket. He folded this neatly and crammed it on top of all his other equipment. His black North Face Coldworks parka would be better suited to moving about in the shadows than a bright white jacket, after all.

Even so, he had to be careful. He had to make sure he wasn't followed and that no one noticed him. He kept his head low, and his eyes peeled, staying off the beaten path and in the shadows before he hit upon a store that sold clothing. He bought a blue bobble hat that matched the one his skinny woman tail had worn. It made him appear less sinister and matched a lot of people on the streets.

He realised as he left the shop that he was feeling quite drained. He could also feel the early warning signs of a hypo approaching. He hadn't eaten well since breakfast and the chocolate bar he'd found in Ingeborg's purse was wearing thin. Tilson knew he needed a proper meal, preferably a high carb one.

The problem was that most of the restaurants or cafes were very much centred on the railway station. Not somewhere Tilson fancied being as no doubt there was a police presence there, too.

Instead, he walked down the small road – Nedre Brekkevegen – to where a slip road led up to the E16, a far more major road. Although pedestrians were not supposed to use it, Tilson only had to walk a couple of hundred metres over the river to where the road disappeared into the hillside and brightly lit tunnel.

To his right was a glass barrier, preventing people from jumping. But this vanished where it met the rocky slope. All he had to do was vault the low wall and make his way down the gentle incline to the unencumbered railway track. Crossing that took him onto the smaller street that led away from town along the coast.

His chosen route did take him within a few hundred metres of the train station, but it was just far enough away that no one paid him any attention. One thing that did surprise Tilson was the sight of a huge cruise ship moving up the fjord beyond, heading to make port in Flåm.

He knew this was a popular tourist destination, but he had forgotten that the deep Fjords make it possible for ocean-going liners to come quite a way inland. And its arrival meant that very soon the town would be flooded with more tourists, making the police's work of finding him next to impossible.

The street changed its name as it bent around the bay. Now Vikjavegen it led away from the centre of the town towards the marina. And nestled on the shore next to it was the Marina restaurant. It was quite upmarket, but it was busy.

Adopting an American accent of dubious origin, Tilson asked for a table for two, saying his wife would be joining him. After a suitable pause, he told the waitress that she was feeling ill and was staying in her room. As such he'd be ordering on his own. Making suitably sympathetic noises, she fetched him a menu.

CHAPTER 11

As Tilson finished his meal, Inspector Frida Skardet was sitting in her car outside the Olsen residence, preparing herself to do something she'd only ever done twice before: break the news to someone that a loved one had died. She had never met Helena, but she knew her by reputation. She was one of the best hunters in the region.

Norway has an enduring culture of hunting. The country's wild reaches offer the ideal atmosphere to practice this time-honoured tradition. Hunting is seen as commonplace and perfectly dovetails with the hearty Norwegians' enthusiasm for the great outdoors. In fact, Norway ranks fourth in the global count of hunters per capita, behind Canada, Finland, and Cyprus.

This can be attributed to the ease of getting to wilderness areas and the past reliance on hunting for sustenance in the face of harsh winters and short, cool summers. The number of active hunters in Norway has stayed around 140,000 for the last two decades, and those who wish to hunt must register in the Norwegian Register of Hunters and pay the fee of about £50 for a hunting licence.

All hunters must provide paperwork showing qualification for hunting in their home country or pass the Norwegian hunting and shooting tests. Additionally, they have to have permission from the landowner before they can hunt.

Helena not only helped local farmers and foresters thin their population of red deer, but she also worked with several of them on the tourist circuit, taking out wealthy Americans and Australians mostly to stalk Moose or whatever large game they could find and had paid for the privilege of shooting.

As she walked up the path from her car up to the three-storey apartment building, Frida also reflected on the other events of the day. The alleged attack on the obvious Russian agent. So many questions there. But her main concern was about the motive. Why mug one person? Why use a gun? Why this one victim in particular? There was far more at play here. The only thing she did believe about the story was the fact the other man involved was British.

It was simply too much of a coincidence that on the same day that this very odd crime should occur, a woman should be killed in the home of another Englishman, albeit this time a dead one. And a relatively well known one in the area.

Like many small towns across the planet, nothing happened in Flåm without all the locals knowing about it or discussing it in the local hostelries. Even she knew of Malcolm Fox. Ex bigwig British diplomat involved in the arms industry and acting as an adviser to their very own *Blodøks* Industries that had a compound up the valley further inland.

This was her patch. Rural, quiet. She dealt with RTA incidents involving people who were usually related, the odd drunk and disorderly friend, and maybe a DUI every now and again. Very few drugs, very little organised crime and never, ever any cloak and dagger security agencies. Until now.

Frida stopped in front of the double doors and pressed the buzzer for flat 7. With an electric hum and a loud click, the door opened without anyone saying anything on the intercom. The detective climbed the two flights of stairs to level three and found the door to Ingeborg's apartment open.

"Come in, *Mamma*, did you forget your keys again?"

Frida lurked on the threshold of the apartment and called out. "*Hallo*? Helena Olsen?"

A woman appeared in the doorway between the hall and the living room. She was tall – at least six foot three – blonde hair worn long but clearly just released from a grip that she held in her left hand. Statuesque, her young face was already marked somewhat by the harsh conditions in which she plied her trade.

"Who are you?"

"I'm Detective Frida Skardet. May I come in?"

Helena bobbed her head and turned into the living room. "Close the door behind you. Don't want the heat escaping!"

She was wearing blue jeans, thick, cream socks and a strappy vest that had clearly had a sweater of some description over the top as the pattern was still imprinted on her skin. Frida did as she was asked and then followed Helena.

The room she found herself in was decorated with animal hides and mounted heads. A traditional Norwegian rug – a *rya* patterned in red, black and white – covered the floor, and two settees faced one another across a simple pine coffee table. Each had sheepskins thrown on them and several comfy cushions scattered along their lengths. Helena was pouring herself a beer from a small fridge hidden in the sideboard. "You don't mind?"

Frida smiled and shook her head. "Shall we sit down?"

"I was just going to!" The tall woman collapsed onto one of the sofas and sipped the beer.

"I'm afraid I have bad news," Frida began. Helena's neutral face fell, and her brow furrowed – several lines appearing on her forehead and around her starling blue eyes. "It's your mother. Ingeborg."

Helena gasped and her right hand came up involuntarily to cover her mouth.

"I'm so sorry. She's... passed on."

Frida had already decided what to tell her. Helena just looked at her as if not comprehending what was happening.

"She was killed in what we think was a burglary."

"I thought it was about my gun permits or something," Helena mumbled. She removed her hand from her mouth and was suddenly as icy as the beer she reached for. She took a swig and then asked, "Who did it?"

"We don't know. We received an anonymous call from a woman about an Englishman in the house of Malcolm Fox." Helena nodded. "She cleaned for him." A single tear rolled down her cheek and stopped in the furrows around her mouth. "A British guy?"

"We don't know for sure. That is what we were told. We are investigating. Rest assured we will find whoever is responsible."

Frida reached forward and stretched her hand out to touch Helena on the knee. "Again, I am so very sorry."

"I will kill this man," Helena said, staring out of the large window that ran across one wall into the premature darkness beyond.

Although Frida dismissed the statement as that of a bereaved daughter, she totally believed the young woman. The police detective simply nodded in understanding and stood, leaving Helena sitting on the sofa, nursing her beer, her grief and her anger.

***

As he sat at his table, Tilson felt a sense of relief wash over him. He had finally found someone with the same model and colour of iPhone as his, and he was determined to get it back. He had been watching the bar at the Marina restaurant for what seemed like hours, nursing the last dregs of his Diet Coke, hoping for someone to come in with the same Midnight Blue phone that had been smashed earlier that day. Just as he was about to give up and leave, his patience finally paid off.

The woman who walked in was middle-aged, with greying frizzy hair and a pair of designer bifocals. She was petite with a chiselled bone structure. She seemed completely unaware of her surroundings as she took a seat on one of the four barstools to await her table.

Tilson couldn't believe his luck as he watched her swipe through her messages and updates on her phone. He knew that this was his chance, and he was not going to let it slip away. As he stood, a minor prickling sensation of guilt crossed Tilson's mind, but he needed a phone and he had to get one without drawing the attention of the police.

He approached the bar, nonchalantly, making sure not to catch the woman's eye. Instead, he focussed on the huge model yacht that stood on a shelf beside the optics of gin, vodka, whisky and so on, trying to give a semblance of being transfixed.

Just as he'd hoped, the woman looked up at him when he got close enough. He pretended not to notice for a couple of seconds and then gave her his best, most charming smile. She almost blushed but managed a coy smile in return while brushing a non-existent stand of hair behind her right ear.

"I'm sorry," Tilson said, still affecting his nondescript American accent. Her smile broadened.

"A fellow American!" she said with a light Texas drawl.

Shit. She was bound to detect he was a fake. He nodded and smiled.

"Did you see this yacht, here, ma'am?" he asked. She looked over her shoulder at the model. "Isn't it magnificent?"

"You like boats?" the woman asked. "I just got off one! That big doozy in the harbour there."

Again, Tilson nodded, now doubting his accent even more.

"Could I ask you a favour?"

"By all means, Mister...?"

"Sam, please." He held out his hand and she took it.

"Another coincidence! My name's Sam. Although mine's short for Samantha, which I doubt yours is!" "Could you take a photo of me with the boat?" He looked down, feigning sudden reserve. "The model one, I mean!"

She laughed easily as he proffered the broken phone. Samantha took it and Tilson pretended to pose, moving very close to the bar where her own phone lay face up.

She brought the iPhone up to her eye but then frowned. She lowered the device and raised an eyebrow. "I think you need to turn this on."

Tilson couldn't help grinning at the inuendo, but the American just stared at him, unaware of what was funny. Samantha handed the phone back to Tilson. He went to take it but then let it fall through his grasp, hitting her phone and sending them both to the floor.

"Oh no," he said, quickly squatting down. "I am. *So*. Clumsy..."

He stood up and placed one of the phones back on the bar. Then he leant forward. "Thank you, Samantha," he said. "I'm so grateful."

He went to move away but then suddenly turned back. "Do you mind if I take a picture of you? For the holiday album."

She looked a bit taken aback at this but then shrugged. "Sure. Why not?"

"Then give me your best side!" Tilson said and took a photo with her own phone that he was now making out was his. No fingerprint of face recognition is needed to do this. The phone made a clicking sound and Tilson stood back. "Something to remember you by, Sam," he whispered.

Now she was startled but managed an awkward, unprepared smile. The camera clicked again.

At that moment, a young male waiter appeared. "Your table, madame."

"Thank you," Tilson whispered and turned to move from the bar, leaving the confused Samantha in his wake.

Once outside, he walked swiftly away from the restaurant and was in the treeline in a matter of moments. No one followed him so he assumed she hadn't looked at the broken phone. For his part, Tilson quickly checked out the thumbnail of the image he had taken in the bottom left of the phone's screen. He pressed on I and it expanded to fill the screen. Now all he needed was a mirror and he'd be into her phone, by-passing the facial recognition lock. He hoped that he would find one where he was going next.

Hjemme Hus was a long, white building of three storeys, and home to eight different apartments, one of which belonged to the Olsens. It was literally only a stone's throw away from the popular Marina restaurant, and Tilson walked there in under two minutes.

He was about to cross the road in high spirits given the benefits of his hearty meal and the acquisition of a new phone, but he stopped dead in his tracks.

Under the solitary streetlight to the building's south facing aspect was parked a Norwegian Police Volvo V90CC patrol car. He ducked back into the treeline to see what would happen. He did not have to wait long. The older woman – the senior police officer, the Tamsin Grieg lookalike – appeared at the door to the building and approached the car, clicking the central locking on the key fob from a distance of a few feet. She climbed in. Sat for a moment.

Tilson watched closely. Was she crying? Then Tamsin turned and key, smoothly engaged her seatbelt and pulled away.

Tilson gave it a few minutes and then resumed his approach to *Hjemme Hus* with less of a spring in his step. The address he had from the driving license had said apartment 7. So, he pressed the buzzer beside that number and waited. There was a long pause.

"Who is it?" a deep but lyrical voice asked in Norwegian.

"Helena? My name is Sam Tilson. I was with your mother when she died."

Another long pause.

"You'd better come up, then. Third floor."

The door buzzed and Sam entered, cautiously taking the stairs, aware this could be a trap.

In a bizarre mimicry of the house he'd entered when finding Ingeborg, the door to the flat was slightly ajar. Tilson pushed it open gingerly with the splayed fingers of his left hand. His right hand was inside the pocket of his North Face jacket, clutching the Vektor.

"Helena?" he called.

"In here!"

Tilson followed her voice down the hall and into the living room beyond. Facing him was a woman of a similar age to him but of what he would describe as Amazonian proportions. Fierce, blue eyes regarded him with loathing and a slight sneer spoiled her otherwise beautiful, rugged good looks.

She was holding a Sauer 404 lightweight bolt-action hunting rifle tight to her right shoulder. It was levelled directly at Tilson. She thumbed the safety catch behind the bold and her finger tightened on the trigger.

"I swore I would kill whoever murdered my mother."

CHAPTER 12

"You only get one chance," Tilson said evenly. "So make sure you shoot the right person."

Helena looked suddenly uncertain.

"The Police said you were at the scene," Helena hissed. "You killed her."

"No," he said emphatically. "No, I didn't."

"I do not believe you."

"She gave me a message. She said, 'Tell Helena I love her'."

The young blonde woman's eyes narrowed. "An obvious thing to say. This will not save you, Englishman."

"She used a nickname. *Lille Bjorn*. 'Little bear'."

Helena frowned as if she didn't understand what was happening. Then she relaxed, he shoulders sagging, and she looked away, out of the blackened window, wondering what to do next.

"I promised her I would deliver the message."

Helena loosened her grip on the trigger.

"*Lille Bjorn*," she repeated in a hushed whisper. Then she sniffed and stood up, placing the rifle back into safe mode. "OK. Talk."

"I shouldn't be telling you this, but I work for the British Security Service."

"You are a spy?"

"I just came her to get Malcolm Fox's diaries," he said.

"I see..." Helena was frowning again. "And these 'Russians'?"

"I think they're here for the same reason. Two of them at least. A man and woman. I think one of them killed your mother."

Tilson took a deep breath before continuing, knowing that Helena was still sceptical and on edge. He needed to gain her trust and convince her to help him in his mission.

"Look, I know it may be hard for you to believe, but I'm telling you the truth," he said, his voice calm and steady. He placed one hand on his heart. "Honestly.

"The Russians are after those diaries for some reason. I don't know why. I don't know what was in them, but they must think they're worth getting hold of."

"Worth killing *Mamma* for," Helena said bitterly, bowing her head.

"The contents of those diaries may be something that could be dangerous in the wrong hands," Tilson said. "Something your mother, I think, knew. Which is why she didn't tell them."

Helena's expression softened slightly, but she still held onto her rifle tightly. "And what does this have to do with her anyway?"

Tilson hesitated. "I have no idea, but I wonder if your mum and Fox were... close?" Helena snapped her head up to stare at him, pulling a face. "Or she was just in the wrong place at the wrong time. The Russians came looking for the diaries and she ended up being killed.

But Fox entrusted her with the diaries, she said. Asked he her to hide them for him."

Helena lowered her gun, placing it beside her, but still kept a cautious eye on him. "Why should I trust you?" "No reason really," Tilson said with an open-palmed gesture. "But we have a common enemy. The Russians killed your mother, and they will stop at nothing to get what they want. If they suspect Fox gave the diaries to Ingeborg, then they may come here."

"Then I shall give them the same welcome," Helena said, patting her rifle.

"Do you know where your mum would have hidden the diaries?"

"No."

"Do you know if there were any copies made?"

"No."

"An electronic version?"

Helena exploded from the sofa, holding her blonde hair tight to her head, eyes squeezed shut momentarily. "Stop, stop, stop!"

Tilson fell silent, feeling suitably abashed. "I'm sorry." He said quietly.

Helena sat down once more, hunched over.

"She didn't tell me anything," she said. "I knew something was going on!"

Then she pressed her hands together almost in prayer. Tilson sat down on the sofa opposite.

"Really. I'm sorry for all this. I am."

Helena looked at him and he could see she was momentarily grateful for the sympathy. In the five minutes he'd spent with her, one thing he did know was that the young Norwegian woman's expressions were often inscrutable.

"Okay, Englishman," she said coming to a decision. "I will help you. But if you are lying, I will not hesitate to pull this trigger."

Tilson let out a silent sigh of relief. He knew he still had a lot to prove, but at least he had Helena on his side now.

"Thank you."

"It will not help us make these diaries magically appear, though," she added. "But we can look together."

Tilson and Helena sat in silence for a moment, both lost in their own thoughts. The weight of the situation hung heavy in the air, the danger they were in becoming more palpable as the seconds drained away. He knew they needed to act fast if they were going to find those diaries and get out alive.

He looked at Helena studying her features carefully. She was tough and resilient, that much was clear. But he also saw something else in her eyes? Pain? Grief? That certainly made sense. He couldn't help but feel sorry for her. She had lost her mother and was now caught up in this dangerous game of espionage.

"I promise I'll do everything in my power to find those diaries and get us out of here safely," he said, breaking the silence.

Helena nodded, her expression still guarded. "I believe you. But we still need a plan."

Tilson bobbed his head in agreement.

"Did your mother give the diaries to you?"

Helena pulled a non-plussed expression and blew her cheeks out. "No," she said and shook her head. "Why would she say that?"

Tilson stared out of the window, but a ghostly reflection of his own face stared back. And across from him, the ghost of Helena "No, she didn't say that," he said. "She'd never place you in danger, would she?"

"Yes, that's true," she said as if it hadn't occurred to her before.

"She could have said anything to send me on a cold trail."

Helena nodded approvingly. "You think like a hunter."

"She must have thought you would know where to look," he said. "Is there anything you can think of?"

Helena sighed.

"The only thing I discovered was that she cleaned Herr Fox's office as well. I don't know if that means they were having an affair, but it might have given them an excuse to be together more?"

Tilson frowned. "In his house?"

Helena shook her head. "No. He had an office in the *Blodøks* compound – just down the road."

Tilson translated the word in his head. Blood Axe. A famous Viking warrior.

"Is that a company? The one he was working for?"

"Yes. It's a technology company. Some say an arms dealer," she tutted. "Whatever. It builds components for naval and maritime navigation systems."

"You sound like a Wikipedia page!"

She looked at her feet. "I just know these things," she sounded guilty.

"It's fine," he said. "Thank you. All useful information."

Suddenly, Tilson was on his feet. Helena looked at him with a raised eyebrow.

"You're going there? Now?"

"I can't let the Russians get the drop on me," Tilson said. "And this is the only time since I got to Norway I've felt ahead of the game."

Helena stood, picking up her rifle. "Then I am coming with you."

"No, I don't think – "

She cut him off. "I was not asking permission, Englishman."

Tilson let a wry smile cross his lips. "It's 'Sam', by the way," he said.

***

The *Blodøks* industrial compound was a stark contrast to the idyllic Norwegian countryside, with its sprawling grey warehouse and imposing chain-link fence. The office windows, positioned at one end of the building, were a small token of humanity in an otherwise sterile and colourless space.

Despite their efforts to hide it behind newly planted conifers, the building seemed to loom over the valley like a slumbering giant, casting its shadow over the nearby river Flåmselvi.

Every day at dusk, the security lights flickered on, casting an eerie glow over the compound. The once unassuming and out-of-the-way building was bathed in a harsh orange light, allowing the CCTV cameras that dotted the perimeter to see at night. These silent sentinels stood guard; their watchful electronic eyes scanning constantly for any potential intruders.

It was clear that *Blodøks* Industries took security very seriously and were willing to do whatever it took to protect their investment.

As they drove to the compound in Helena's battered, dark grey RAV 4 from 2013, she told Tilson all she knew about the place, which wasn't much.

"Some claim it is a secret government facility, conducting experiments on unsuspecting citizens," she said, staring through the windscreen. "Others believe it is a front for a powerful criminal organisation to hide their illegal activities."

She shot Tilson a look because she could no doubt feel his sceptical gaze.

"You think the English-speaking world has the monopoly on conspiracy theory nutjobs?" She gave a slight laugh. "I am a professional hunter. I meet more survivalists who want to hide in a cabin or a bunker than you have had your hot meals."

Tilson laughed now. "I bet."

Despite the moment of levity, he couldn't shake off the feeling of unease he'd had since leaving Oslo. He still had no idea really what was going on. He was grasping at straws. The diaries were clearly hot property, but had anyone in MI5 known that when he was sent to recover them? And how did the Russians already know he was coming? This was a dangerous mission, and he couldn't afford to let his guard down.

He glanced at Helena, who was driving steadily with a determined look on her face. He couldn't deny that he was grateful to have her by his side. They reached the foot of the access road leading up to the compound, Tilson signalled for them to stop.

"We should go on by foot," he said.

Helena parked the Toyota like a pro; she drove it across the snow-covered grass and up against the trees, its grey bulk now hidden in the shadows. They both grabbed their packs from the back of the car and Helena took her rifle, slinging it over her shoulder. Tilson checked the clip of ammunition in the Vektor. It was full: fifteen rounds of 9mm held in a staggered formation.

They nodded to each other and set off up the slope, keeping to the shadows afforded by the pines. It only took a few minutes to climb the incline, so they were in range of the gates. Helena used the Zeiss sights from her rifle while Tilson used his trusty Steiner 10x50 Military Marine Binoculars. He could see guards patrolling the area, and the security looked tight.

"Let's skirt round," he said in a low voice. "You go down here, I'll head round the other way. We need a blind spot."

She bobbed he head, shouldered her rifle, and set off even more silently than Tilson himself. The footfall of a hunter.

As they separated, the guards in their black uniforms, thick coats and furry hats seemed oblivious. Tilson darted across the road and down into a drainage ditch. This gave him perfect cover as he approached the perimeter. Every now and again he would stand back to be able to look over the parapet and check his position. Satisfied that the guards weren't looking his way or that the lenses wouldn't reflect the security light and give him away, he'd scan the fence with the binoculars.

He continued to do this as he was forced to abandon the ditch and clamber to slightly higher ground on the same level as the compound itself. Fortunately, there only seemed to the two guards on the main gate and no patrols. Just over halfway round, Helena came up behind him, silent as an owl in flight. She almost startled him, but he wasn't going to give her the satisfaction of knowing that.

"Anything?" he whispered.

"The fence is the same height all the way around. There are no dark areas. The lights show everything to the cameras," she sighed. "How about you?"

"There's a large yellow bin for gritting the road that's close enough to the fence to use as a way of reaching the top. I'm surprised how big it is."

"They used to be smaller, but we had a problem with vandals," Helena whispered. "They kept tipping them up. Brainless idiots. So, they made them too big to lift – 500 kilos or so." She shrugged "Problem solved."

"Right," Tilson replied. "Well, lucky us. Come on, I'll show you where it is."

Helena followed as Tilson led the way back around the way he'd come and into the ditch once more. When he reached the right section, he stopped. She tapped his shoulder and pointed at the gates, only a couple of dozen feet away.

"You can climb the fence, but you will be seen!"

"We'll need a distraction," Tilson said in hushed tones.

"You want to draw the guards away?"

"Yes, and that's the only way. Over the fence and into the warehouse."

Helena patted his back like an old friend, a mischievous glint in her eyes. "Leave it to me."

Before Tilson could protest, she had taken off her jacket and had placed it on the ground along with her rifle. Then, she tore at her shirt, exposing some flesh above her chest and, without a backward glance, set off towards the guards at a run.

She approached the two men and started shouting to them in rapid Norwegian, gesturing wildly. Tilson couldn't make out what she was saying, but he could see that she was putting on a show. And it seemed to be working. The guards were totally focussed on Helena rather than their surroundings.

Tilson took this opportunity to crawl across the ground between the ditch and the grit box. Then, double checking Helena still had the guards' rapt attention, he vaulted onto the lid of the box and leapt for the fence, getting a double ended grip on the top cable. He hauled himself up and over, to land like a cat on the other side.

However, he was still bathed in the orange glow of the security lights, and then he thought he saw a guard looking his way. Fearing he was discovered, Tilson sprinted for the shadows of the nearby warehouse. He tried to pull the Vektor from his pocket, but it kept catching. He was sure he'd be spotted any minute.

CHAPTER 13

Tilson should have had more faith in Helena. The guards had opened the gates and let her in. One of them had even taken off his coat to drape around her bare shoulders. Then they led her towards the small hut that served as a sentry box during the day, controlling the barrier just inside the gates. Inside she sat down and Tilson thought he could see her crying. He had not had her pegged as quite the actress, but she seemed to be playing the role of a damsel in distress extremely convincingly.

He watched from the shadows as the guards fawned over Helena, completely oblivious to his presence. He couldn't help but smile at her clever ploy. She was clearly resourceful and quick on her feet.

They actually made a good team, she and Tilson. He was grateful once more to have her by his side in this dangerous situation. But he couldn't afford to waste time extolling her virtues. With a deep breath, Tilson focused on the task at hand, stuffing the Vektor back in the pocket, this time making sure it was more easily accessible. He had to find a way into the warehouse and retrieve the diaries before they fell into the wrong - Russian - hands.

He made his way around the warehouse, keeping to the shadows and trying to avoid any security cameras. Tilson knew he'd have to find a way of dealing with their recordings in due course, but as no one had raised the alarm, he assumed no one was monitoring them, so he pressed on.

Soon, he found what appeared to be a back entrance with a porch. He tried one of the doors, but it didn't open. Tilson tried the other door, but it was locked as well. He cursed under his breath, frustration evident in his tense body language. He needed to find a way in and fast. He couldn't risk getting caught and having the diaries slip through his fingers. With a determined expression, Tilson made his way around the building, his senses on high alert. He needed to find a weak spot, a vulnerability in the warehouse's security.

And then it presented itself in the form of Helena and a guard, walking towards the main door. "Thank you for letting me use your bathroom," she was saying, her voice raised, presumably in an effort to let Tilson know what was happening.

"Not a problem," the man replied in accented Norwegian. Tilson couldn't place it. The guard pulled a lanyard from within the black fleece waistcoat he was wearing and tapped it onto a small plinth to one side of the doors. A high-pitched tone of approval sounded in the cold, silent night and the doors swung open.

Tilson quickly made his way towards the open door, slipping inside before it could close again. He found himself in a large reception area, a desk inset with screen showing the camera feeds at its centre. He'd have to deal with them afterwards. Helena was his focus now. She had split the guards up and taking out the one she had brought with her now seemed the obvious thing to do. If Tilson could establish where he was.

Behind the desk, a corridor split in two, going left and right. But which way? It was dark in the building and the guard could be lurking anywhere. Then the tell-tale sound of a toilet flushing told him that they were down the left-hand corridor. Silently, he drew the Vektor, positioned himself behind a tall, potted rubber plant and waited.

"This way," the man said in the darkness and Tilson could suddenly make out a slight silhouette, black on blackness. As he passed the pot plant, Tilson moved out of the shadows and dealt a blow to the back of his head with the Vektor. The guard moaned and collapsed, holding the back of his head. Tilson quickly patted the man down, removing anything and everything from his pockets, finally pulling the lanyard from around his neck.

"What...?" he managed.

"Quiet," Tilson hissed. "Up!"

He grabbed the man's nearest arm and hauled him to his feet. "Now, show me the janitor's coset."

Helena was watching as the drama played out before her. She had done her bit and now Tilson had to do his.

The guard managed to gesture towards the other corridor, mumbling.

"You got your phone?" he asked Helena. "It'd be handy if we could see."

She fished out her phone and switched the torch on. In its harsh light he could see the wall of the corridor and a sturdy door set into it. A sign in Norwegian read: Ancillary Personnel Only.

Tilson held the lanyard to the door mechanism and the latch clicked open. He pulled the door towards him and then thrust the man inside before shutting and locking the closet door once more.

"Come on," Tilson said, getting out the phone he'd taken from Sam in the bar earlier. With it, he lit up the corridor ahead. "Any idea where Fox's office is?"

Helena followed him. "My *mamma* was the one who came here. Not me."

Ahead was a set of double doors with vertical glass slats in them. Shining his torch through one of the windows, Tilson could make out component desks and machinery assembly points. This was the "factory floor", not where the offices would be if the outside of the building and its windows were anything to go by.

"Look!" Helena was pulling at his sleeve. She was pointing her own flashlight at a stairwell, again with a locked door and a touch pad beside it. Hurriedly, Tilson employed the lanyard once more, allowing Helena to pull the door open and head up the stairs, two at a time, Tilson on her heels. On the first floor, she turned to him.

"I'll take this one. You go on up!" she said. Tilson nodded. "How long do you think we have before the other guard comes, Sam?"

"Not long if he's not stupid," he said. And with that he gave an encouraging smile and took off up the next staircase. "Shout if you find anything!"

On the top level, a shorter corridor stretched away to his left, with doors off it on either side. Tilson came to the first one and illuminated it with his torch. It had a name on it. Lars Nilsen. This would make it a hell of a lot easier, he thought, moving onto the next door. Marius Berg. He ran to the next. And the next. No sign of Fox's name.

As he ran down the corridor and almost jumped the whole flight of steps in one leap, Helena called out to him. "Sam, I have found it!"

"Coming!"

She was hovering in the doorway of an office at the far end of the hall, which was longer than one above it. Tilson joined her and together, they swept their phone lights about the room.

"What are we looking for?"

"Any place that he could have hidden some diaries," He replied. "I guess the size of notebooks. A5 maybe? I have no idea what they look like." Tilson made a mental note that the next time he was sent on a wild goose chase he'd find out in advance what the goose looked like.

Together, they combed through the room, checking every possible hiding spot. Drawers, cabinets, under the desk; they searched everywhere. But it seemed like their efforts were in vain.

However, just as they were about to give up hope, Helena noticed something strange while searching the sideboard that ran down one wall of the office.

"One of these isn't as deep as the others," she said, waving her torch at an open cupboard that contained a few bottles of alcohol: gin and whisky as well as the ubiquitous Aquavit.

Upon closer inspection, Tilson could see that she was right. The back panel of wood was only a few inches away from the front. As he watched, she pushed this panel backwards and it came loose.

Urgently, they moved the bottles and Helena lifted the false back away to reveal seven or eight small notebooks, all the thickness of a bar or soap, bound in a dark red material.

She let out a sigh of relief and smiled at Tilson, who smiled warmly back.

"Jackpot!" he said.

Tilson gestured for her to pass him the diaries and she did so, peering over his shoulder as he brought his torch to bear on their pages.

He flipped through the sheet of paper, confirming that they belonged to Malcolm Fox. They did have his name on the front page of each alongside some dates. Each one seemed to cover approximately a year since his retirement from the Joint Intelligence Committee liaison position with the Olso Embassy. He'd have to take a closer look later.

"That's them," he said. This time he smiled at Helena and she smiled back. Tilson's quick thinking and her own determination had paid off. But they couldn't celebrate just yet. They still had to make it out of the building undetected. They found themselves staring at each for just a moment too long. Tilson broke the spell. "Let's go."

He stuffed the diaries into his Hard Ware rucksack and moved to the door, checking the corridor before ensuring Helena was behind him. Then he pressed on, hoping they could avoid another encounter. As they made their way back towards the stairs, Tilson's mind kept flitting back to the fact that he should have been more prepared.

The two of them descended to the ground floor, ready to make their escape before the other guard arrived. But, as they hurried down the stairs, they heard someone calling out in the reception area to his buddy.

"Viggen? Where the hell are you? You better not be shagging that woman!"

They reached the ground floor just as the sound of footsteps approaching echoed along the corridor. The other guard was coming.

Tilson timed his run and barrelled into the other man just as he was coming around the corner from reception. The two men fell to the ground in a tangled heap. Tilson regained his footing first and just as he had with the first guard, he hoisted him to his feet and frog marched him to the janitor's closet.

He asked Helena to open the door with the lanyard and she took it from his neck. The first guard was inside, looking up at them, blinking. Tilson shoved the second man inside to join his partner before slamming the door shut again.

Helena ran off now, heading for the exit.

"Come on!" she yelled; her voice taut with stress.

Tilson followed her into the reception area. "Wait," he hissed, pointing at the desk and its screens. "We've got to wipe the recordings."

He crawled under the desk and found a pair of Dell tower computers acting as hard drive stores for all the video footage.

The only way to totally destroy data on a computer is to physically destroy the disc. Up until his MI5 training Tilson had believed a magnet, or a magnetic field would do the trick. But, his instructor had said, you'd need a magnet so strong that it wouldn't really be feasible.

Instead, he'd been told to either break up the entire computer with an industrial metal shredder. Or, if one those wasn't readily available, to break the discs by snapping them into pieces, then drilling and burning.

Although burning is a solid way to damage the disc, if there's a possibility of advanced forensic recovery, then using thermite – a composition of metal powder and metal oxide that causes an exothermic reaction – is the best option.

As he didn't have any of that either Tilson was hurriedly taking the back off the PCs to reveal their inner workings.

Helena looked on impatiently. "Hurry," she said.

"We should be OK," Tilson replied, running his tongue along his bottom lip as he concentrated on finding the discs in the semi-darkness. "There's no one to raise the alarm now. You did a great job."

He heard her make a harrumphing sound in the darkness. "I told them I was assaulted," she said. "That someone was trying to take off my clothes."

Tilson nodded as he retrieved the first disc. "Right. That's why you took your coat off!"

"They were nice men," she said. "I feel bad."

Tilson was onto the second PC. "We've only locked them in a closet!"

Helena cocked her head to one side. "True."

Tilson emerged from under the desk triumphantly.

Helena unlocked the main door with the lanyard, and they burst out into the cool night air. Now they had the diaries belonging to Malcolm Fox, he could go home. He just hoped the Russians were off his trail.

They ran through the open gates, their hearts racing with adrenaline. As they reached the safety of Helena's Toyota, she turned to Tilson her face illuminated and happy even.

"That was... interesting," she laughed. "I think I even enjoyed it!"

Tilson smiled broadly and shook his head in disbelief at her enthusiasm. "I'll make an agent of you yet," he replied.

Again, the look lasted a moment longer than it might, but this time it felt OK. Tilson felt a wave of gratitude for Helena's help. They climbed into the Toyota, and she steered the 4x4 out of the shadowy trees and onto the main road, switching on her headlights as she did so.

As the RAV 4 sped off on its return journey to town, neither of them noticed a second vehicle - a black Skoda Yeti - detach itself from the darkness beyond the access road and start to follow them, its own headlights extinguished.

CHAPTER 14

Earlier that night, Frida had driven home having been forced to release the supposed victim of the assault, the Finnish man, Antti Isotalo. From the moment she'd watched him walk cockily away from the station and down to a waiting car with a blonde driver, she'd known that there was more to the sudden crime spree happening in and around Flåm. She could feel the underlying connection between the so-called assault at Kjosfossen station, as well as the break in and subsequent murder at the Fox house.

They were like pieces of a puzzle waiting to be put together. And the key to the puzzle, she was certain, was Isotalo. Her gut was telling her he was a Russian up to no good and that meant either some stupid super-power confrontation had spilled over into her back yard of peaceful Norway, or organised crime was trying to muscle in on the area. Either way, she wasn't having it.

As soon as she got home, she decided to phone one of her old contacts, someone who could provide her with more information. Morten Balke had been a bit of a mentor to her on the secondment to the PST. An older man who was probably gay but never spoke about it, Balke had taken a shine to Frida and guided her through her introduction to the intricacies of security work. They caught up every now and again, but on this occasion, it was business not pleasure.

Balke agreed to help. He said he would run the image of Herr Isotalo through facial recognition and see what popped up. If he did prove to be an agent of a foreign power or some gangster hitman, he would send one of his own agents to help her.

"A promising young woman, as it happens," Balke had told her over the phone. "Reminds me of someone."

They'd laughed together and Frida had thanked him before hanging up.

"Supper in 15 minutes," she called up the stairs.

She'd immediately sent Balke the police image by text and went into the kitchen to start preparing dinner for her and her son. Her thoughts were consumed by the investigation and the looming presence of Antti Isotalo over it. She couldn't shake off the feeling that there was something bigger at play here, something beyond her control. But she told herself that she would get to the bottom of this, no matter what it took. And preferably without Balke sending a younger model taking the glory.

Was that a flash of jealousy for the unnamed woman's age, or the fact she was doing exciting things in Norway's second city? Or even that he had Balke's attention and support? Frida knew deep down it was a combination. The PST commander had always believed in her; he had seen something in her that many others had not, and she was grateful for his guidance.

But then she'd returned to her hometown, fallen in love, had a son, got divorced, and settled into the run-of-the-mill investigations that populated her tiny part of the world. The possibility of a Russian spy operating in her country was both thrilling and terrifying. She knew she had to be careful, but she also couldn't let fear hold her back.

"Tomas!" she bellowed.

Eventually, Tomas appeared. His hair was a scruffy tangle of medium length mousey dreadlocks. An equally grubby "black metal" t-shirt emblazoned with the logo of the band "Mayhem" was half tucked in to black jeans personalised with a few holes at the knees. After they'd eaten, Frida went back to pouring over the statements and crime scene reports from today's bizarre mix of crimes. Tomas returned to his Xbox.

She couldn't decide if the Russian reporting a British guy attacking him or the preliminary crime scene report from the Fox house was the stranger of the two. The first was certainly implausible and smacked of a clumsy attempt to frame someone or at least cause trouble for them. But the crime scene at the house spoke of two intruders.

The door had been forced by one person and the house had been searched. A second person had come in the same way and cleaned up most of the kitchen. One set of footprints close together in the snow led away from the front door and the other – more like the stride of a long jump - headed into the forest. Had they been together and split up? Or had they entered at different times?

At 10pm she turned on the TV to see if they had made the news. Indeed, a reporter was standing in the driveway of the house belonging to Malcolm Fox, speaking to camera with the familiar yellow, blue, and white tape demarking the crime scene behind him. She moved across to the kitchen, still listening, to make a cup of cocoa.

Suddenly, her phone rang, making her jump. The ID told her it was Balke. Frida felt a frisson of anticipation.

"*Hallo*, Morten."

"Seems you might be right, Frida," Balke said in a serious voice. "As ever." He snorted a short laugh down the line. "Although we have no real proof, this Antti Isotalo is suspected by us of being a Russian illegal, living in Finland and working as an operative for the GRU across Europe. Our boarder control records show him entering and leaving Norway over a dozen times in the last few years. So, whatever it is, it may well be that his operation is something long-term."

Frida was standing at the stove, the pan of milk in front of her bubbling over, splashing on the hob. She quickly turned the heat off. "GRU?" she repeated.

"Yes," Balke replied. "Real name: Kiril Volkov."

"At least that's easier to say," Frida joked humourlessly. Balke ignored this.

"One more thing you should know. Might help you in the short term. Often, when we have noted Volkov's entry to the country, he has been accompanied by another suspected Russian operative. A woman by the name of Lyuba Kozlova. I will send you her passport details which has her Finnish alias and her photograph."

Norway shares just one non-Schengen Area land border, and that happens to be with Russia itself. The Border Agreement of 1949 between Norway and the then Soviet Union ensures that laws and codes of conduct to do with cross-border traffic are adhered to.

The Norwegian Border Commissioner was set up as part of the Norwegian Police Service one year later headed up by a civilian commissioner. In this instance "Civilian" has always meant a high-ranking army officer who has recently "retired". His or her Deputy's position is taken by the chief of the Garrison at Sør-Varanger, a military base in the far north-east of Norway close to Russian territory and charged with the protection of the 122-mile border.

HEAVEN'S FIRST LAW

Historically, the relationship between the forces of the Norwegian and Russian Commissioners has been one of co-operation and open dialogue. That has changed in recent years due to Norway having itself added to Russia's Unfriendly Countries List. As such, it tended not to be the way of infiltration favoured by Russian agents. Instead, they made their way in via third party nations, usually under a false or illegal passport.

"Thank you, Morten," Frida said breathlessly. "I am so grateful." She fell silent for a brief moment as something nasty occurred to her. "May I ask, why in the short term?"

A sigh at the other end of line. Was it disappointment? "This is beyond local police now, Frida," Balke said. "I am going to send you some help. Well, she will be leading the investigation now, but she will need your support and that of your officers."

"*Javel*." Frida breathed in sharply as she said this. It was a slightly passive aggressive phrase indicating disbelief or displeasure. It was out her mouth before she could catch herself.

"Don't be naïve, Inspector Skardet," Balke was suddenly brusque. "I will sort everything with Chief Kielland in the morning."

The call disconnected and Frida swore loudly.

She jumped up and went to the stairs once more. "I have to go out. Back in the morning!"

Outside, Frida quickly found where she'd parked the Police Volvo and unlocked it as she approached the driver's door. About to climb into the driver's seat, a feeling she was being watched washed over her. She turned, the skin on her back and neck prickling. There was nothing there.

Berating herself, she got in, slammed the door, and started the engine. Her trip was urgent, but there was no need for the siren or lights, she thought. However, in the morning, she'd be replaced by some new girl. Someone who didn't know the area. Frida wanted to put this to bed before that happened. Somehow.

The drive down the E16 was quiet. No other vehicles around. The clock on the dashboard of her car read 10:48pm as she passed the village sign of Flåm. Everyone would be inside doing normal things: watching TV, eating, drinking. Perhaps she should have been one of them. A regular job on a boat, or in a cafe? Maybe a tanner or a tour guide?

"You're losing it, Frida" she said to herself.

Once in centre of town, she slowed her vehicle to a crawl and started methodically patrolling the streets. As she passed, she looked into every house and garden, peering into every alley and forest boarder. Her mind was now racing with the new information she had received from Balke. Every now and again she stopped the car and leapt out, thinking she'd seen something. But every hope was a false one. She was literally jumping at shadows.

As she drove past the railway station with the huge bulk of a cruise ship looming over it, Frida spotted a group of teenagers hanging out near the closed restaurant. She recognized some of them as troublemakers who had caused problems in the past. For now, she had much larger concerns.

Then it hit her. She could use them!

She swung the car around in a wide arc, the tyres crunching on the snow. As she approached the group, they all gestured at her and started to move off. Frida wound down the driver's window.

"It's OK," she shouted.

Frida's heart was pounding as the group of teenagers approached her. She knew she was taking a risk by involving them in the investigation, but she was desperate for leads. She had to solve this case before Balke's new girl arrived and took over from her. She bridled at the thought of a younger woman swanning in and giving her orders. And she certainly wouldn't let someone else take credit for her hard work.

The six boys and two girls eyed her warily. She recognised the leader of the group, Rikon. He swaggered over with a smirk on his face and a smell of marijuana following him. Frida knew the boy from a few run-ins he'd had with her constables, and wondered if he might be a valuable source of information.

"*Hei, hei*, Rikon," she said, trying to keep her voice calm. "Just wanted to ask if you've seen anything strange tonight. Anything out of the ordinary?"

Rikon's smirk turned into a frown as he glanced at his friends. Frida could see the wheels turning in his head, trying to decide whether to trust her or not.

"What's in it for us if we have?" he asked with a sly grin.

Frida knew he was trying to play her, but she couldn't afford to let him get the upper hand.

"I'll pretend I don't smell the weed and search you for illegal drugs," she replied. "How about that?" Rikon's face fell, and he exchanged a hesitant glance with his friends as he weighed his options. After a few moments of tense silence, he finally spoke up. "We saw something strange near the forest earlier," he said, avoiding eye contact with the detective. "Up near *Leinafoss Kraftverk*."

"And what were you lot doing up at the hydroelectric plant?" she asked innocently. She knew perfectly well there was an old portacabin in a layby there that was used for petty drug deals, teenage drinking and untalented graffiti displays.

"Just hanging out," Rikon said without much conviction.

"And what did you see?"

"A car," the teenage boy replied.

"Wow," Frida commented. "That is strange." The girls in the group sniggered at this but Rikon got angry and turned to them.

"Shut up!" he exclaimed.

"Please," Frida said. "Focus."

"It was parked up. You know? Not just on the side of the road. Like it was hidden or... or waiting for something."

Frida nodded. "Very good, Rikon. Anyone in it?"

"No."

"Did you see what sort of car? What colour?"

"It was dark," he said, trailing off.

Frida laughed. "Don't tell me a master thief like you didn't try the doors."

Rikon frowned and again this got a laugh from some of his gang.

"So, you got close enough to see what the car's make, probably its model."

"It was Toyota, OK? RAV 4. Maybe black. Maybe dark blue. There was only that orange light..." Frida thought for a second. There were no orange lights at the hydroelectric plant.

"You were up near *Blodøks*?"

"It was where the road slopes up to it, yeah."

Frida nodded. "Thank you," she said. "You are all model citizens."

And with that she gunned the accelerator and pulled away with a screech of tyres burning through the ice on the tarmac.

CHAPTER 15

Helena looked out the window and saw nothing untoward, just the church that Tilson had used earlier and the road ahead. The first flakes of a new snowfall made her flick the windscreen wipers on. She turned to Tilson who was intently focused on one of Fox's diaries, illuminated only by his phone. The car swayed a little on the bumpy road, causing Tilson's arm to jostle and the light to sway back and forth, making it obvious he was having difficulty reading.

"Sorry," she said. "The road is not great, and my car is old."

"It's fine," Tilson replied, still concentrating on the pages he was reading. "I just need to find out why these diaries are so bloody important. Why have people died..."

It sounded like he couldn't finish the sentence, like he'd realised he was being insensitive but didn't know what to say, Helena's heart clenched at the Englishman's words. Helena should have felt the bitter sting of grief. But she was sanguine. Then her fingers trembled, allowing her passenger to notice her weakness. She took a deep breath, asking for strength from her mother.

Without warning the roar of another engine filled the car and Helena was blinded by a car's headlights on full beam, blazing in her rear-view mirror. A second later, the pursuing vehicle rammed them from behind, causing the Toyota to skid on the road. Helena fought hard to control the car, her hand no longer trembling.

"What the fuck?" Tilson had dropped the diary in the footwell and was taking out the Vektor from his jacket pocket.

"Is it them?" Helena asked. "The Russians?"

"Yeah," Tilson said angrily. "It's them. Or someone with a misplaced case of road rage."

He cocked the weapon and pressed the button inset to the door that opened the passenger window.

With another snarling sound, the car behind hit them again, but this time they were ready. Helena sped up, making the impact less dangerous. Tilson loosed a single shot, but nothing changed. They were relentless pursuers.

Ahead of them, she could see a sideroad: Ryavegen. Ironically it loosely translated as "clear road". It led primarily to Håreina *stasjon* – another stop on the *Flåmsbana* railway – but it then continued up the side of the valley, linking a few remote farmhouses to the rest of the village. She had memorised the local area map and knew it went up through the forest to the peak of Lysegrovi.

Although it began as a decent road surface, the more it wound up through the forest to the mountains in a series of tight bends, the more it deteriorated into a farm track. Ultimately, it was a dead end. But before the road petered out in a mountain meadow by a barn, there was a small river, hewn from the rocks over which ran a rickety, old bridge. You had to cross it very slowly due to its instability. Too fast and you'd plummet into the ravine.

"I have an idea," she said and turned the wheel sharply.

The other car went zooming past the side road, unprepared for the maneuverer because they could not have known about the change in direction. Helena saw the bright red lights of its brakes shining in her wing mirror. The black car behind them reversed and then came after them once more, up the gentle slope of the street.

One 90-degree turn to the right and then a sharp left took Helena and Tilon past the station itself and onto the hill road proper where the gradient became steep very quickly. The car passed a handful of large farm buildings as they continued their ascent, trees now zipping past on both sides.

She gunned the Toyota up the incline, and the grey RAV 4 slipped a little in the icy conditions. Her manoeuvre had won them about thirty seconds, and they were now about a hundred feet ahead of the other vehicle.

"Where we going?" Tilson asked, looking over his shoulder.

Helena hurriedly explained her plan and she could see her passenger grinning by the dashboard lights. He was handsome, she supposed. And he seemed like a nice guy. But she was not really one for relationships.

Sexual or otherwise. It all got messy.

"If we do that, how are we getting back down?" he asked.

She frowned.

As a teenager, she had been a wild spirit, roaming the rugged countryside and competing with local boys in sports and sharpshooting. She herself had suffered the feckless fumbling of some of them, with none of them ever really showing any interest once the deed had been done.

"We walk," she replied with a smile.

However, when she grew into a woman, she left behind any adventures between the sheets and was then disappointed to find that no man could match her in any other aspect of her life, either.

Her mother always said she was a force to be reckoned with. Although she didn't totally believe this, she certainly felt unmatched in her prowess with a weapon - be it rifle, pistol or knife. Her confidence was as solid as a glacier in winter. And because of that she found no one appealed to her as a lover. Perhaps that's why she felt a pang of interest in this British spy.

"I like this plan," Tilson joked. "I'm excited for it."

She was intrigued by Tilson's skills and charm, not to mention he was easy on the eye. He seemed to possess a unique combination of strength and intelligence, and she found herself actually admiring him.

She tutted. What was she doing?

At that moment, a 21mm Gyurza round, designed to penetrate body armour, smashed through the back window with the sound of a thunderclap. The glass completely collapsed from the window, and the bullet, its velocity only slightly reduced from its normal 1,400 feet per second, continued on, through the car, putting a neat round hole in the windscreen.

"Shit!" Tilson placed a gentle hand on Helena's shoulder. "You OK?"

She nodded; her teeth gritted in a rictus smile. Although she handled weapons every day, she definitely didn't like being on the receiving end.

The car continued to speed up the forest track, Helena's heart racing as she gripped the wheel tightly. The situation was getting more dangerous by the second. Tilson's hand was still on her shoulder, his presence providing some comfort in the chaos. But she knew they couldn't outrun the other car forever.

"How far to the bridge?" Tilson asked urgently.

Helena shook her head, uncertain. "I think a few kilometres."

Tilson looked at her, his face set in a resolute expression of resignation. "We won't make it," he said. "Not without slowing them down somehow."

He unclipped his seatbelt and a tiny alarm started pinging on the dashboard. Then he clambered over the seat and into the back of the car, silencing the annoying sound.

"Be careful!" Helena implored him.

"I'll try." Tilson turned and flashed her a smile that she caught in the rearview. Then he turned back to the road receding behind them and the ominous black car, its headlight still partially blinding her as she drove.

Helena's double-handed grasp of the steering wheel tightened as she manoeuvred the car through the treacherous road conditions. The car shuddered and swerved, but she managed to keep it on the road. To either side were now deep ditches that would take the meltwater down to the river in spring. For now, though, they were steep precipices in which snow had drifted in some depth.

If she hadn't grown up in a landscape like this and knew all too well how to handle winding roads like this one, then she was sure they would have crashed by now. Although, the GRU agents seemed to be doing OK. She hoped the increasingly treacherous weather would play to her advantage. With another skid, her knuckles turned white with the strain of another tight bend. She had to get them to safety, no matter the cost. Tilson glanced back at Helena his expression seeming to be one of admiration.

"You're doing great," he shouted above the noise of the over-revving engine and the skidding wheels.

As he flashed her a reassuring smile, she couldn't help but feel grateful to have him with her on this joyride from hell.

The car lurched to the side once more as Helena took the second hairpin bend in the road almost exactly at the 300m contour line. The car dislodged snow and chunks of frozen mud throwing them into the air, like coarse confetti at an ogre's wedding. Glancing over her shoulder once more, she saw the Englishman taking careful aim with his handgun.

"Let me know when we get to a straight bit," he said coolly.

"Of course," Helena replied. "Two more bends if I remember it right.

Then we hit the straightest stretch for some time."

Another shot rang out in the night, but no bullet hit them. Helena wrenched the steering wheel to the side, taking the next bend sideways. She wrestled the wheel back under her control and rammed her foot on the accelerator making the most of the black car not being directly behind them for a brief moment to put some distance between them.

Ahead, picked out in the glare of the headlights, was the last turn.

More gunshots rang out as she spun the wheel once more.

"Get ready!" she called.

The Russians' car not being directly behind them, provided a momentary sense of relief. However, Helena knew they couldn't let their guard down. She took advantage of the lull to peer ahead and examine the upcoming turn. Her heart racing, she braced herself for more gunshots as she spun the wheel once more. Tilson, now in a better position on the back seat, steadied his gun on the rear headrest.

The Toyota skidded around the bend, following the same trajectory as it had on the previous corner. But its position relevant to their pursuers now gave the Russians following them a different advantage. Instead of only having the back end of the RAV 4 as a target, now the driver's side of the Toyota was exposed to them. One of the GRU agents unleashed a volley of gunfire.

One of the shots found its mark, taking out one of the rear tyres with a loud bang. In milliseconds the solid black rubber was turned to shredded strands of latex.

The blowout caused the Toyota to become imbalanced, with the rear of the RAV 4 swinging away from the disintegrated wheel. The car spun like a top, with Helena frantically gripping the steering wheel as she fought to regain control. The bullet had struck the tire with such force that the Toyota was now skidding along on three wheels, leaving a nasty trench of stinking, burning rubber in its wake.

The spin intensified, throwing Helena back into her seat hard, her seatbelt locking her in place. Tilson, however, was not so fortunate. He was hurled across the back seat and hit his head on the nearside door. Desperately trying to grab onto something, he dropped his weapon and reached for the handle above the door. As the spin increased, his hands failed to connect with the grip and he fell back the other way, ending up in an uncomfortable heap in the footwell of the back seat.

The car, still spiralling violently, left the road and careened into the air. For a moment Helena almost felt weightless as the car not only turned about its axis, but also began to roll. The momentum took the car a certain way over the deep ditch that ran alongside the track before it plummeted down. The Toyota managed one and half complete revolutions before it hit the ground, flying into an equally deep snowdrift. Even though the impact was somewhat cushioned by this, her head was thrown sharply against the steering wheel, and she was only saved from a nasty concussion or fracture by the car's crash safety system engaging.

The collision left them in a disorienting silence, the only sound being the hiss of the driver's airbag deflating and for some reason the ticking of an indicator. Helena was the first to regain her senses. She was hanging upside down in her seat, her head throbbing from the impact, her nose and chin feeling numb.

Suddenly, with a sickening creak, the car slid backwards out of the drift and down the last few feet to the bottom of the ditch, its underside angled up at the road above. With a crunch, the car came to a halt, its headlights shining into the night sky beyond the dark triangular shadows of the pine forest.

Helena let out a ragged breath and twisted awkwardly to check on Tilson. She saw his body was now sprawled on the ceiling of the car above the backseat.

"Sam! Are you okay?" she asked, her voice sounded genuinely concerned.

He did not respond, and his body was dreadfully still. Helena unclipped her seatbelt to be able to get to him. She braced against the roof and lowered herself before getting the right way up. Then she reached out to the unmoving body and ran one hand down his face, quickly pulling it away when she felt something wet and sticky. In the partial light of the headlamps that were somehow still working, she could see the thick red stain of Tilson's blood on her fingertips.

CHAPTER 16

Helena looked at her fingers tinged in red and then back at Tilson.

"Oh my god," she breathed, fearing him dead. "Sam..." But then he groaned and attempted to raise his head.

"I think... I think I've been... better," he replied, wincing as he tried to sit up. Now she could see the gash on his head that ran across his brow as if he was a boiled egg someone had tried to open. "What... about you?"

"I'm fine," Helena assured him. "But we have to get out of here!"

As she kicked her door open, she heard the black car skid to a halt on the road some 20 feet above her. The sound of car doors being slammed told her she had only moments. She ripped open the passenger door after it refused to budge and then thrust her arms inside, reaching for Tilson.

Helena's heart raced as she looked up to see the two Russian agents silhouetted on the precipice above. She knew they were after the diaries she and Tilson had taken from Fox's office at *Blodøks*. But she wasn't going to give up without a fight. She felt the butterfly touch of Tilson's fingers stretching desperately to reach hers. She reached in a bit further and grasped the Englishman's hands in hers, slowly pulling him through the open door.

They fell to the ground together, Tilson wincing as his head brushed the icy ground.

A female Russian voice raised in anger assailed the quiet of the night. Apart from the slowly dimming headlights of her car, that were pointing away from them, there was no light to illuminate Helena and Tilson.

"Torch," muttered Tilson. "They're getting a torch."

Helena realised what the implications were, and she left him lying there, protected by the side of the RAV 4, and crawled round to the boot.

Through the broken rear window, she pulled her hunting rifle and an ammo bag.

She quickly loaded the gun and pointed up at the ridge where a torch light was now approaching, illuminating the female GRU agent in even more detail. She steadied her breathing, gently closed one eye and sighted down the barrel of the Sauer 404 lightweight bolt-action hunting rifle.

The shot rang out louder than a nuclear explosion in the silence of the nighttime forest. Snow and mud erupted into the air at the feet of the GRU woman. She immediate dropped to her stomach, out of sight of the Norwegian huntress.

For her part Helena reloaded the rifle. "Get whatever you need," she whispered to Tilson. "I'll keep them busy!"

Another shot and a nasty ricocheting sound from the tree she'd just taken aim at.

Tilson rolled over onto his stomach and moved forward to the passenger door. It was buckled and there was no way he'd be able to open it. Instead, he picked up a nearby rock the size of his fist and rammed it into the corner of the window. He turned it, applying as much pressure as possible and the glass shattered.

Then he half scrambled through and retrieved his Hard Ware rucksack with the diaries in them along with his equipment. Then he reversed out of the front and re-entered the car via the door Helena had opened. He was breathing hard from the effort, the cold of the snow and ice coupled with the shock making him shake.

Another shot. Then something unexpected.

"We only want what you took from office, tovarich." It was the male Russian. The black haired ugly one. "Why you help this English, Helena Olsen?"

The blonde answered him by chambering another round and sending it zinging off another tree at the top of the ditch. Tilson finally located his dropped Vektor and grabbed at it like a drunkard reaching for his glass.

"Hurry up!" she hissed. He picked the gun up before wriggling out of the car for the final time.

Tilson nodded, wincing as he stood up. They had to act fast.

"L-let's go," he said, his teeth chattering.

Slowly, they retreated from the vehicle, using it as cover until they were in the darkness. Then, with Helena supporting Tilson, she led the way uphill, the two of them trudging through the snow, trying to find a way out of the ditch, heading deeper into the forest.

Helena's years of training in the wilderness came to the fore. She knew forests like old friends and was determined to lead them to safety. The snow made their progress slow, but they knew they had to keep moving. Gunshots rang out behind them, but Helena knew they were too far away. They sounded as if the Russians hadn't moved from the car wreck. What, then, were they shooting at?

Another volley of shots echoed through the quiet forest. They may be far behind them, but the unlikely duo didn't stop; they couldn't stop.

They had to keep moving, keep running.

Tilson felt a little like a ragdoll, propped up by the woman's strength, but his face was set with the sort of determination to keep going usually only demonstrated by the military or competitive athletes. Helena approved. They wouldn't stop; they couldn't stop. They had to keep moving, slowly and quietly hoping to put as much distance between them and the Russians as possible, and hope that they would eventually find a way out of this nightmare.

***

Kiril Volkov and Lyuba Kozlova lay on the frozen, muddy bank, overlooking the site of the crash some twenty feet below. The frozen ground beneath them was rough and cold, sending the occasional shiver through their bodies, despite the thick coats they wore. The snowflakes falling from the dark sky melted on their skin, leaving them damp and numb.

The icy air stung their cheeks and noses, making it hard to breathe. But they couldn't take their eyes off the site of the crash. They had the Norwegian woman and the Englishman pinned down at last. For the more inexperienced Lyuba, the tension was palpable.

"Now what?" she asked her partner in Russian. Volkov sighed. "Kill them."

Lyuba snorted. "That is your solution to everything," she said. "And I like it."

"We were given orders for two outcomes when it comes to those documents," he reminded her. "We retrieve them, or we destroy them."

Either way, anyone who comes into contact with diaries, we kill.

"What if they do not have the documents?" Lyuba looked at her partner with concern.

"They have them!" Volkov said as if he were addressing an especially slow child. "They took them from the munitions factory."

"But what if that was a dead end?"

"Then what were they doing in there so long?"

"Just searching? Look, Kiril, all I am saying is -"

Volkov cleared his throat spat loudly on the ground, cutting her off.

"And all I am saying is I am in command of this operation, tovarich. You would do well to remember that."

He lifted his chin in a sharp movement to indicate the car crash over the ridge.

"So, let's do this!"

He crawled as close to the edge as he dared and then peeked over.

Reluctantly, Lyuba followed his lead.

They both peered intently into the chasm below, only the muted lights from the Toyota's headlights shedding any light on the scene - a frozen, unmoving tableau.

If Vilkov was right, they were finally going to get their hands on those classified documents. They would be heroes. Despite his shortcomings, the older Russian knew what he was doing. He was a bit "old School" and some of the younger agents made fun of his Soviet ways. But so far, they had partnered on three occasions and their relationship was a good one. He tolerated her insubordination in return for the benefits of working with a younger woman.

Vilkov's performance in bed had been a shock to her. Often in their line of work it paid to sleep with one's superiors. But he had been anything but perfunctory. He knew his way around a woman's body. Probably trained for it, Lyuba joked to herself. But he was considerate and not at all a chore. Perhaps knowing he was punching so far above his weight kept him on his toes.

"Stop fucking daydreaming," her charming partner said. "You've got the torch, shine it down there so I can get a clear shot!"

She was still relatively new to the world of espionage and violence, but she had taken the idea and practice of killing like a lioness. She'd already taken two lives on his mission alone. Making it three or four didn't matter if it was vital to the success of their mission. She looked over at Vilkov, her partner and mentor. She saw the dark determination in his eyes playing alongside a twinge of slowly abating annoyance.

Lyuba brought out the powerful and versatile SureFire X300 flashlight from her pocket and held it up for Vilkov to see.

Although not of Russian design or manufacture, the Ultra WeaponLight is built to be mounted on handguns and longer weapons. It features a high-performance LED that generates 1,000 lumens of stunning white light focused by a Total Internal Reflection lens to produce a tight beam with extended reach and significant surround light for peripheral vision.

If anything could pinpoint their prey in the darkness below it was this. It would also act to temporarily blind them, being so bright as to overwhelm all aggressors' "dark-adapted" vision.

She shuffled forward and held the torch over the ditch, pointing at the car wreck below. At the same time, Vilkov rose to a crouch and aimed at the car, firing four shots at the underside of the Toyota. Then he ducked back down again and Lyuba extinguished the light.

HEAVEN'S FIRST LAW

Vilkov had been doing this sort of thing for years, and she trusted his judgment. Without another word, they performed the same manoeuvre, this time with both of them opening fire.

The sound of gunshots echoed through the cold air, mixing with the ever-increasing howl of the wind and the crunching snow beneath their boots as they moved.

One of the bullets – Lyuba couldn't tell whose – hit the fuel line connecting the tank to the engine. It's a truly disappointing experience when you first see a car hit in this way. Generally speaking, car fuel tanks don't really explode. Movies and TV shows need to be visual spectacles and lead the audience to believe that all manner of vehicles explode. Not only that, but they also soar into the air once the gasoline is ignited.

Alas, this simply isn't the case. For an explosion to take place, you need oxygen, so certainly cars that have just been filled up won't become a fireball even though it seems counterintuitive given the amount of fuel a car can hold.

The bullet that pierced the pipe under the Toyota had simply caused petrol to start leaking out on to the car and the ground around it.

It was now that the pair of Russians could try shooting again in an effort to ignite the petrol with a spark possibly caused by ricocheting off the metal structure of the car. And for that to be spectacular, you need to give it a few minutes. They had a job to do, and emotions had no place in their line of work, but now Lyuba was impatient. A few minutes took hours to pass in these situations.

Finally, the two stood up and opened fire again. This time, they did cause a spark. With an impressive whoomph, the fumes and liquid ignited simultaneously. Within moments, the inside of the car had been set ablaze and the wheels were starting to smoulder. The fire illuminated the immediate area and the flames lifted into the air above, catching a couple of pine trees in their flickering dance. This lit up the sky for some distance and was accompanied by the acrid black smoke from the rubber and plastic of the tyres and interior.

Vilkov was already making his way clumsily down the slope, the incline making it difficult to control both his footing and his momentum. Lyuba followed more cautiously, sweeping her Vektor and the SureFire torch around in arcs to cover their rear and to see if anyone was running away in the darkness.

No one was, but something caught her attention.

"No bodies," called Vilkov from beside the burning car. He sounded disappointed.

"I think I see why," Lyuba replied. In the torchlight she could see the signs of two people leaving the scene, with one looking like they had a limp. "One's injured," she said. "So, they can't be far away."

"Search the immediate area, I'll look in the car. Then we better go. This fire might be seen."

***

Frida found not one but two sets of tracks at the foot of the *Blodøks* access road. One was on the left, approaching the incline and the other was on the right, suggesting the occupants of these vehicles were not operating together. Each one was facing a different way and had approached from a different direction.

She was squatting by the first set of tracks, following their arc. It led out of the treeline and onto the road, turning round to travel back to town. The other, as far as she could see, had come from out of town and parked deeper into the trees before pulling out and heading in the same direction, perhaps following the other car.

Despite speeding all the way to the location, she had missed the cars whose imprints she was now examining by a minute. If she had been there earlier, she would have seen Helena's Toyota pursued by the Skoda Yeti turn up the forest road.

With not much else to go on, Frida started walking up the hill towards the arms company compound. As she reached the top of the road where it levelled off, she saw immediately that the gates were open.

Drawing the Heckler & Koch P30s semi-automatic handgun she had taken from the locked compartment in the Volvo, she approached the entrance cautiously, eyes alert for any movement. Her instincts told her she was way too late to this party, but it didn't mean she would rush in.

The gun was light in her hands, due to its polymer frame and this variant of the sidearm was fitted with an external ambidextrous thumb safety. This was very useful for "southpaws" such as herself. Although it did add a few grammes to the weight of the weapon it certainly didn't impede its efficiency or indeed efficacy. The handgun had only narrowly missed out when the UK itself was looking for a replacement for its long-standing Browning L9A1, with the eventual winner of that coveted job going to the Glock 17.

Passing through the well-lit gates, bathed in orange, Frida was perplexed. Assault, murder, car chases, now something weird at *Blodøks*. Finding no one around and with a cursory check of the sentry post, she moved on to the main building, stepping carefully and turning every now and again to cover her rear and any place someone might be hiding. On the ground by her feet she saw the lanyard Tilson had dropped earlier and picked it up. She pressed this against the entry system and the glass door in front of her swung open.

Once inside the reception area, it was very dark, but she quickly located the light switches and turned them all to on. With the customary flickering of strip lighting, the whole place was bathed in faux natural light.

"Anyone here?" Frida shouted. "Police! I am armed. Show yourselves!"

No one appeared, but she could hear muffled voices coming from someplace nearby. She moved through the area past the reception desk and into the hall, cocking her head to listen. The sound was coming from her right. It soon became apparent there were at least two people locked in a janitor's closet.

Again, making use of the reclaimed lanyard, she opened the door to the tiny anti-chamber and two men clad in black and looking extremely sheepish came tumbling out. One of them had a slight head injury. But they seemed none the worse for that.

Explaining in garbled sentences they told of her of the man and woman who had tricked them and locked them in the closet. Frida guessed – wrongly – that this was her pair of Russian illegals from Finland. She had no idea yet that Helena Olsen was now so heavily involved.

In Norway, there are three emergency telephone numbers, one for each of the Fire, Police and Ambulance services. Those being 110, 112, and 113 respectively. The number 111 was never used as an emergency number as it can be "dialled" simply by telephone wires knocking together and sending the three separate pulses down the line to the exchange in the local loop. Although the technology has moved on the numbers have never changed.

Frida walked outside, leaving the two men to search the building, and hurriedly dialled 112.

As had happened with the call from the stationmaster earlier that same day, the call was routed via the tiny police station in Aurland and relayed to her own base at Lærdal. The young constable on the other end couldn't quite believe what she was saying.

"A break in?" he queried. "By foreign spies?"

Frida confirmed that this was indeed the case and that he needed to call out everyone he could. They needed to put a stop to this outrageous incursion on their sovereign territory before it went any further.

No sooner were the words out of her mouth than she saw a bright light in the sky to the northeast. A fire on the mountainside. "Too late" she muttered angrily. "Too bloody late."

CHAPTER 17

Making their way through the dense forest was slow and laborious. Helena could feel the weight of the situation bearing down on her as much as the fatigue that was seeping into her muscles. She had never expected to be caught up in a dangerous game with GRU agents but here she was, with a wounded stranger in tow, and those agents hot on their trail.

Tilson stumbled on an exposed tree root and Helena caught him, her grip strong and sure. They had been walking for what felt like hours, although she knew it could only be 20 minutes or so. The adrenaline was keeping her going despite the biting cold and exhaustion. However, she knew they couldn't keep this pace up forever. They needed to find a safe place to regroup and figure out their next move.

Finally, they reached a small clearing where the trees thinned, but this only meant that the snow fell even harder and faster here.

Staring hard into the thick forest behind them, Helena tried to make out any pursuers in the darkness. There was a faint glow from the fire of what she assumed was the battered old Toyota.

Satisfied no one was about to ambush them, she set Tilson down against a tree. He managed a weak smile.

"Sorry," he said. "I'll be fine in a minute."

They both knew this was a lie. His open wound was a problem. Freezing weather is known to slow down blood flow and worsen circulation. This means far less oxygen reaches the wound, making it more susceptible to bacteria and infection. And if frostbite set in, it would cause delayed healing at best and at worst tissue necrosis and sepsis.

"We need to see to that," Helena said, waving a hand at Tilson's forehead. He nodded mutely. "I have a first aid kit..."

She unshouldered her own backpack and took out the neatly packed Tupperware boxes she used for all her equipment: rifle cleaning kit, dried food, Hexi burner mini stove with waterproof matches, and a very well stocked plastic container of medical supplies.

Helena would be the first to tell anyone on an expedition that it's not only about having the kit with you, it's also understanding how to use everything inside that kit as well as cultivating a level of mental preparedness so you can help yourself — or others — in a hurry. She had taken a first aid, emergency preparedness, and critical injury course before she'd started her first job.

She pulled out a silvery foil survival blanket and placed it over Tilson's shivering body. Then she passed him a flask of hot tea and he drank thirstily from it. The warmth of both would help ease the shock. Then she handed him a couple of Tramadol painkillers. These were seriously strong, but she reckoned Tilson could handle them and was unlikely to develop any opioid addiction as a result.

Helena quickly opened the first aid kit and began to clean and then dress Tilson's wound. She had done this countless times before, but it still made her stomach twist in knots. Shooting was one thing, but blood and guts had always made her a little nauseous. Stupid for someone in her profession, but she knew that if she didn't act fast, the consequences could be far worse.

She worked efficiently, her hands moving with practiced ease. It was never her intention to end up in a dangerous situation like this, but she was grateful for the knowledge and experience she had gained.

When she finished bandaging Tilson's wound, she could see the relief in his eyes.

"Thank you," he said, his voice barely above a whisper.

Helena smiled, trying to reassure him. "We will be okay, Sam," she said confidently, though she wasn't entirely sure if she believed it herself.

One thing she did know for sure was that they had to keep moving, to stay one step ahead of their pursuers.

Taking one last look at Tilson, who miraculously did appear better already, she helped him to his feet and they continued on through the forest, leaving the little clearing behind.

"Besides," she added with a stupid grin, "I am going to need you alive to fight Russians! Deer I can deal with, even Moose. But these KGB people?" She snorted and shook her head. "No."

Tilson laughed. "You mean GRU," he said. "There hasn't been any KGB for years."

"Whoever they are, this is your department," she told him, half joking.

After a few minutes heading uphill again, they were back deep in the dark forest. Helena could feel Tilson was more certain in his footing and becoming less of a burden to her. As a result they were making much better progress.

The trees began to thin out as the steep mountain side plateaued into what during the summer was pasture but now was a blanket of snow. Helena stopped. She could see a small, blackish square standing out from the white maybe a couple of kilometres away.

"What's happening?" Tilson asked, suddenly more alert.

Helena was pretty sure that what she had glimpsed was one of the small number of hunters' huts that dotted the remote landscape across the region.

"Our accommodation," Helena replied.

"Good food? The finest wines? Great dancing?"

She looked down at him. "You are definitely feeling better, Herr Tilson!"

He grinned. "Thanks to you."

She hoped it would be a suitable refuge from the elements – no missing roof tiles or a tree through one wall. In the sometimes gale-force winds that whipped across the mountains around the municipality of Aurland come the colder seasons, both of these were real possibilities.

Only ten minutes later, they passed one of the final trees before open ground. It wasn't quite as dark here as it was in the forest, the whiteness of the snow dissipating enough of the night for them to see outlines. Helena pointed to the left, indicating a shadowy structure standing some 80 feet away between two coniferous trees of equal height.

Her heart lifted at the sight of it, nestled between two trees and hidden from view by thick foliage. She could feel Tilson's relief as they approached the small, wooden structure. It may not have been luxurious, but it was shelter from the harsh elements and a chance to catch their breath.

Praying it was empty of both people and wildlife, Helena cautiously approached the door and pushed it open. Finding the cabin deserted, she quickly ushered Tilson inside and locked the door behind them.

She could see that the building was still in decent condition. The roof was intact and there were no obvious signs of damage. She helped Tilson to an old wooden cot bed in the corner.

"I'm much better," he protested.

"You will be," she replied, rustling around in her backpack once more. "But not yet."

Reluctantly, Tilson nodded and sat down on the small, wooden bed.

"We can both rest here," she said, handing him back the foil blanket. "I'll keep first watch."

Tilson nodded, grateful for the warmth and the chance to recuperate.

"If those bastards come anywhere near, I'll wake you," she assured him as he closed his eyes. "We might even get lucky," she added. "They might not find us."

Tilson did not reply. He was already asleep.

Helena stepped up to his slumbering form and brushed his hair from his eyes – just as her mother used to do to her when she was a little girl, what seemed like a lifetime ago.

***

Frida was heading down the road back to town, repeatedly ducking her head down to get a better angle through the windscreen on the fire that was burning high on the hillside to her right. She followed the same route Helena had taken earlier and started up the precipitous forest track with a sense of both outrage and trepidation. Luckily, the Volvo V90CC patrol car was a decent 4 x4 and designed for just this type of terrain. It climbed the hillside easily, making short work of the hairpin bends, its bright LED headlights picking out every detail of the once dark trees.

As she neared the site of the fire, she slowed the car to a crawl, keeping the headlights on full beam to spot anything untoward and to dazzle anyone who happened to be lurking in the shadows.

Rounding the final bend, she found something alright, but nothing lurking in the shadows. Parked haphazardly across the road ahead was a black Skoda yeti. Its driver and passenger doors were wide open, its own headlights shining at the side of the road, pointing to where the tongues of flame were licking at the snow-covered trees.

Frida brought her patrol car to a halt and surveyed the scene from the relative safety of her vehicle. Then, satisfied that there didn't seem to be anyone about, she opened the door and stepped out, gripping the Heckler & Koch P30s semi-automatic tightly.

With the gun carefully aimed at the ground ahead of her, Frida moved slowly toward the car. Norwegian law dictated that she should call out a warning to anyone she suspected of being hidden inside the vehicle, but right now she was convinced this would be a bad move. And after the day she'd had, she really didn't give a damn about the rules. No one else seemed to be playing by them so why should she?

She wrinkled her nose as the smell from the fire reached her nostrils.

She knew it well. Plastic and rubber. A car. Was this a simple RTA, then? Just like she was used to? Every fibre of her being told her not to believe it for a second.

As such, her last steps towards the driver's door of the Skoda were fast and light, the detective bringing the P30 up to window height. She could see straight away that the car was empty. She breathed a sigh of relief.

She circled the vehicle, scanning for any indication of what had happened there. But there was no one in sight. Just the burning trees and the eerie silence of the night. There was no doubt in her mind that this was related to all the other series of escalating events in Flåm.

But why would someone leave their car in the middle of the road and run off? And what was their connection to the fire? Frida's mind raced with possible scenarios; her detective mind dulled by the lateness of the hour. She knew she had to investigate further, but she also didn't want to leave her patrol car unattended. Deciding to call for backup, Frida retraced her steps to the Volvo and was just reaching inside for the radio when she heard voices nearby.

She froze.

There were two of them. Calling to each other from over the very ridge that their car was illuminating like an outdoor theatre. They were Russian. And now they were getting closer.

"*Jesus Kristus*," she breathed.

She tried desperately to steady her breathing as it fogged irregularly in the frigid air. There was no doubt in her mind she was now in grave danger. Then she saw a figure emerging over the embankment, silhouetted by the flames behind it. She knew it had to be the Russian man she'd met earlier. Kiril Volkov.

Without thinking, she raised the Heckler & Koch and shouted for them to stop.

The figure of Volkov stopped in place. He also had a weapon, but it was held loosely and pointing at the icy ground.

"Armed Police!" she shouted, her voice cracking. "Drop the weapon!"

The man just remained stock still and Frida wondered if he'd heard her.

"If you do not drop it, I will open fire," she added.

Again, this elicited no response. Shit. She had only discharged her weapon a handful of times in her 20 years on the force. And only one of those was actually aimed at another person.

She tried a different tack. "Drop the gun, Volkov!"

She may have imagined it, but she thought she saw him jolt at the mention of his real name.

Frida's finger tightened on the trigger, ready to defend herself if necessary.

When they came, the double tap of bullets fired by Lyuba hit both Frida and her patrol car; the first skimming the bonnet and zinging away harmlessly into the bark of a tree some 30 feet away.

The second, however, found its mark. The round sliced through the thick blue coat, Police issue jacket and shirt before slamming into flesh just above Frida's hip. It continued through her lower torso and exited the body leaving a fist sized hole in her back. She was thrown back, her body flipped by the impact, and fell to the ground behind the Volvo, face down.

CHAPTER 18

Frida lay on the ground, her body wracked with pain and her mind racing with fear. She knew she had to act fast if she wanted to survive this encounter with Kiril Volkov and his blonde accomplice. But her injuries made it difficult to move, let alone defend herself. The voices of the two Russians grew louder as they approached cautiously, unable to see her behind the patrol car.

She clenched her teeth, determined not to give up without a fight. With a surge of adrenaline, she pushed herself up onto her elbows and dragged herself back to the Volvo. She left a trail of dark red blood in her wake, staining the snow pink as they mixed.

Her mind raced as she fought to stay conscious. She knew that she couldn't give up now, not after coming this far. With a surge of adrenaline, she willed her body to push through the pain and move towards the Volvo. She couldn't let these shitheads win, not when she had come so close to arresting them and finding out what the hell was going on in her sleepy little backwater.

As she dragged herself along the ground Frida left a trail in her wake, the snow stained pink from the mixture of white frosting and her own deep red blood.

The pain was excruciating, but she refused to let it slow her down. She gritted her teeth, grinding them hard in an effort to keep moving, to keep fighting.

With every ounce of strength she had left, Frida finally made it back to the Volvo. She could see the weapons box in the backseat and knew that was her only chance at taking control of the situation. She closed her eyes and tried to block out the thudding ache that told her she was losing blood at a frightening rate.

Ignoring the desire to just give up and rest, she reached into the safebox, and pulled out the other gun it housed. She felt a moment of relief, knowing that she now had at least a fighting chance.

"You had your warning!" she shouted. "You think I can't take pain, you fuckers? I've given birth!"

Using the support of the car door and the driver's seat she wrestled herself into a semi-standing position, aiming the gun between the door and its frame.

She could see the two of them now- the Russian Volkov and his girlfriend - each with a sidearm raised, coming in her direction. The last vestiges of her strength were ebbing away as she struggled to stand, her entire body shaking from the pain and exhaustion.

In her weakened state, she knew she couldn't last long. But she refused to give up, knowing she had to do whatever it took to protect herself and to get back to Tomas. With a determined look on her face, she aimed the gun between the car door and its frame. As the two figures approached, lit up by the Volvo's headlights, Frida could see the fear and hesitation on their faces.

They had underestimated her. But she had endured the most excruciating pain to bring a new life into this world. And now, she was ready to do the same for her own life. She screamed in defiance and pulled the trigger, hesitating no longer.

The weapon she had retrieved from the locker was not another Heckler & Koch P30s. This was its bigger, noisier, deadlier cousin: the MP5 submachine gun.

Developed back in the 1960s, the MP5 is arguably the most widely used weapon of its type in the world with over 100 variants. Over forty countries for their military or law enforcement requirements.

Despite the German manufacturer developing a successor to the MP5 – the UMP – before the turn of the Millennium, and even though it costs more, the MP5 maintains its crown.

Technically, it can fire approximately 800 rounds of 19x9mm parabellum cartridges at just over 1,300 feet per second. But none of that mattered to Frida. All she cared about was the effect it had on the two Russians. They dived back down the ridge, taking cover from the submachine gun spitting death at them.

Frida slumped into the driver's seat and rammed the car into reverse, spinning the wheel to perform a 180-degree turn. Even with treacherous, icy road conditions, the Volvo's special winterized tyres allowed her to complete the manoeuvre with almost no skid.

She slammed her foot on the accelerator and hurtled back down the snowy road, her mind still reeling from the intense encounter with the two GRU agents - now receding in her rearview mirror.

She knew she couldn't let up now. They could easily be following her in the Skoda. She gripped the steering wheel as if it were lifebelt in a treacherous sea and she was about to drown.

But she refused to let herself give up. She had to make it back to Tomas, and she would do whatever it took to do that.

Frantically, she reached for the radio, dropped it and had to find it again. Every movement should have been agony, but her brain had long since stopped paying attention to the pain receptors.

She held the handset to her mouth, taking a deep breath and then screaming into her radio.

"Detective Skaret. Urgent assistance needed. Shots fired! Officer wounded!"

It came out as a jumble of words, but she dropped the radio, hoping she had done enough.

She applied the Volvo's brakes to take another corner, but her reactions were shot, her strength starting to fade, her injuries taking their toll on her body. She felt heady as if drunk or high. Everything seemed to be moving in slow motion, her vision blurring.

The patrol car did not complete the turn, instead ploughing off the road and through the forest for a moment before slamming into one of the pine trees head on. Frida blacked out from the impact and slouched in the seat, blood oozing from her wound.

Then the radio crackled to life, and the voice of her fellow officer, constable Lars Lindberg, 20 miles away in Aurland filled the car, responding to her call for backup, reassuring her that units were on their way including an ambulance. The noise made Frida look up one last time, and moan something incoherent before surrendering to the darkness.

***

The snow was falling more and more heavily now, blanketing everything in a thick layer of white. Volkov's black jacket was almost invisible under the fresh powder, but the mud stains still stood out; smears of shit on a white sheet. He cursed under his breath again as he tried to brush off the excess snow.

He stared up angrily at the parapet above from which he'd been forced to launch himself when the Norwegian policewoman had opened fire with a bloody submachine gun!

"*Súka*," he growled – "bitch". Then he spat on the ground to emphasise his displeasure. He was angry. Not just with the situation or the fact he'd been outgunned. It was a general rage caused by the fact this was not how he had envisioned this mission going.

This was supposed to be a simple mission. "Easy", Control had called it. Vital, but nothing to worry about. You go in, you come out. No problems.

Well, they had fucking problems now.

The car had stopped burning only a few minutes earlier, even though the trees above it were still ablaze, hissing and cracking as the heat from the flames met the snow on its branches. It was lighting up the sky like a bloody beacon.

He looked across at Lyuba who was staring into the smouldering wreck, almost transfixed.

"What?" he asked in Russian.

Lyuba pointed. "There," she said, "In the footwell. The diary!"

Volkov trudged over to stand beside her and looked into the charred vehicle. Sure enough, there was an A5 sized notebook. Its cover was blackened, and the corners of the pages had been burnt away, leaving a singed outline the colour of ripe bananas.

He glanced over at Lyuba, wondering if she was thinking the same thing. They may yet be able to salvage this disaster if they could make it back to GRU control in Finland with the very document they were sent to retrieve.

The diary.

Volkov was amazed. After all the chaos and destruction, the diary was still intact.

Lyuba suddenly darted forward to pick up the charred notebook.

"Be careful, *Žópa*," Vilkov said. Although meaning "brat" or even "arse", the term he used was a playful Russian slur, actually used as a term of endearment amongst loved ones in a joking albeit affectionate manner.

Lyuba smiled at him gratefully and touched the frame of the car gingerly to check its temperature. Even through her gloves the heat must have been palpable as she snatched it away, grinning at the older man.

Now taking care not to make contact with the metal, she reached into the car and carefully pulled the book out, trying not to smear the pages with her soot-covered gloves.

Volkov watched her with eager eyes, her breaths coming out in short puffs in the cold air. She stood tall, offering the diary to him, hopping from one foot to the other like a child who had done a good painting in class and wished to show it off to her parent at the school gate.

He nodded, acknowledging that this was a win for them. Then he took the notebook gently and opened it, quickly scanning the pages, his heart racing with excitement.

This was it. This was the information they had been sent to retrieve. The reason they had risked their lives and caused so much chaos. And now, it was finally in their hands.

But there was a problem. The diary was written in English. Despite speaking it pretty well, neither of them had the skills to translate it verbatim. They would have to hand it over to their superiors. He closed the diary and looked over at Lyuba. She was still staring at him, waiting for his next move.

All he knew was that now they had opened fire on the Norwegian Police they would be surrounded and outgunned in a matter of hours. If they were lucky, they could simply vanish off the radar of law enforcement, but they needed to get out of there, and fast.

"We'll take the car and drive up the mountain," he said. "We need to find the British agent and eliminate him. His whore, too." He tucked the diary into his jacket.

"How?" Lyuba looked into his eyes, searching for reassurance.

"We think like the enemy," Volkov replied, starting to make his way back up the slope.

"I don't understand," she called after him. "What does that mean?" Volkov stopped walking and turned to her, grinning maniacally in the firelight casting shadows from above. "It means, *Žópa*, that it is time to bring out the big guns..."

***

Flight DY1319 from London Gatwick to Bergen Flesland Airport was a Boeing 737-800 operated by Norwegian Air Sweden. The airline is known for its iconic red and white livery, often referred to as the "red nose".

Designated SE-RPL, the aircraft entered service in January 2020 and had another feature unique to the airline that never fails to catch the eye. Adorning the tail fin of each of the 171-strong fleet is a large portrait of a Scandinavian hero. In this case, it was the Norwegian sculptor, Gustav Vigeland most associated with the magnificent array of his statues in Frogner Park, Oslo.

On this particular flight, the Boeing was only half-full, carrying less than 90 of its full complement of 186 passengers. However, for one passenger in particular, the number on board was of little consequence.

Sitting in seat 8F, Ebony Fadipe was focused on her final destination and the vaguest of missions that awaited her. Camille had already booked her a hire car, a five-seater Audi Q2 automatic, for pick up out of hours. This meant the late hour of her arrival did not affect her plans for the onward journey.

The flight touched down in Bergen, Norway's second city, close to midnight. Despite the late hour, Ebony felt wide awake with a heady mix of anticipation coupled with a healthy dose of fear. This was her first field operation after all.

She had taken more time to select her outfit than she had taking in Anne's hurried briefing. She had finally chosen to dress as practical as possible - trainers (not ones she would miss if they got messed up), jeans, and the thickest, warmest coat she could find. Her hair was tucked under a large, green and yellow woolly hat with a blob of faux fur at its peak.

Her one change of clothing - accompanied by extra knickers and some toiletries - was found in the small cabin bag she now swung gently to and fro as she passed though the baggage reclaim via customs and out into the main arrivals hall.

A large but very firmly closed coffee shop, Espresso house, was situated to her right and ahead the car hire offices. With the lack of passengers and the day almost over it was not difficult to spot anyone lurking around who didn't look like they really belonged. In fact, there was only one man that jumped out at her. He was sitting at one of the tables outside the cafe, no food or drink in sight, and no book, his chin resting on his hands as he stared into the middle distance.

Ebony frowned. Was he a spook? An enemy agent? Or simply a backpacker fresh off a redeye from somewhere exotic? As she got nearer to him, she examined the man in greater detail. He was thick set but certainly not overweight and had a comma of dirty blond hair that fell over his eyes. He was wearing light grey canvas trousers and solid, black boots with a thick, parka style jacket in dark Navy blue. He might even be a native, she supposed. He could even have been on her flight. But then why was he sitting there and not heading home?

Ebony walked past the man, her heart beating a little faster. She had been trained to be cautious and always on the lookout for potential threats. And something about him was off. A gut feeling telling her that he was trouble. As she passed the man's table, he suddenly looked up at her, his piercing blue eyes meeting hers. In that moment, Ebony felt a shiver run down her spine.

She quickened her pace, trying to put some distance between them. But as she approached the car hire office, she allowed herself a swift glance back at the man. He was now standing up, his eyes following her every move. She could feel his gaze burning into the back of her head.

Collecting her keys to the Audi, she stole a surreptitious glance over at the cafe table. The man was nowhere to be seen. Maybe it was just her imagination, she thought to herself as she headed to the exit.

The designated parking lot for the rental agency was unusually dark. There were poles that had lights mounted on them but only half seemed to be working, casting a gloomy atmosphere over the area.

Ebony moved along the row of cars until she spotted the Audi with the right license plate number. It was a nondescript metallic grey but looked almost new. She unlocked the car, threw her small bag in the back, and then climbed into the driver's seat, looking about for how to start the vehicle with the help of the warm interior lights overhead.

Just as she figured it out and closed the door, without any warning the passenger door was thrown open and a figure loomed in, holding a gun.

It was him.

Ebony's heart raced and her eyes flicked from the automatic he was levelling at her - a Glock, she thought - and the key she was holding in her hand, ready to start the car.

As she tried to work out if starting the engine and making a run for it was a death sentence, the man climbed into the passenger seat and shut the door, plunging the Audi's interior into darkness.

CHAPTER 19

When Tilson opened his eyes, he found himself in cold darkness. The first thing he did was check the time on his Omega watch. The glowing dial and hands told him it was already past 4am, which meant he had slept for only a little over five hours.

His head was throbbing from the injury he sustained during the car crash, but he felt grateful to have someone like Helena by his side to patch him up. He wondered if he would have made it through the night without her. He was very grateful to be with such a capable woman.

As he sat up, Tilson could hear the howling wind outside, as if it were a crazed wolf circling around their small hunters' hut, but never quite closing in for the kill. Despite the cold weather, the makeshift building seemed sturdy and well-built. The only source of cold air was from the small gap between the door and its frame.

Helena, who had insisted on taking the first watch, was now fast asleep in the corner of the room. He couldn't blame her. She must have been just as exhausted as him - if not more so - having lugged him up the mountainside. He berated himself. Perhaps she hadn't just conked out; perhaps she had realised the Russians would never find them given the weather conditions and had settled in for the night on the hard floorboards.

Tilson's eyes wandered around the hut and landed on a small wooden stand in the corner next to Helena. On it sat a white porcelain basin, slightly larger than a breakfast bowl. He assumed it was used for washing or cleaning kills, or maybe both. A faded tea towel hung from a nail on the side, with childish images of Norwegian folktales printed on it. In the middle of the wall beside his bed stood a small iron wood burner, with its chimney pipe disappearing into the ceiling. Surprisingly, there was a small pile of chopped firewood on either side of the alcove it sat in.

Silently, he pulled the phone he had stolen from the bar in Flåm from his pocket, turned it on and checked for a signal. No joy. He frowned but then saw his ruck sack sitting on the floor beside the cot bed. He quietly reached across and down, pulling out one of the diaries. Perhaps the

phone would be useful for something else...

The notebook he'd selected was – like the others – A5 in size, approximately 4 cm thick, and bound in a tough material the colour of a good Claret. It was the type of notebook you could buy from posh stationers or fancy book shops. Opening the cover, he found the name "Malcolm Fox" written in pen – a real fountain pen, not a biro – on the first page and then a year: "2018/2019".

This appeared to be volume 1 and as Tilson read the journal, this was confirmed by its contents. Although he was not a fanatical diarist and not every day was covered, when he did write, it would be an essay length entry, detailing his thoughts – often quite philosophical about events at the Embassy that triggered memories or long-held beliefs. Fox clearly thought he needed to get these down on paper for some reason and he even mentioned having never kept a diary before. Instead, he referred to the journal as his "thoughts book".

In the early part of the book Fox wrote of how he had left the Joint Intelligence Committee and taken up a post at the British Embassy in Oslo. However, as the pages turned, the diplomat seemed to become increasingly melancholy in his writing.

It transpired his wife, Barbara, had died a year or so before he moved to Norway and one of his children, Simon. He had been killed on active service in Iraq back in 2003. Fox's surviving child, Ellie, he wrote about a lot. She seemed to have cut all links with her father as Fox mentioned wishing she would call or visit. Indeed, this estranged daughter seemed to be the catalyst for his increasingly cathartic admissions.

At first, he mentioned very little about his time as a spook, but as time wore on, he started mentioning names and operations, missions, and codenames. Just in passing to begin with, late in 2018.

Finishing his documenting of the first volume had taken just under ten minutes, and Tilson knew he had to speed up before Helena awoke.

One by one, he pulled the diaries from his Hard Ware rucksack and flipped through them with haste, skim reading where he could.

He was becoming increasingly aware that the temperature had dropped significantly. By the time he'd finished, the chill in the air was seeping through the cracks in the door, relentlessly creeping into Tilson's bones. He knew the only thing protecting him from the freezing temperatures was the survival blanket given to him by Helena. As he rose from the one-person cot, he made sure not to disturb her peaceful slumber.

He couldn't bear to see her shiver in the cold like he was. Quietly, he made his way to the door, his booted feet barely making a sound on the floorboards.

With a keen eye, he inspected the tiny gap between the door and its frame. The frigid air was finding its way in, making the small space feel even colder. He ran a finger up and down the slit in the wood to check his findings. Tilson was grateful for one thing - the drift outside seemed to be blocking most of the gap, only allowing a small amount of wind to whistle through the top and only marginally through the sides of the door, approximately 10 centimetres from the top.

Still careful not to wake Helena, Tilson tiptoed back to the cloth hanging from its makeshift hook. He gently removed it, knowing it was their only barrier against the unforgiving cold.

Returning to the door, he stuffed the cloth into the tiny gap at the top, hoping to minimize the draft and maximize the little warmth they had left. He was determined to make their shelter as cozy as possible, with the stove and wood.

The details of their surroundings were not lost on Tilson. The howling wind, the icy air, and the ever-present threat of the cold; all these factors could contribute to a feeling of hopelessness and desperation. His Royal Marines training refused to let it break him. He remembered his platoon sergeant saying that every positive action you took showed your determination to stay alive. Making their temporary home a place that was safe and warm was a good start. Tilson turned and gazed at Helena's peaceful face. She was so practical and resourceful. Resilient and caring.

He knew he'd do anything to protect her now.

"*God morgen, min kjære,*" Helena mumbled and followed this with a stretch. Even with her thick clothing Tilson could tell her body would be flexible and graceful like a Siamese cat.

Tilson grinned. She'd called him "My dear".

"Morning, sleepyhead," Tilson replied, confident in his familiarity.

He threw his arms around his chest several times, patting himself warm

"I was just going to light a fire."

Helena looked up at him quizzically. "We will not be seen?"

Tilson jerked his head at the window. "Not in this!"

Helena took in the snow and nodded. "A whiteout," she said. She was referring to a specific weather type that Tilson was familiar with from his Arctic Warfare training.

Often, regular snowfall or blizzards are mistakenly referred to as whiteouts, but in a genuine one a blizzard engulfs the landscape and blurs the boundaries between objects and landmarks. In severe conditions, one may experience a loss of movement, confusion, and an overall reduction in the ability to function.

The sky and terrain blend together, leaving no visual cues for navigation or orientation. Shadows disappear as light is scattered equally in all directions by a continuous layer of white cloud and snow.

For those traveling in a true whiteout, there is a significant risk of becoming completely disoriented, and anyone driving is forced to stop because roads become almost literally invisible.

"Those Russians will never be able to find us in the storm," she said.

"No," Tilson agreed. "So, let's get cozy!"

Within minutes, Tilson had lit the fire and Helena was cooking fish from a tin on her Hexi burner stove.

Really, the situation was dire, and they both knew it. They were stranded in the middle of a blizzard with no way of getting help. They were both exhausted, and it was only a matter of time before they would have to face the harsh reality of their predicament. But, strangely, for now it was like being on a camping trip. Albeit a rather cramped one.

They could push those dark thoughts to the back of their minds.

Once they had eaten, Tilson opened his Hard Ware rucksack and took out the diaries once more. With a sinking feeling in the pit of his stomach he realised one was missing. How had he missed that? He sighed and sat on the cot. Helena looked at him from the floor.

"What's wrong?"

"We're missing one," he explained, waving the diary he was holding in the air. "I must have dropped it when we crashed."

Helena rose and came to sit beside him. Timidly, she put a hand on his knee.

"Don't be hard on yourself, Sam," she said soothingly. "This has been crazy. So dangerous."

Tilson shook his head. He was angry with himself. But Helena was right. This mission had gone from something relatively straightforward to bloody World War III in the space of a day.

"You have most of them. Perhaps if we look through them, we can find something?"

Tilson looked up at her. Still so positive. It was certainly an attractive quality. He nodded. "Sure."

"Get under the blanket," she ordered him.

Dutifully, Tilson climbed under and then watched her as she retrieved a candle from the backpack and set it up on the washstand. She lit it with one of her waterproof matches and then returned to the cot.

"Move over," she said. "That is my blanket, you know!"

They had agreed to let the fire burn down, letting the room heat up and then slowly get cold again before relighting it. This would keep the temperature bearable for longer, rather than chuck all their fuel into the burner for one hit of extreme heat.

Tilson and Helena huddled together under the covers, trying to keep warm and focus on the handwritten journals, but it was proving to be a difficult task. Eventually Helena put the diary down and blinked in the candlelight.

"I am not great with English," she confessed.

"You don't have to read them," Tilson said. "It's not like it's your job."

"I know," she said and wriggled a bit further down the bed, to rest her head on his chest. "I just like to help."

"Without your help, I'd have been..." he trailed off.

"Fucked?" she asked innocently.

Tilson snapped his head round to look at her in mock horror. "I was going to say 'lost'!"

Helena smiled. "That, too."

They laughed easily and Tilson felt the sexual tension between them becoming palpable, and with each passing moment, it seemed to grow stronger. With the fire now just ash, the only source of light was the candle, its flickering flame casting shadows on the walls.

Tilson was dazzled by the way Helena's aquamarine blue eyes sparkled in the candlelight, and the way her lips curved into that beautiful smile.

He found himself drawn to her, wanting to be closer to her. Their laughter echoed in the small cabin, creating a sense of comfort and warmth in an otherwise bleak situation. She looked up at him.

"No girls like me in England?" the Norwegian asked.

Tilson watched her intently. She was teasing him. "Must be," he said. "But I suppose I just never met one."

As they gazed into each other's eyes, the walls that they had built up around themselves began to crumble. Lying in the semi-darkness, both their hearts raced as they tried to ignore the growing attraction between them.

The warmth of their bodies pressed together, their breath mingling in the cold air. In that moment, they were no longer just friends, but two people who had found solace in each other's arms. The flickering candlelight casting shadows on the walls only added to the intimacy of the moment.

Tilson's hand reached out to caress Helena's cheek with the back of his fingers. She closed her eyes and leaned into it, and he moved his hand down to her chin. He pulled it gently toward him and she moved her head, letting her mouth open a fraction as he bent down to kiss her.

As the kiss between Tilson and Helena intensified, their passion for each other could no longer be contained. The heat between them grew more intense, igniting a fire within them that they had been trying to ignore.

Tilson pulled away, breathless, and took a moment to look into Helena eyes. "I've wanted to do that for a while now," he admitted, his voice filled with sincerity.

Helena's smile grew wider, "We've only known each other a day," she laughed, kissing him again.

Tilson felt a little stupid.

"It's OK," she said, her cheeks flushed with desire. "I feel the same."

They continued to caress each other's lips with theirs, bodies becoming entwined as they lost themselves in each other. Nothing else mattered in that moment. The cold cabin, the harsh conditions outside, and even the mission, all seemed insignificant as they focused on each other.

Tilson couldn't resist the urge to further explore Helena's body, unfastening her coat and sliding his hand down her back and stomach, sending shivers down her spine.

"Do you think," Helena asked breathlessly, a grin on her moistened lips. "That we should be getting naked when it is so cold?"

Tilson at once responded by rolling off her. "You're right," he said in a considered tone. "We shouldn't."

A microsecond of silence followed before he took her in his arms again and kissed her even more deeply and full of longing.

It felt like they were trying to make up for some imagined lost time they had, in fact, never squandered. Their hands roamed freely, exploring every inch of the other's body as they shed the outer skin of thick clothing.

Finally naked, Helena squealed in delight and hit him playfully on the leg, letting her hand stay there before gradually moving it up his thigh to cup him gently. He gasped.

There would be no turning back now.

Each caress brought with it a new sensation, a new shudder or intake of breath. The fire within them burned brighter with each passing moment, and they were lost in their own world, oblivious to everything else around them.

As the time melted away, the candle eventually flickered out unnoticed leaving them in almost complete darkness. But even without the light, their connection only seemed to intensify. Their bodies found comfort in each other's embrace, their laughter filled with a new kind of joy. They had found warmth and solace in each other, something that had been missing from their separate and isolated lives.

Tilson felt that he was falling for Helena, and he couldn't deny the emotion any longer. It was a strange realisation, one that both excited and scared him. But in that moment, all he wanted to do was hold her close and never let go. As the dark night seemed somehow to thicken in the snowfall and the wind still howled, Tilson and Helena drifted off to sleep, tangled in each other's arms, covered in the blanket and their discarded clothing.

CHAPTER 20

Helse Vest RHF, also known as the Western Norway Regional Health Authority, is a governmental organization responsible for managing the hospitals in the counties of Rogaland and Vestland. Headquartered in Stavanger, this authority oversees five health trusts and nine hospitals. One of these is the privately operated Laerdal Hospital in the town of the same name.

An Air Ambulance had taken Frida Skardet's body away from the scene of her crash and flown straight up the coast, landing on the helipad behind the two-storey white building in less than 15 minutes and outflying the blizzard approaching from the northwest.

Frida's hospital room was a peaceful oasis amidst the chaos of the small town. The walls were painted a soothing shade of pale green, creating a calming atmosphere for the patient. Three plush chairs were carefully arranged in the room, providing a comfortable space for visitors to sit and offer their support. One chair was placed next to Frida's bed, allowing her loved ones to be close by during her recovery.

The other two chairs were positioned across from each other, creating a cozy sitting area in one corner of the room.

Frida slowly woke, her mouth dry, her side numb but still throbbing with a disconcerting sensation that she knew should be pain. As her eyes adjusted to the light, she could see a handful of intravenous drips feed tubes hanging down from a metallic stand hanging above her head.

Her memories were foggy, but she knew she had been attacked by the Russian agents. She vaguely recalled getting into the Volvo and performing some hairbrained escape down the road, but after that...

Suddenly, she felt a rush of anxiety. What about Tomas? She attempted to move and winced as her side strongly disagreed with the action. Instead, she turned her head. Surely, she'd be able to summon a nurse to help her with a nearby button?

Then she saw her little boy asleep in the chair beside her bed. She almost cried. He was OK.

She turned her head back to the front and tried again to sit up. This time she cried out involuntarily and she heard a soft voice next to her.

"*Momma?*" It was Tomas. "*Momma, Kristus*, I thought you were dead." He jumped up the hot tears flowing from his face with abandon as he told her how worried he had been and how he had been praying for her recovery.

Frida couldn't hold back her tears either and she gestured for him to come to her. Despite her life-threatening injury, she hugged her son tightly.

They stayed like that until the door to her room opened and a nurse came in, busying around the patient and making notes on a data pad. Tomas stood back, looking at his feet. It was only then she noticed he had put on a proper shirt – long-sleeved with a collar. Her big man.

Just then, the Police Chief Ivar Kielland appeared in the open doorway. He had a grave expression on his face as he came in, but he managed an encouraging smile as he drew closer to his officer. It was clear that he was deeply concerned for her well-being.

"Detective bloody Frida Skardet!" he said in a booming voice. "You had us worried there for a while!"

Frida felt a sense of relief wash over her as she saw him. She had always been close with Chief Kielland, and she felt that she could trust him with her life.

"But it's a miracle you're alive, Frida," said Chief Kielland. She tended to agree. A gunshot wound to the abdomen was usually fatal. She looked down at her bandaged stomach and remembered the pain she had experienced when the bullet had pierced her skin.

Tomas shifted uncomfortably and Kielland seemed to notice him for the first time.

The nurse swept from the room without a further word, closing the door behind her.

The Police Chief tried to lift the mood.

"But look at you!" he said with a smile, coming forward to stand by her bed. "Your mother, eh?" he said, turning to address Tomas. "Six hours in surgery and she looks like she's been on a family picnic!"

"Thanks, Chief," Frida said quietly. "You saved my life."

"Not really me," he admitted. "It was Julie who found you. She did a quick patch up job and got you down to the railway station where there was enough room for the helicopter to land."

Frida smiled. Julie Solberg was a bit of a protégé of hers.

"It was her quick thinking that saved you. She called in the Air Ambulance, knowing there wasn't enough time to get a normal one. Plus, with the blizzard…"

He trailed off, and Frida could sense there was something wrong.

"What?"

"Well, it's the weather conditions, Frida. The storm means we had to call off the search for your attackers. The blizzard has made it impossible to track them down."

Until then, she had been feeling groggy and detached from reality, but now a righteous anger was building in her. Kielland knew very well the look that had crept onto her face.

"I'm sorry, Frida," he whispered. "There was really nothing we could do."

His words were like a cold bucket of water thrown in her face.

The storm had put a halt to the search for Russians. The bastards who had put her in this hospital bed, fighting for her life. Frida's mind raced as she thought about the consequences of not being able to find them. They could strike again, targeting innocent people. She couldn't let that happen.

"We found a car up the track before the blizzard hit properly," he continued.

"The Skoda?"

Again, Kielland looked a little uncomfortable. "A Toyota," he said. "Helena Olsen's car. It was burned out. In the drainage ditch. It had overturned in the crash."

"What?" So, she was too late. They had already struck again.

"No bodies, but we saw some tracks leading away from the wreckage."

Frida breathed a sigh of relief. But how was Helena involved in all this? Had she really meant it when she'd sworn revenge?

"What was the Skoda?" Kielland asked.

"The car the Russians were driving."

"Russians," Kielland repeated. "That explains it."

Frida was feeling tired. The exertion of all this was draining her.

"Explains what?" she sighed.

"They're sending someone to take over. Said this is all now a matter of National Security."

Right on cue there was a knock at the door. Kielland turned and opened it.

Standing there was a stunning young woman in a Police uniform. The rank insignia on her epaulettes – two stars with golden borders – told Frida she was equal to her, despite being at most 30 years of age. Her eyes were an amazing – almost yellow – colour, her skin was a deep tan and the hair under her Police baseball hat was beautifully styled into tight curls. She could have been a model.

"*Hallo*," she said cheerfully. "Chief Kielland?"

"Who are you?" the burly policeman man asked, rubbing his grey moustache in irritation.

Amazingly, she performed an immaculate salute. Frida almost laughed.

"*Politioverbetjent* Hedda Riki," the newcomer said. "I'm here to take over *Politioverbetjent* Skardet's case."

Frida couldn't help but sneer. She was through trying to be nice. So, this was the golden girl that Morten had sent to clear up her "mess".

"Right," Kielland replied. "Well, I was just paying my respects to the very woman, here."

Hedda's eyes opened a bit wider. She couldn't have realised the woman lying in the bed was the same woman she was ousting from her job.

Her mouth formed an "O", but she managed to clamp it shut and come forward, extending her hand. "I am so glad to see you're well," she said.

Frida regarded the hand and then waved it away, wincing in pain even though she didn't need to. There was no way she was moving to shake hands with this interloper.

"I wouldn't go that far," Frida said. "Sorry?"

"I am not exactly 'well'," she said through clenched teeth.

Hedda nodded, biting her lip. "Of course not. I meant no dis – "

"None taken," Frida cut her off, a tight smile now set on her face.

Kielland stepped between them, like a boot thrown between two squabbling alley cats.

"Shall we continue this as we head back to Flåm?" he said, taking his fellow officer by the elbow. "I am sure we have plenty of time in this weather!" He allowed himself a short laugh.

Hedda stopped and turned, frowning at the Police Chief.

"But Sheriff! Haven't you heard? The storm has passed, it's clear skies out there." She pointed to the window.

"You must find Helena," Frida said urgently.

"The Olsen girl is a missing person and of course police resources will be given over to that," Hedda said in an even but icy tone. "Our most pressing concern is the threat to National Security you have uncovered."

She smiled and added, "You've done well, Frida."

"Oh, fuck off!"

Everyone turned to face Tomas, who was standing at the foot of his mother's bed, red-faced, fists clenched. "She almost died and you're talking to her like she's a moron!"

Hedda looked as if she had swallowed some cold sick. Kielland tried to hide a smile as he continued to propel the young detective from Frida's room.

Tomas hung his head as the door closed. "Sorry, *Momma*," he mumbled.

Frida laughed. "Come here, my lovely boy!"

Tomas moved across the room and sat by his mother's bedside once more, holding her hand.

"You," she said squeezing his hand tightly, "Are a chip off the block. I couldn't have put it better myself!"

***

Ebony's hands trembled on the steering wheel of the Audi A2 rental.

She let her gaze stray from looking straight ahead to glance at the man in the passenger seat.

"It's all good," he said. The accent was British, possibly a slight Scottish burr. "My name is Jed Kavanagh. I'm MI6."

The name sent a jolt of recognition through her. Had she heard of him somehow? Maybe she'd seen his name in one of the old files she'd been indexing back in the little ICE office at MI5?

Whether she knew him or not, one question seared her mind.

"What are you doing here?" she demanded, fear turning to anger. "You scared the fuck out of me!"

Kavanagh glanced down at the fourth generation L131A1 Glock 17 Pistol - and lowered it to his lap.

"My apologies," he said without conviction. "I needed you not to shout out or run away. God knows who could be watching."

Ebony spun her head to peer out the side window and then back over her shoulder to look out the rear. She couldn't see anything in the semi darkness of the parking lot.

"What are you talking about? Who's watching us?" She grimaced. "Start making sense or I swear to god, I'll use the pepper spray in my bag!"

It was the one bit of equipment of any use that Anne had requisitioned for her. Although some of the gadgets and gizmos dealt by spy quartermasters in the movies were so farfetched as to tip into the realms of science fiction, both foreign and domestic Services still had some interesting kit developed for clandestine activities.

The pepper spray in question was contained in a small perfume spray with Channel branding. It was small - an exact copy of a 20ml Eau de Toilette Purse Spray -and good for maybe two squirts to an assailant's face.

"Fair enough," Kavanagh said. "I followed your boy from Oslo."

"Why? On whose orders?"

"I can't tell you that. But I'm here to help." he sighed. "But I lost him at Myrdal."

"So did we," Ebony admitted. "Well, a waterfall not far away. We think he lost his phone, or it was broken - either accidentally or on purpose."

"Right," the man said, rubbing the back of his neck. "That's why you're here."

Ebony smiled sarcastically. "I can't tell you that, Jed."

"Touché." Kavanagh grinned. "Well, while you've been in the air, the world has gone to shit in the sleepy little town of Flam. So, we'd better get moving."

Ebony didn't like being given orders by this man she didn't know and certainly didn't trust.

"I was just about to," she said. "Following the orders from my boss."

"Then our orders dovetail nicely, eh?"

She put the destination into her phone and as it worked out the route, she started the engine and pulled away from the airport, heading for National Road 580.

"Just over two and a half hours," she told her new companion. "But

I'm sure we can shave some time off that!"

"I think we'd better," Kavanagh retorted.

"Tell me how the world went to shit, then," she said.

Kavanagh looked at her. "Well, we've got some time so I can go into all the gory detail."

Ebony pulled a face. "'gory'?"

As they drove through the dark streets, Kavanagh explained what he'd been hearing about in and around the small port town. Ebony was aghast at what she was hearing. She had always known Tilson was a bit of a pain, but he had seemed... she hesitated at such an old-fashioned word. Honourable? Although, even for a commando, this sounded like a whole new level of chaos to her.

While Kavanagh continued to fill her in on the details, she felt a sense of dread wash over her. This was not the type of mission she was trained for. In fact, she wasn't trained for any type of mission. But she didn't have time to dwell on this.

They were on their way to Flåm, and Ebony knew they had to act fast when they got there. She was grateful to have Kavanagh by her side, even if she didn't fully trust him. They were both on the same team, working towards the same goal, right?

"You don't think Sam had anything to do with the housekeeper's death, do you?"

"No idea," Kavanagh said, sinking his teeth into one of the duty-free chocolates Ebony had purchased at Heathrow. "But I'd say it sounded more like the sort of thing a GRU agent would do rather than an MI5 rookie."

Ebony felt the sting of defamation and an uncharacteristic twang of esprit de corps sparked within her. "He's a Royal Marines Commando, you know," she said in her colleague's defence.

"That is true," Kavanagh conceded. "So, maybe." Ebony frowned. That wasn't exactly what she'd meant.

"Well, I'm sure he wouldn't do it unless it was to save his life – or another's."

They fell into an uncomfortable silence for the next few minutes as they drove through the dark, deserted streets of Bergen's hinterland, Ebony felt a sudden frisson, a sense of foreboding. Was the Norwegian backwater aware it was about to become a battlefield? And if they were, did they know what a brutal one it could become?

But she was determined to face whatever came her way. She was an agent of MI5. And Kavanagh seemed capable. Perhaps together they could be a force to be reckoned with.

Ebony pushed the Audi to its limits on the icy road heading for Flåm. She was determined to do whatever was required to save Tilson from whatever sticky situation he'd managed to get himself into.

CHAPTER 21

Several hours earlier, Volkov was driving up the track, concentrating hard on the road ahead through the wild sweeps of the windscreen wipers. The Skoda Yeti was complaining as the Russian over-revved the engine and it kept slipping back a few centimetres for every few metres it managed to climb.

The snow was coming down hard now, large flakes splattering on the glass in front of the driver. They built up almost as quickly as the previous ones were pushed aside, Making sticking to the road increasingly difficult.

Lyuba was leaning out of the rear passenger window directly behind Volkov, squinting into the snowstorm, small ice particles forming on her eyelashes. She was shining the SureFire X300 flashlight into the forest beside her. It was on that side that the old Toyota RAV 4 had gone over the lip of the drainage ditch. She was hoping to catch a glimpse of the British agent or his female accomplice. But even the 1,000 lumens of stunning white light it produced was being diffused in the storm so much, it was only illuminating the closest trees.

She was wondering what Volkov had meant by thinking like the enemy and calling in the big guns. She hadn't asked him because he seemed to be in a foul mood. Best to keep quiet and not appear to question him.

If truth be known, the Russian agent was starting to doubt their mission. It had all gone wrong when she'd found the cleaner in the British ex-diplomat's home. She didn't care so much about killing the woman. She was simply collateral damage. She hated weak women; the ones who had to have a man come and help. No. It was the fact that her decision to phone in an anonymous tip about the MI5 agent had backfired. If she hadn't done that, the body might have lain undiscovered for days.

She knew this is what would be crossing Volkov's mind like a deer with a limp. He had been gracious so far in not bringing it up although she had never really found herself applying that word to the behaviour of Kiril Volkov.

With a sigh, she brought her head back in the car, shaking the ice and snow from her hair before winding the window back up. The conditions were worsening by the minute and Lyuba assumed their target was slipping further away with each passing moment.

She knew that Volkov was a skilled agent and a professional. That didn't stop her feeling a sense of real unease. He was a like a pan of milk left on the heat. All seemed quiet and still - everything under control - but then he could suddenly boil over causing damage and destruction to anything in his way. Usually, it was she who managed to tame the volcano, but in this instance, she was the root cause and she doubted she would be able to placate him.

The Skoda Yeti was struggling to navigate through the heavy snow, and Lyuba was wishing it wouldn't. Every slip and skid made the man in front swear under his breath. She winced at every expletive, as Volkov's frustration continued to grow.

Lyuba's thoughts were interrupted by a sudden swerve of the Skoda Yeti, causing her to grip onto the door handle for dear life. Volkov had slammed on the brakes as they came upon what looked like a wall of some sorts blocking their path, the snow and ice making it nearly impossible to see.

"*Pizdets*!" Volkov screamed the worst possible curse, sending flecks of spittle flying at the inside of the windscreen.

With a sense of dread creeping over her, Lyuba placed a cautious hand on Volkov's shoulder and prepared her most soothing voice.

"Don't worry, *lyubov' moya*," she said - my love. "I will take a look."

She opened the door and climbed out, slamming it behind her. The cold was breathtaking, but if anything, it was a relief to be out of the car, away from him.

She had to hold her head down and lean into the wind it was so strong. She approached the dark wall, her head turned against the snow that was whipping into her face.

When her hands touched the wall, she could tell it was a relatively modern farm building of some sort constructed from a corrugated plastic of carbon material. She leant against the wall and gradually felt her way along it until she came to a door. As she was about to open it, she wondered if the British agent or his accomplice would be there, staring back at her.

Instead, she was even more startled by the strange vertical pupils of a goat. Many goats, in fact, all suddenly crowding at the door that had a metal mash across the bottom half. They started bleating, asking for food.

Lyuba cautiously opened the lower grille and stepped into the dimly lit barn, pulling the door to, behind her. The goats bleated and crowded around her, belligerent in their hunger. She couldn't help but feel relieved and a bit amused by the situation. Fucking goats! She laughed out loud and started feeling along the interior wall for a light switch.

When she found it, the flickering strip lighting 20 feet above showed her there were some 50 goats standing, lying and wandering about on dirty straw that was strewn across the floor as bedding and potential food.

The moment the lights came on, the goats all came running to her, as if she was their messiah. They were bleating so loudly she was sure Volkov would hear them.

"All right!" she said. "All right!"

She may have been a GRU agent now, but she'd grown up on a farm in her native Saratov *Oblast*.

To her right was a fenced off area the goats could not reach. Stacked on its concrete floor were a dozen or so bales of fresh straw, a trio of hay bales for fodder and a few sacks of what she assumed were livestock pellets - the goat's main food.

She waded through the throng that had gathered around her and climbed over the fence, noting a long, shallow trough attached to it. The noise was becoming almost unbearable, echoing off the plastic walls of barn, joining with off-key howling of the wind in a cacophony that was giving her a headache.

Lyuba grabbed one of the sacks and noted an old sickle sticking out from a wooden kitchen cabinet that stood incongruously a few feet away.

She grabbed the tool and sliced the sack open with its slightly rusty blade. It was sharp enough, though, for the job and pellets of animal feed started falling to the ground.

She hoisted the bag onto the fence and let its contents cascade down into the trough where the goats were all now lined up to feed. They fell silent as they started eating and Lyuba smiled.

As they eagerly chomped away at the meal, she took a moment to catch her breath and collect her thoughts. Volkov's frustration and anger were still palpable back in the car, and she knew she had to find a way to salvage the situation. But for now, she was content to be surrounded by these innocent creatures, away from the tension and danger of their mission. She smiled to herself, grateful for this unexpected moment of peace amidst the chaos.

"There you go!" she said. "Auntie Lyuba's here to make su -"

She was cut short by Volkov who had appeared behind her through another door. he spun her round to face him and slapped her hard across her face.

"What the hell are you doing, you stupid bitch?"

Lyuba turned her head back to face Volkov. "What the fuck was that for?" she asked her eyes flashing with anger. "I was shutting these stupid animals up!"

"You left me in the car," he hissed. His breath was hot on her face. But Lyuba did not flinch.

"I was coming back, you big baby!" she said, smiling at him now. "Jesus!"

They looked at each other for a moment and then Lyuba stepped easily away, walking over to the other door.

It was a larger one, actually two doors – like a garage. They could park the car there overnight. Take shelter in warm straw and get the British agent the moment the storm abated.

"Was it too dark out there on your own?" she teased, hoping she had judged the situation correctly.

"Shut up," he said loudly, but his voice was more relaxed.

He had obviously had the same idea. Perhaps she would escape his wrath this time.

It was not meant to be.

After he'd driven the Skoda into the barn and closed the doors behind it, he searched through the farm supplies and looked in every locker, drawer, and cupboard. Lurking at the back of one of the cabinets where Lyuba had found the sickle was an unmarked bottle of clear liquid. It had no label, but Volkov took what looked like a home-made stopper from the neck of the bottle and sniffed at the contents. Then he took a small sip and swallowed.

"Moonshine!" he said with a glint in his eye.

"What we need is food," Lyuba said, trying to avert her partner drinking on an empty stomach.

Volkov looked at her with something approaching hatred. Then he looked past her, and a nasty smile came to his mouth.

"No problem, *Žópa*," he said coming forward and taking the sickle from her. "You love these goats, *pravda*?" Then he climbed over the fence, grabbed the nearest animal between his legs and, as it bleated in terror, slit its throat.

He looked up at Lyuba with a cruel smile. "I love goat, too. Now, build me a fire!"

Lyuba had watched in horror as Volkov slaughtered the poor creature without a second thought. Was she next?

She berated herself as she realised - not for the first time - that she was working with a man who had no real regard for life, be it animal or human. He was a killer. He took pleasure in it. She was an agent. She'd worked hard to get where she was. But she knew she had to keep her cool and play along if she wanted to survive this night let alone the mission.

It was astounding how quickly he had switched from anger to excitement at the sight of the moonshine and blood. But she knew better than to question his actions, especially when he was in this state.

She plastered a fake smile on her face as Volkov gleefully took out his phone and called Control. Despite the blizzard, he managed to get through. He requested an assault team to help them finish the job followed by immediate exfiltration.

When he hung up, he'd even looked happy. "They're sending a sub," he said excited by the prospect. Then he set to butchering the unfortunate goat that he'd dragged from the pen and was bleeding on the concrete floor.

The only wood in the barn was the kitchen cabinet so she duly broke that up with an axe she found in a nearby cupboard. As opposed to the rusty, old sickle, the axe looked brand new. She took out her anger and resentment on the furniture until she had some decent sized kindling and some larger pieces that should last long enough to cook the goat meat.

As they sat by the fire, eating their makeshift meal, Lyuba's mind raced with thoughts of how she could get out of this situation. She had been so naive to think that working for the GRU would be any different from her life on the farm, and the burly Slavic farmhands who had teased and sometimes abused her.

Volkov finished his handful of meat and wiped the fat from his lips with the back of his hand. But then he reached down and ripped another chunk from the carcass. But it was not for him. To Lyuba's disgust, he tossed it into the goats' pen. A couple of them squabbled over it but the bigger of two won the competition and started chewing.

The balding man laughed maniacally. "Fucking cannibals!" he exclaimed and took a swig at the last dregs of the moonshine. "Did you see that?"

Still laughing, he took another piece of meat and did the same thing.

Again, one of the goats managed to get the prize and started chewing.

Volkov rolled back on the straw bale. "Stupid fucking goats," he said.

As the moment passed, he leant forward, elbows on his knees, hands clasped together. He looked across the fire at Lyuba and smiled lasciviously.

Lyuba couldn't believe what he was doing but felt powerless as he stood up and came over. He reached down, pulled her to her feet, and stated to sway, dancing drunkenly around the fire as he nuzzled her neck.

Then he stopped and stood back, admiring the woman's body.

Volkov's lustful eyes bore into her, his hands reaching out to touch her. She was exhausted, but she knew she had to play this carefully. She pushed him away, her voice firm and resolute.

"Not now, Kiril, please" she said. "We should rest. We have to be ready for the assault team."

He ignored her protests and quickly unzipped her jacket and moved onto her shirt.

But Lyuba was not one to give in easily. She pushed Volkov away, her eyes blazing with defiance. She knew she had to placate him, but she refused to let him have complete control over her. She was not just a helpless pawn in his sick mind games.

"We need to focus on the mission," she said firmly, trying to regain some semblance of control over the situation. "We can't afford to be distracted by this."

But Volkov was way beyond listening to reason. He grabbed her forcefully and pulled her towards him, his breath reeking of alcohol.

"Who cares about the mission?" he slurred, his hands roaming over her chest and down into the band of her trousers. "We have all the time in the world."

He pushed her to the ground and started unbuttoning his trousers.

Lyuba scrambled to stand up she spied the axe resting against the sacks of animal feed.

But then he had her again, his arms clamped around her stomach. She couldn't let him have his way with her. She was a trained agent, and she would not let him break her. Taking advantage of his drunken state, she managed to push him away and grabbed the axe.

"I said 'no', Kiril," she said, brandishing it threateningly. "Now back off, before I chop your wood!"

Volkov stumbled back, a look of anger and confusion on his face. Lyuba held her ground, her eyes never leaving Volkov's as she waited for him to make a move. She was ready to fight if she had to, but she prayed that he would back down.

"This isn't you, *lyubov' moya*," she said quietly. "Now sleep it off. I'll keep watch. From the car."

She snatched the car keys from the side where Volkov had left them along with his phone. Then she opened the Skoda, climbed into the driver's seat, and shut the door, Volkov watching her through the windscreen. Finally, she clicked the button on the fob to activate the central locking. She was safe.

CHAPTER 22

The Russian Navy's Northern Fleet has long relied on submarines as its dominant force. However, the current contingent has been aging for some time, raising uncertainty about its efficacy. To answer these concerns president Vladimir Putin ordered the production of a generation of models to keep up with NATO forces.

These include the *Yasen* Class nuclear-powered cruise missile submarines, which are considered to be Russia's most advanced and formidable vessels. They are highly regarded for their stealth capabilities, even being compared favourably with some contemporary

Western submarines. The US Office of Naval Intelligence reckons the *Yasen* Class is the quietest, least detectable, of modern Russian or Chinese models.

Designated K-560, the *Severodvinsk* is the lead vessel of that class. Again, it is much admired – and feared – by Western military strategists and senior officers alike. It was even singled out by the Naval Sea Systems Command's program executive officer for submarines, as a tough potential opponent. Indeed, the Pentagon was completely in the dark when the *Severodvinsk* slipped into the Atlantic Ocean unnoticed and managed to evade all attempts to find her for several weeks in the summer of 2018, her maiden deployment.

With a length of 456 feet, the *Severodvinsk* is a formidable submarine. If its seven-blade screw back propeller was placed on the ground beside the iconic Big Ben clock tower in London, the impressive warship's length would tower over it by some 140 feet.

At that moment, the *Severodvinsk* was moving stealthily through the icy waters of Aurlandsfjord. The 18-mile-long inlet is a branch off the main Sognefjorden, Norway's longest and deepest fjord. That said, this little offshoot is over 3,000 feet below sea level. However, its width is generally less than two miles making navigation reasonably tight for such a long boat.

Defying Norway's territorial boundaries, the boat proceeded towards a tiny beach on the shore, north-east of Flåm. This was where the four-person unit of elite Spetsnaz operatives were to be released. They would go ashore before dawn, the crepuscular semi-darkness serving as the perfect cover for their covert mission. It also allowed the ship to complete its journey without drawing any attention.

As the *Severodvinsk* cut through the frigid waters of Aurlandsfjord, its crew worked tirelessly to maintain its stealth capabilities. Despite being deep in Norwegian territory, the submarine remained undetected, a testament to its advanced design and technology. The Spetsnaz team on board the vessel was preparing for their mission. They were Russia's elite special forces, trained for covert operations and skilled in various forms of combat.

Their primary goal was to disembark and meet up with two GRU agents who were on a top-priority and extremely clandestine assignment. It was inconceivable that even the new, belligerent Russia - which had invaded Ukraine just over a year before - would dare to be discovered in Norwegian territory unless the operation was of crucial significance.

There was only ever one time a Russian sub had been spotted in a Norwegian fjord and that was back in the Autumn of 1990, when a minisub containing a four-man team from the Navy Special Operation Command was seen to surface briefly in the waters of Jarfjord, near Kirkenes. It remained there for several minutes before silently diving back beneath the surface.

This was a far more major incursion.

The *Severodvinsk* has risked coming to broadcast depth only a few hours earlier, around 3am local time, deploying the antenna for its *Kora* satellite communications system. Only breaking the surface of the fjord for mere minutes, the captain was given the message that their mission had changed. Initially, he'd brought his boat into these waters for the simple task of exfiltrating Volkov and Lyuba, Now, he had been ordered to pass on the need for an assault team to assist the GRU agents in finishing the mission to the commandos attached to his ship.

The rest of the crew had been told that the future security of their country depended on their success. As such, they were all ready to risk everything for the motherland.

Now on the final approach to their deployment zone, the crew were tested to the extreme, silent running at a speed that never topped 14 knots – around 15mph – half what the sub's would usually operate at when submerged silent. This was due to the depths of the waters and navigation hazards such as submersed rocks and mud banks. There were also the local, small vessels to consider along with the cruise ship moored nearby. Although that wasn't expected to leave until later that day and by then, if all went to plan, the team would be back on board along with the GRU agents.

The design of the ship was sleek and menacing. An inky black colour, the boat's "conning" tower was located almost at the bow, itself thin and tall. All the sub's communications equipment protruded from the upper hull of this raised section: the Anis Park Lamp radio direction finder, MRKP-58 Radian ESM/radar mast, and the non-penetrating electro-optical periscope – along with the Kora antenna the Russians had used earlier.

Forward of this point and sitting just behind the main navigation bridge with its five windows, the tower contained an innovation for Russian subs – an escape capsule, the VSC. When the Kursk disaster occurred in August 2000, Russian submarine design had to change. An explosion onboard caused the vessel to sink to the bottom of the Barents Sea, killing the entire 118-strong complement of men. Ironically, it was Norwegian rescue divers who opened the outer hatch, finding the airlock flooded. They also found a chilling note from the Captain saying simply; ""None of us can get out".

Since then, newer Russian submarines have been fitted with a detachable pod that can float to the surface when detached from the main body of the tower for retrieval of personnel. Unbelievably the VSC can accommodate the entire crew of the *Severodvinsk* in its cramped space.

On this occasion, the VSC would not be deployed, but the four-man team of special forces soldiers would use it to exit the submarine via its airlock hatch before using scuba equipment to reach the shoreline and infiltrate inland to the forest where the GRU agents were waiting for them.

The four men now preparing their gear in a compartment beneath the hatch were seasoned members of Spetsnaz 420th Marine Reconnaissance. Initially, this unit was made up of soldiers from anywhere in Russia, but the fact that they were deployed exclusively to the Northern Fleet meant that – in the process of training - problems arose with acclimatisation to the wintry conditions and low water temperatures. Residents of areas further south, in warmer climes could not get used to the harsher, colder operational environment. As such, the unit is only drawn from the populations of Russia's northern regions.

In the first stage of the selection process groups of volunteers would be landed from a helicopter some 200 km from their base, and made to march back across the tundra, testing their aptitude, both physical and psychological, for these conditions. Only then could 420 MCI recruits head onto pass selection and become Commando Frogmen – known colloquially as the "Sea devils" by the Russian Navy. They receive training in diving and mountaineering, the latter to facilitate their ability to scale the steep sides of Norwegian fjords.

The leader of the group was *Kapitan-leytenant* Nikolay Aliev, a 33year-old former Olympic swimmer who missed team selection due to his military service and the doping scandal that surrounds the Russian team, meaning they could not compete under their country's flag. He was blond, square-jawed, and athletic with brown eyes and a sly sense of humour.

Around him were the three non-commissioned soldiers in his unit. *Starshina* 1st Class Dmitriy Nikitin, a 35-year-old body-building nut standing at 6 foot 4 inches to his bald head, Maksim Kuzmin a badass, 30-year-old sailor who had been in and out of trouble his whole life, a street brawler with a broken nose and many scars to show the knife fights he'd survived, and finally Artyom Shevchenko a newly minted Sea Devil, just 24 years old and fresh-faced with a tight smile and a buzzcut of chestnut hair.

Kapitan-leytenant Aliev gave the order, and they donned their drysuits over their black combat fatigues before checking one another's rebreathers, facemasks and air supply tubes. With the divers' signal for

"OK" all round, Starshina Nikitin led Shevchenko up the short ladder to the airlock hatch. Once they were inside the chamber and the door to the inside of the sub was closed behind them, water started to fill the space.

They waited for the pressure to equalise with the exterior waters and then opened the second hatch to the outside and half-pulled themselves and half swam through it into the almost freezing waters of the Aurlandsfjord. Nikitin returned to the hatch and closed it once more. He then waited with Shevchenko bobbing nearby, as the procedure was repeated and his commanding officer and Kuzmin joined them in the open water.

With the outer hatch secured once more, they steadily made their way from the lurking shadow of the base submarines and headed towards the shore some half a kilometre away. By Aliev's divers watch it was just after 0600 local time. They had two hours at least before dawn.

The group moved slowly and cautiously, their eyes becoming quickly accustomed to the dark, murky waters of the icy-cold fjord. As they swam, their training kicked in, each member moving in perfect sync with their partner, their bodies cutting through the icy water with ease. The mission was a dangerous one, and they knew that their success depended on their ability to work as a team. But for the Spetsnaz, this was not an issue.

They were the best of the best, and they had been handpicked for this important task. As they approached the shore, the group could see the rocky, muddy bed of the fjord sloping upwards. The shoreline was treacherous, with large boulders and sharp rocks littering the beach. They knew they had to be careful if they were going to make it to their target undetected.

Crouching in the water, each man scanned the shoreline with their night vision goggles, searching for any signs of a potential threat. But it was quiet and still, with only the sound of the slowly abating storm, the wind whistling quietly and the gentle lapping of the water against the shore. Satisfied that there was no one around, only then did they creep forward, shedding their scuba gear and hiding it - along with extra rebreathers and dry suits for their GRU comrades – securely among the large sea rocks.

Now clad in their dry combat fatigues and armed with their weapons, they were ready to move forward. The group slipped up the beach, their steps silent and their movements calculated. They were well-trained and experienced, and they knew the importance of stealth in completing such an infiltration mission. They were parts in a well-oiled machine, each member knowing their role and trusting their teammates explicitly.

The VSS Vintorez sniper rifle slung on Aliev's shoulder was his trusted companion, a weapon he had used in countless missions before. But like the others, he had also equipped himself with a more rapid-fire weapon. His brand-new AK-15 was a force to be reckoned with, and Aliev knew he could count on it in case things got heated.

Shevchenko, on the other hand, had chosen the AKS-74U, a compact assault rifle that was perfect for close combat. And then there was Kuzmin, the burly soldier who preferred the Pecheneg machine gun. Its sheer power and accuracy made it the ideal weapon for a man of his size. Finally, their commanding officer carried an AS Val assault carabine, a weapon known for its stealth and precision. Together, they made a formidable team, each one an expert in their own right.

Above them on the road, a lorry's engine complained as it ploughed through the thick snow, leaving a trail of muddy slush in its wake. The icy air was thick with tension as the four Russian soldiers huddled together, their weapons at the ready. They were prepared for anything, of course, but none of them was keen to be discovered so early in the mission.

The dangerous looking foursome waited in the semi-darkness as a lorry braved the snowy conditions of the E16, its headlights never penetrating far enough into the snow flurries to reveal the Russian Sea devils hiding nearby. Once it had driven safely past and its red rear lights had become hazy pink pinpricks in the white darkness, Aliev signalled they should move up, cross the road and start climbing the hillside to their rendezvous point.

CHAPTER 23

When Tilson woke up he found Helena naked but for her coat, looking at one of the diaries. It was much lighter outside now and she was reading without the candle or the
flashlight from her phone. She noticed he had opened his eyes and turned to kiss him before sitting back up again and putting the diary away.

"I still cannot read this very well," she said. "It is his memories from his earlier life, written out during the years of his retirement. I can tell that. But the names and what he says? They mean nothing to me."

Tilson laughed. "I'd be worried if they did!"

She turned to smile at him, and his heart felt as if he'd been jolted by a crash cart. They had found something special in the darkness of that night, and it was something they both knew they couldn't ignore. From that night on, they were no longer just friends, but something more.

Tilson couldn't believe how quickly things had escalated between them, but he didn't want to stop. He had never felt this way about anyone. It was heady. He berated himself. He was being a classic giddy schoolboy, not a trained Royal Marines Commando and MI5 operative.

However, he knew they had to talk about their situation. They couldn't just ignore the fact that they were stranded in the middle of nowhere, with only each other for company.

"I don't want to ruin this moment," Tilson said softly, "but we need to talk about what happens next."

Helena nodded. Her eyes were suddenly serious. "I know," she said quietly. "We can't stay here forever."

Tilson took a deep breath. "When the storm breaks, we should split up. You know these mountains. You should head back to town."

"What? And leave you here? She asked incredulously.

"No. I'll lead the Russians away. I'm trained for warfare and tactics in these very conditions."

"That may be," Helena said, pouting slightly, "But as you say, I live here. I know this land. I am staying with you, Sam."

She was right. But he didn't want to endanger her any more than he already had. She turned to look at him with her scintillating eyes.

He grinned. "You win," he said.

"Good," she replied. "I like to win!"

Their eyes locked and Tilson was suddenly aware of how powerfully intoxicating a woman she was: beautiful but with such inner strength, and an ability to lead just as proficiently, if not better, than he had. She was an inspiration. He felt the need to kiss her again and he went to lean in for a final embrace before they got dressed.

Before he could make contact with Helena, a bullet smashed through the window, shattering both the glass and their snowbound romantic dream simultaneously.

"Get down!" Tilson was on his feet, shielding her as she lay down, breathing hard.

"My rifle," she said.

Tilson looked across the tiny cabin and saw it leaning against the far wall. He crawled over and passed it to her. She cocked the weapon and moved across the floor to the other corner, from where he could see through the broken window.

"What are you doing?" he asked. She was now standing, totally naked aiming the hunter's rifle in the direction of the window, standing well back in the shadows.

"Get dressed!" she hissed. "Hurry! I will cover you."

As she finished speaking, she thumbed the safety off and fired her first shot into the white blur beyond the hut.

A second and third shot rang out, the sound of them deadened by the snowy blanket that covered everything around the secluded hut. But inside, the staccato burst echoed like thunderclaps rolling up a valley. In the snowy silence, Tilson could feel the vibrations of each bullet penetrating the wooden walls.

He quickly threw on his clothes, his movements fluid and precise, before switching places with Helena. She was equally efficient, her movements graceful yet purposeful as she dressed herself in record time. He drew his eyes away from her to check his ammo, grimacing at the low number. Only 13 rounds left. He would have to be selective and make each shot count. He couldn't afford to miss. Not when their lives were on the line.

But the consequences of this mission weighed heavily on Tilson's mind. He knew with absolute certainty that if an agent of a friendly state were to take a life with an illegal firearm, even in self-defence, it would result in a severe prison sentence. The weight of this knowledge hung heavy on his shoulders, a constant reminder of the dangerous game they were all playing.

Helena, with her sharp mind and quick reflexes, had already understood this. She had shown it the night before, when she effortlessly aimed her weapon at the trees surrounding the GRU agents. Her actions had been calculated, precise, and ruthlessly efficient.

But there was more to Helena than her deadly skills.

She was a complex and intriguing woman, with a past that he realised that he knew nothing about. Her piercing gaze held a hint of sadness, a pain that she tried to hide behind a tough exterior. Obviously, the fact she'd only just lost her mother. Yet, despite her tough exterior, there was still a warmth in her voice that drew him in.

She had a way of making Tilson feel like he was the only person in the world - but he had to remind himself that indeed he had been the only one in her world for the past 12 hours. Nonetheless, it was a rare quality in his line of work, where trust was a luxury and vulnerability could be fatal.

He was struggling with surprisingly strong emotions, a mix of desire, admiration and a nagging sense of danger. She was like a flame, beautiful and alluring, but he felt she was still capable of burning anyone who got too close. And yet, he couldn't resist her pull. Together, they did make a formidable team, it was true. Both with their own strengths - and weaknesses - but together they seemed unstoppable. He couldn't imagine this mission without her by his side.

For sure, this had become a dangerous mission, but it was one Tilson was trained for. In fact, he'd literally signed up for when he joined the Royal Marines after his A levels a decade ago. Queen - King, now - and country. But she hadn't. She was a civilian. And one who should have felt out of her depth. But she took every twist and danger on without complaint.

Tilson felt Helena's body press against his from behind, as she aimed her rifle through the broken window. He knew she was a skilled hunter, but this was a different kind of battle. They were fighting for their lives.

As another bullet smashed into the woodwork around the shattered pane of glass, he felt a pang of guilt for bringing her into this situation. Technically, of course, he hadn't. She'd insisted. But he could have left her behind at any point. Instead, he'd used her – in every possible sense.

"I saw them both behind that group of trees," she whispered in his ear. It sent an excited shiver down his spine. She was waving the muzzle of her Sauer 404 at a clump of a dozen younger, shorter pines on the edge of the tree line about 30 metres away.

Although dawn was still an hour away, the sky was clear and the daylight was already creeping over the horizon, illuminating everything in a strange, dark ochre glow. Tilson watched carefully and after a second, he saw a flicker of movement. Then there was another shot and this time he spied the tell-tale muzzle flash.

"They're not advancing, he said. "They're both in that clump of trees, both shooting."

As he spoke a bullet impacted the door of the hut, several feet to his right. "And not with any great accuracy, either."

"Why?" Helena asked. "They wanted to kill us last night!"

Tilson nodded. Why, indeed. Then it hit him, and he felt a cold chill in the pit of his stomach.

"They're keeping us here," he said.

"Maybe they wait for us to run out of ammunition." Helena said.

He pondered this and then shook his head. "I don't think so. They might know how much I have by the Vektor's clip size, but they have no way of knowing how many rounds you have in your bag."

"So why, then?" She took careful aim and returned fire, hitting one of the trees and sending splitters blooming in the freezing air.

"I think they have back-up coming."

There was a nasty silence as this sunk in. Tilson now knew they couldn't hold out forever. They needed a plan, and fast.

"Helena, we need to retreat," Tilson said quietly in a lull between gunshots. "We can't stay here any longer."

She nodded, her eyes blazing with determination. "If they are in front of us only, then we can go the other way," she said.

"They'll see us using the door."

Helena grinned at him. "We make a new door."

She moved to the back of the hut and examined the wooden boards from which the wall was constructed. she gave one a hefty kick with her boot and it gave a little.

"If we can take two of these out, we can squeeze through," she explained. "But they cannot know what we do."

She held up the rifle and mimed hitting the butt of it against the wall.

"Every time I hit the wood, you shoot."

So that is what they did, Tilson counting down from random odd numbers - 3, 5, 3, 7, 9, 5 - and then Helena sashing the stock of her rifle into the planks as Tilson aimed as well as he could into the group of trees and fired.

After the sixth attempt, one of the boards was loose enough for Helena to yank it away, revealing a thick, mossy substance that acted as insulation for the hut. She quickly tore that aside, too, allowing them both to see the white virgin snow and lightening blue sky above.

She gave a thumbs up and they repeated the process. This time it was much faster to remove the board and in only three shots, they were ready to leave.

"You go," Tilson said. "Get as far as you can using the hut to block their line of sight. I'll use my last rounds to keep them thinking we're both still inside. I'll follow when I see you signal to me. OK?"

She nodded earnestly and then slid through the gap in the rear wall, turning back to glance at him as soon as she was outside. She gave a thumbs-up, which he returned, and then started running, staying low and quiet as she went.

Tilson returned to the window and really tried to aim as best he could. There is some debate about the effective range of the Vektor.

Russian official statistics would have you believe it is an incredible 150 metres. Tilson didn't believe it for a minute. It was far more likely to be half or even a third of that figure. Nonetheless he waited for another shot from the GRU agents to spot the muzzle flash. Then he took careful aim and pulled the trigger, controlling his breathing to make the shot fly as true as possible.

His patience was rewarded by a scream. It sounded like a woman. This was followed by a string of Russian expletives and a volley of shots that suddenly stopped. Tilson guessed the man had exhausted his magazine and was having to reload, or even taking the opportunity to check out his wounded comrade.

When he turned to look through the makeshift exit in the hit, he saw Helena crouching in a dip in the landscape and partially hidden by a snowdrift. She saw him looking and gave a curt wave to say she'd reached the extremity of the Russian's field of view.

He moved to stand at the hole and shot through the window, not really caring where the shot landed, just that they would not approach just yet, thinking they were still there.

Then he spied a coil of reasonably modern climbing rope hanging from the wall above the makeshift wash basin. He grabbed it, and put it over his head and one arm, wearing it like a bandolier. Then he squeezed through the gap and darted across the snow field to where Helena was waiting for him.

As he went to ground beside her, he could see the dip was actually the water channel of a shallow stream, now frozen solid. With the snow drift above it, they would be able to crawl along its length unnoticed. Tilson quickly relayed this to Helena, and they started leopard crawling away from the hut, almost at right angles to it, following the stream's course north northwest, downhill.

Behind them they could hear the occasional thump of gunfire from the Russians, but as the minutes past they became quieter.

"If we get far enough, there are more trees on that side," Helena whispered, pointing ahead of herself. I think my apartment is at the foot of this side of the mountain!"

She turned and smiled at Tilson.

"Home and dry," Tilson replied with a wink.

Then he saw Helena's face freeze before the smile faded from her mouth as if erased by Photoshop. Tilson turned to see what she was looking at and once more he found himself wondering if this mission was never going to go their way.

Making their way steadily across the snow-covered meadows was a group of four men in polar camouflage fatigues, all carrying nasty looking weaponry. The way they moved told Tilson that they did not want to be discovered. This meant they weren't Norwegian forces. They could only be the back-up he thought the GRU were waiting for.

"Spetsnaz," he said with a growl.

They were now in deep shit.

CHAPTER 24

Flåm's tranquil façade was bathed in the soft glow of dawn, a coastal town seemingly untouched by the chaos that lay beneath its surface. As she navigated the Audi through the quiet streets, Ebony's mind raced, struggling to piece together the unfolding events. She had been so sure that Tilson's mission was a straightforward one. That he was living out his dream of getting away from the boring women - and Gareth - at ICE.

Then the bloody GRU had raised their ugly heads. And now there were too many missing pieces to the puzzle, too many unanswered questions. But with the pressure of the Russian threat looming over them, she knew she had to keep going, forgive Tilson his desire for action and maybe even save his ass. Finally coming to a halt near the station— the last place they had been able to establish Tilson hadn't reached - an uncomfortable feeling settled in the pit of her stomach, nasty little butterflies casting a shadow of uncertainty over her thoughts.

As they waited anxiously in the car, Ebony considered the possibilities. Kavanagh's lack of conversation only added to her mounting frustration. She had no idea what to do next, but she couldn't shake the feeling that they were missing something crucial. Her thoughts turned to the police reports, the only thread they had to follow. The lack of electronic surveillance - her speciality - was a major obstacle, but she was determined to find a way to track Tilson's movements.

Finally, Ebony broke the silence. "OK," she said with a huff. "What's our next move?"

Kavanagh, seated beside her, gazed ahead with an inscrutable expression. Finally, he responded but his tone belied a veiled trace of sarcasm, "You tell me," Kavanagh said, still gazing ahead of him.

"What's your brilliant plan?"

She frowned. He was belittling her. She sighed. So what if she wasn't a seasoned field agent like him? She still had her more than capable mind. She didn't need GPS trackers and social media feeds to help her think.

She methodically recounted the sequence of events they had pieced together from the police reports.

"We have the murder of the Fox's cleaner and the break-in at the arms manufacturer where he was working. Then there's the daughter of the cleaner, Helena. Her car was found abandoned on the mountain road, having been in an accident. And then there's the shooting of a police officer close to that."

As she spoke, a sense of unease settled in her stomach. It was clear that Tilson was on the run, but she wondered if any of these horrific events was down to him. Everyone was chasing after him. Certainly, she could feel all these events were connected, but the missing pieces were still eluding her. Tilson was a soldier. He wouldn't be afraid to use violence to protect himself. But had he killed the cleaner? Shot at the Police?

Kavanagh remained annoyingly stoic; his focus unwavering. "So?"

A plan began to coalesce in Ebony's mind. "We should head to the accident site."

Kavanagh nodded in agreement. "Let's go then!"

Driving to the site of the accident, the crisp morning air carried with it an undeniable sense of foreboding. Or so it seemed to her. The mountains felt as if they were looming over her, and the winding road, flanked by dense forests and towering cliffs, seemed to coil tighter with each passing mile. Kavanagh seemed unaffected, an enigmatic smile on his lips, like a kid on a school outing.

Her thoughts spiralled like a squirrel trapped in a cage, and she couldn't shake the nagging feeling that Tilson might already be dead. An unsettling premonition gnawed at her, but she pushed it aside.

Upon reaching the accident site, Ebony found herself at the edge of a barely passable mountain road, surrounded by thick pine forest.

They both got out and examined their surroundings. The abandoned car—a battered and forlorn relic—rested in a ditch in a snow drift. It was burned out and the area around the vehicle had been marked out by blue and yellow tape that also bore the word "Politi".

There was no clue as to what had happened. The car had a few inches of snow on it and any sign of tracks, or a fight had been drowned in the beautiful blanket of white. There were tyre imprints all over the road showing that there had been a lot of activity recently – after the snowstorm. But not much else.

"No sign of our boy," Kavanagh offered unhelpfully.

Ebony rolled her eyes. "No shit, Captain Obvious," she said.

Kavanagh frowned now. It was an unpleasant sight. He looked like a thunder god who'd given his clap to someone else.

Ebony pretended to be oblivious to his dark look and climbed back into the car. No sign. She looked up the mountain. If Tilson had been here, what would he have done? As she'd pointed out to Kavanagh earlier, Tilson was a former Marine. Royal Marine, she corrected herself with a slight smile.

She rolled the window down. "Get in, matey. I know where he is!"

The moment the passenger door closed, she started the car with the touch of a button and slipped the automatic into drive. If he was being chased, he'd go uphill, into the snow, into the wilds. He'd think that his training would be better than that of any pursuers. And he was probably right, to be honest. With her hesitancy gone, she put her foot down and the car sped away from the crash site, further up the snaking forest track.

***

Just under a mile away to the north, Tilson and Helena were racing through the snow-covered trees, their breath blooming in the freezing air and disappearing over their heads like smoke from a speeding steam train. They had crawled away from the Spetsnaz troops, but they could hear shouting in Russian nearby. Not only the soldiers but Tilson also recognised the voices of the GRU agents.

Their retreat had been masked by the course the stream had cut into the rock over millennia and they were now slowly making their way down hill on its frozen surface, slipping on the surface as they ran but using the rocky outcrops to either side to steady themselves.

Behind them, the calling voices of the Russians were getting closer. One of them – probably from the Spetsnaz troop, he thought – had figured out their escape route and they were now properly on their tail and not sweeping the landscape in the hope of spotting them. He needed to bring this to an end. He needed the Norwegian police.

Ahead, Tilson could see another stream flowing downhill towards him meet with this one. The two joined together and then flowed as a larger watercourse down the mountain at right angles. When they paused briefly to catch their breath, he pointed it out to Helena who looked flushed from the exercise.

"What?" she asked.

"That confluence of rivers," he said. "They'll assume we've followed it."

Helena raised an eyebrow. "But I guess we won't be doing that?"

He grinned at her cynicism. "No."

When they reached the meeting point of the two rivers, Tilson called a halt again and took off his backpack. His plan was to throw something down the ravine to make the Russians believe they had definitely gone that way, while they would head uphill and then down again the other side.

Rummaging through his backpack, Tilson retrieved his Steiner 10x50 Military Marine Binoculars, took careful aim, and hurled them as far as he could downstream with all his might. They flew about 25 metres into the air and then came down, bouncing once on a rock to the righthand side of the motionless river and then landed a further five metres on in the ice with their lenses pointing up at the sun overhead. They glinted satisfyingly in the sun.

"Nice throw," Helena said, nodding in admiration.

"Cricket," Tilson said. "I'm always in the outfield."

Helena looked at him. "I have no idea what you are talking about," she said.

"Come on," Tilson urged, his eyes scanning the forest as he prepared to lead Helena on their ascent. "We need to move quickly."

As they began their climb up the other small stream, Helena tapped him on the shoulder. "They'll work it out, you know."

Tilson grimaced at her seeming admiration for the enemy. But she was right. They shouldn't underestimate them and indeed, they would work it out.

"They will," he said turning back to continue his climb. "But we'll be long gone by then."

"I hope you are right!"

With resolute determination they moved away from the deceptive path marked by the binoculars, heading up the steep slope. The race against time had intensified, and the outcome remained uncertain.

When they heard the Spetsnaz Sea devils and their GRU counterparts coming over the crest of the other water course, Tilson and Helena quickly took cover behind a suitably large rock. They watched as the six figures made their way down the stream to the point where it met the one that they had followed uphill.

At the point of convergence, the Russians stopped and there followed some pointing, and then finally an excited cry from one of them. It sounded female so probably the GRU agent. More pointing and then the team split. One of the soldiers went with the agents downhill, while the three remaining Spetsnaz started to clamber up the other stream towards where the MI5 man and the Norwegian huntress were hiding.

"Shit," hissed Tilson.

The chase was getting more intense with each passing moment. Tilson knew that they were on their heels and the stakes were higher than ever. The thrill of the chase was exhilarating yet terrifying at the same time.

He glanced back at his partner, Helena, and saw the determination in her eyes. They were in this together, and they had to make it out alive. This had truly become the cliché of a deadly game of cat and mouse.

Tilson's mind flickered back to all the Tom & Jerry cartoons he watched as a kid. It was ironic how he used to root for the mouse, and now he was playing that part himself. But he also remembered how the mouse always managed to outsmart and defeat the cat. He grinned at this ridiculous thought. "Never have a sense of humour failure" was another of his platoon sergeant's sayings. He knew that in this scenario, he had to channel his inner mouse. That said, Tom was never armed with an assault rifle.

Taking Helena's hand, Tilson led her towards the rocks, using them as cover from their pursuers. The adrenaline was pumping through his veins as they climbed, their hearts racing with every step. They had managed to gain a lead of about 80 metres, but they couldn't let their guard down. The chase was far from over, and they had to keep moving if they wanted to survive.

Suddenly, gunfire erupted behind them as the Russian operatives spotted them. Bullets whizzed past as the staccato bursts struck trees and rocks, ricocheting, and sending splinters of wood and chips of rock into the air. Tilson and Helena had to keep moving, zigzagging through the forest.

Tilson scanned ahead. They were coming up on the crest of the hill. Once down the other side, at least they would be out of sight and out of range.

"Over the other side," he gestured at the top of the hill. "We'll be heading downhill towards your flat, right? If we can make it there, we can bring in the police and Norwegian army."

Helena nodded but she didn't seem very certain. Tilson pressed on regardless. What else could he do?

However, as they reached the crest of the mountainside, Tilson saw that there was no other side. Instead, a narrow ridge ran along a clifftop and beyond that, a vertical drop. He spun round to look behind them. The Spetsnaz troops were closing in fast, and the only way forward was over the crag and down the sheer drop to the freezing fjord below.

CHAPTER 25

Helena was looking desperately from side to side, back at the approaching Russians and then over the edge of the cliff. She and Tilson shared an anxious look. There seemed no way to go further, no escape route left. They might have been trapped but for the only option now left to them.

"We'll have to go over!" he said to Helena. Without waiting for a reply, he hurriedly started unravelling the rope from around his torso. Helena watched with growing anticipation, realising what it was Tilson had in mind.

"Are you crazy?" she asked.

"We have to be. Sometimes." Tilson said, securing the rope to a solid looking tree. Then he emptied the contents of his Hard Ware rucksack and put together a makeshift harness from his black North Face Coldworks parka and the buckle from his belt. Finally, he placed the iPhone he'd taken from the other Sam in a sealed sandwich bag and stuffed it into his trouser pocket.

As he worked, Helena unshouldered her rifle and aimed it back in the direction of the Spetsnaz troops. She was ready when the first member of the Russian special forces team appeared over the ridge, Helena loosed a shot at him, causing the man to go to ground.

"No time for that," Tilson called. "Come on!"

He gave the line a couple of solid tugs to test the strength. It appeared solid and he hoped it would hold both simultaneously. Then he motioned for Helena to go first, securing her into the harness.

"Stay at right angles to the rock face until you pass the lip of the cliff," he instructed. "Like abseiling. Then slowly let yourself hang. feed the rope through the belt buckle to go down."

She nodded, biting her lip and started moving backwards over the edge of the escarpment.

With no more gunfire, the Spetsnaz troops started closing in, their shouts growing louder.

Helena was already beginning to descend the sheer rock face, the icy fjord waters below growing closer with each inch of rope she fed through the metal clasp. Her safety was his main concern, and he was determined to get them both out of this dire situation alive.

As soon as she was far enough down, Tilson followed. But he had no harness. He was simply going to climb down the rope. Royal Marines were experts when it came to ropework. In training they must master a 30-foot Rope Climb, on the Tarzan Aerial Assault Course that sounds like exactly what it is and on Bottom Field Assault Course, as well as for the famous Regain.

The last is an exercise performed while traversing a rope between two points. Royal Marines Commandos are required to stop halfway, and then to hang from the rope. They then have then had to "regain" the traverse position on top of the rope. It's a manoeuvre that tests and builds both technique and strength. It was something of an area of pride for Tilson. Even so, his heart pounded, and he fought hard to disperse the fear of the approaching Russian special forces.

He followed right behind Helena, keeping a vigilant eye on the brink of the cliff above them for their pursuers. His muscles were straining with the effort of holding his own weight and that of his backpack. The rope was cutting into his palms, and the cold air made it difficult to keep a steady grip. But he couldn't afford to lose focus, not with the Russian special forces closing in on them.

He also reckoned that they both knew the rope could snap at any moment, sending them plunging into the icy waters below. But they also knew that it was their only chance. With no other options left, they had to trust in their skills and each other. And to be fair, they were both making good progress.

Then he heard a shout from above. As they rappelled slowly down, the Spetsnaz team had reached the cliff's edge, spotting the rope instantly. One of the soldiers - perhaps the officer - was leaning over the lip of the crag to speak with them.

"You have nowhere to go, Captain Tilson," he said. The Accent was quite thick. Possibly from the Archangel region. "We can pull you back up and we can discuss the diaries, yes?"

Tilson stared up at the handsome man, blond haired and square-jawed. He gritted his teeth and quickened his descent, reaching Helena at the foot of the rope just as the officer swore at him and then turned to order his men to pull the rope up.

Helena and Tilson knew they were running out of time, but they had also run out of rope. There was a 50-foot drop to the dark surface of the icy fjord below.

Helena looked at him. For the first time her eyes were clouded by doubt. Then with a sickening lurch, Tilson felt the rope being hauled upwards. They only moved a foot or so, but it wouldn't take the elite soldiers very long to pull them up all the way.

Tilson made a gut-wrenching decision. He reached into his backpack and pulled out the Øyo Nordic Hunting Knife. Helena's eyes now widened in sudden fear. He attempted a reassuring grin, but it came out as more of a sneer. She tried one in return, equally unsuccessful.

"Do it," she whispered.

Tilson nodded and cut the rope in one smooth action.

The two figures plummeted down, their clothing and hair swept above them like the gossamer tails on a pair of very odd fish. The fall seemed to last an eternity and then they smashed into the frigid, semi-frozen waters of the fjord, The shock of the cold water hit them like a physical force, stealing their breath away. As they sank beneath the surface, they could hear the shouts of the Spetsnaz troops fading above. The darkness closed in around them, and they struggled to swim upwards, weighed down by boots and clothing and equipment.

Gasping for air, they broke through the water's surface, their hearts racing. They were battered and bruised, but they had escaped the clutches of the Spetsnaz team, at least for the moment.

Around them, the nautical activity on the inlet continued, oblivious to the dramatic escape that had just taken place. Fishing trawlers and kayaks bobbed on the water's surface, and the bustling atmosphere provided a strange sense of safety. There was no way the Russians would open fire now.

Tilson and Helena swam towards the shoreline, the adrenaline still coursing through their veins. They stumbled ashore and collapsed to the frozen ground, still gasping for air and on the verge of total exhaustion. They lay on their backs on the frozen ground, shivering from the shock of the cold water and the adrenaline still coursing through their veins as they struggled to regain their composure.

Tilson finally managed to speak, his voice trembling with a mix of relief and exhaustion. "We need to get up!"

He turned himself over and leveraged himself up into a position resting on all fours. Then he drew his knees into his chest and pushed himself to stand up. Then he moved over to Helena and extended his hand to her. She made an effort to grab it but ended up just slapping his hand and had to try again.

This time he caught her and lifted her into his arms.

"Your place or mine?" Tilson joked, his teeth chattering.

Helena managed a lopsided smile and started to lead the way across the stony beach. She seemed as eager to put distance between them and the pursuing Spetsnaz troops as he was. Together, they struggled onwards, their bodies aching from the ordeal.

As they made their way inland, they found themselves on a busy main road that led to the heart of Flåm. By now the town was now beginning to awaken from its slumber and from the blizzard. Snowploughs had already cleared the roads and the streets were gradually filling with people – tourists and locals – going about their daily routines. It was a stark contrast to the desolate wilderness they had just escaped.

They hurried across the busy road, dodging cars and pedestrians, their clothing still soaking and clinging to their bodies, half frozen stiff, half dripping leaving a trail of slush as they passed. Their appearance drew curious glances from the locals, who had no idea of the perilous situation these two had just escaped.

Finally, Helena pointed to the familiar shape of her three-storey apartment building. They had only met there a day or so before and yet they had been together since, inseparable. And now their "meet cute" would serve as the perfect sanctuary, Tilson thought, a place to regroup and plan their next moves.

Once inside the apartment building, they made their way to Helena's flat. She reached above the door frame and found the key nestling where she'd left it.

When they opened the door, they were hit by an odd, slightly pungent smell. Helena tutted.

"*Momma* was gutting fish," she said, wrinkling her nose. "Must be the dustbin."

Mentioning her mother didn't seem to affect Helena, and Tilson marvelled once more at her fortitude. He closed the door behind him and walked into the living room. Its warmth and homely décor offered a much-needed respite from the cold and the relentless pursuit they had endured.

Tilson collapsed onto the same couch he had occupied before, his wet clothes soaking the fabric. Helena eyed him and then went to fetch some towels, which she then returned with and threw at Tilson.

"Get undressed," she said. "I am certain we can find you some clothes."

"You're so direct," said Tilson archly. Then he gratefully began to dry himself off. The warmth of the apartment and the hot shower that awaited him felt like a dream and Helena was already pulling off her own clothing, leaving a trail as she went into the bedroom.

"Stay there," she ordered him. Then she tuned on her heel and retreated into her bedroom, shutting the door behind her.

Tilson frowned at her apparent coyness. "I thought we could wash each other's backs!"

Then he realised he was being insensitive. Perhaps she needed space. "Sorry!" he called and removed his soaking trousers and underwear.

He rubbed himself vigorously with the towel, his circulation slowly returning to normal but his skin still feeling pinched and taut.

As he waited, he gazed around the room idly. He put on the TV and listened to the news. It was all about him. Or at least the two GRU agents and him. He looked at the various hunting trophies and then found a bookshelf behind the door. Its top shelf held several photos of Ingeborg Olsen – in a restaurant for a birthday, out for a walk in the summer sunshine, on a boat with a fish. Tilson found it mildly curious that there didn't seem to be any pictures of Helena. Perhaps she was one of those women who hate images of themselves.

After a couple of minutes, he went up to the bedroom door and rested his ear against its surface to listen. He hoped he wouldn't hear her sobbing, but instead he detected the distant sound of the shower like tropical rain on a roof of pantiles.

He was sure she wouldn't mind him coming in. He was still numb in places and eager for the feel of hot water on his skin. He turned the handle and pushed gently on the door. It opened slowly. "Coming in," he called.

Strangely, the room was in darkness, the only light coming from the door to the ensuite that was open just a crack. He moved towards the light and steam coming from the bathroom. But then something caught his eye. He turned slowly, unable to process what he was looking at.

The light from the door was falling across the pillow end of the double bed. At first, he thought Helena must have put the shower on and then collapsed from exhaustion onto the bed. What he'd seen in the corner of his peripheral vision was the reflection of light from the pale skin of someone lying in the dark. He moved forward, so focussed that he didn't hear the shower being turned off.

There was a woman lying on the bed. Weirdly, she kind of looked like Helena. Statuesque and blonde. But her features were more manly; she had a square jaw and larger features, especially her nose. Her body was more thick-set, and her hair was cropped into a jagged page boy look beneath which was a neat gunshot wound to her head.

Tilson stood there, dumbstruck, staring at a woman on the bed. His mouth opened and closed a couple of times like a guppy and then he managed to speak.

"Whose body is that? And where the fuck did it come from?"

His eyes strayed from the prone form, and to the bedside cabinet where an Anglepoise lamp stood with a few books on guns and a large photo of two women. Tilson could see almost immediately that the first woman was Ingeborg: older, shorter. It took him a minute to realise that the other woman was not Helena but this woman lying before him albeit a few years younger and with longer hair.

He became aware of Helena having entered the room behind him.

"I can answer the first question," she said in a dry monotone. "It's me."

Tilson frowned. "What?"

"Well, obviously not 'me'," she said with a slight snort. "But the *real* Helena Olsen."

Now he turned, feeling like someone had severed his spinal column, his legs weak and shaky, his head tingling with a rush of adrenaline.

The woman he thought he knew - had slept with - was standing before him in the doorway with a large aqua towel tied around her chest and another, smaller one covering her hair. But the contents of her linen cupboard were not his main concern. It was the fact she was levelling a Vektor semi-automatic at him that really had his focus. This time, it was SR-1MP equipped with Picatinny rails for the quick-detach suppressor that was pointing at his head.

"Hello, Sam," she said. "My name is Kira Kostina. I am an agent of the Federal Security Service of the Russian Federation."

CHAPTER 26

Tilson's heart raced as he processed the shocking revelation. He had been deceived, manipulated, and now, standing before him was the enemy, pointing a deadly weapon at him. The room seemed to close in around him, and the air grew heavy with tension. He took a step back, his mind racing to make sense of the situation.

"You're... FSB?" he stammered, his voice a mixture of disbelief and anger.

Kira Kostina, the woman who until seconds before he'd trusted implicitly as Helena Olsen, maintained a calm demeanour, her steely gaze fixed on Tilson.

"That's right, *min kjære*," The use of the Norwegian term of endearment she'd used in the hunter's hut smarted. She saw his reaction.

"Don't be cross, Sam," she said. "It was lovely."

Tilson's mind raced as he tried to piece together the puzzle. It was clear that the woman he had known as Helena had been an imposter, part of an elaborate ruse to deceive him. But why?

She indicated the body on the bed with her free hand. "As to where the fuck she came from, well, I am assuming my gorilla counterparts in the GRU had something to do with it. I suspect Lyuba. She's a misogynist. Mother abused her, apparently.

"Anyway, when I arrived, she was dead. I put her on the bed. I got blood all over my nice top. I was just changing it when that Police detective turned up, telling me my own mother was dead.

"She was the one who told me about you. I knew MI5 had sent someone to pick up the Fox diaries, and it made sense the man she was telling me about was you."

"How did you know?" Tilson asked, trying to keep calm. "I mean how come the FSB – and the GRU for that matter – were aware I was coming?"

"Ah. That I can't really tell you, Sam. Sorry."

Just for a split second, the FSB woman's attention faltered and the Vektor shifted its aim. Tilson's instincts kicked in, and he lunged to the side, attempting to knock the weapon from Kira's hand. But she was quick and agile, sidestepping his attack with ease. A silenced shot thudded on the wall above the incriminating photo.

He froze, realizing the deadly consequences of his impulsive move. Kira had proven herself to be a highly skilled operative, and he was at a severe disadvantage – literally naked before her.

"Enough games," Kira said coldly, her finger tightening on the trigger. "We need to talk."

She waved her free hand towards the sitting room. "Shall we go through? Sit down? We'll be much more comfortable," she smiled once more. "And you won't be tempted to try anything stupid again."

As Kira took a step closer, her weapon trained on him, Tilson's mind raced as he weighed his options. He needed to buy time, to figure out Kira's true motives, and to find a way to escape her clutches.

He started to move but looked over his shoulder as he did. "Why are two rival branches of Russian intelligence both out here, each one unaware of the other?"

"Please, Sam!" she laughed. "I was very much aware of the rival branch." She had a playful tone to her voice now, but it was still laced with menace. Tilson shook his head. She had played him like a fiddle.

"But why both?" he insisted.

He was now standing in the living room, "Sit," she ordered. He sat.

"Can I put on some clothes?" he asked. She ignored this and sat opposite him just as she had done when they first met.

"How are the diaries?" she asked. "Ruined, I presume?"

"Paper and water don't mix very well," Tilson confirmed.

"Let's see, shall we? Take them out of your bag." She leant forward and made sure the Vektor was so close she couldn't miss if he made a threatening move.

Tison reached slowly for the sodden back pack that had created a large puddle on the living room rug. Inside, his hand clamped onto a damp notebook, and he brought it out, holding it out for Kira to see. It had been swollen by its dip in the fjord, its pages separated and curly, like the petals of an ornate orchid.

"Open it," she said.

He put the diary on the table and opened it to a random page. The fountain pen ink had run so much as to make the writing illegible. "Well," she said. "That's that." She sat back and stared at Tilson.

"When you turned up, you caught me searching this place for those!" she laughed. "I thought this would be very easy."

"So why lie to me? Why not just shoot me?"

"Oh, Sam," she said like a mother disappointed in her child. "We are very different. The FSB and the GRU. Didn't they teach you that at MI5 school?"

"Not that different," Sam said.

"Perhaps not on the surface," Kira said enigmatically. She leant forward again, but this time apparently in an effort to be sincere. "The GRU have always been the soldiers. Assassins. Cold blooded. Spetsnaz is the pinnacle of that."

"And the FSB are cuddly teddy bears?" Tilson asked.

"Well, you found me cuddly, didn't you?" She was smiling a genuinely warm smile it seemed.

Tilson was very confused by her behaviour. But then, maybe that was the point. He'd been caught in the classic honeytrap, had stupidly fallen for a woman he barely knew, and now his feelings were all over the shop.

"The point is, we are different. Certain parts of the FSB, at least."

"Look, whatever it is you're trying to say, just spit it out," Tilson said coldly.

She reached forward and touched his bare knee. "I'm sorry I deceived you, Sam. Genuinely. When I said that I felt it, too? I meant it."

There was an awkward silence. Neither knew what to say. In the distance a police siren wailed. Tilson wondered if it was anything to do with the GRU agents or Spetsnaz troops traipsing all over Norwegian soil.

"Some of us are not convinced a war with NATO is the best way forward," she said slowly and carefully. "The GRU are blunt instruments. Their bosses want conflict, many even believe it is Russia's destiny.

"Personally, I think it would be our doom, so I'm not going to go around killing MI5 operatives," she said and then smiled coyly at him.

"Especially when they are cute."

Tilson was amazed by what he was hearing, but hid it well. The thought crossed his mind that she was trying to recruit him. Would she be that direct? That stupid?

"What I am telling you would have me executed for treason," Kira said, now very serious. "But what I want to do is maintain the status quo.

The diaries were crucial to that. If you'd seen what was in them..."

She trailed off and then shook her head as if to dislodge an unpleasant thought. "Anyway, luckily for you I managed to... distract you."

Suddenly, she stood up and motioned with the gun for him to do the same. Tilson rose.

"What now?"

"Now, I lock you in the bathroom, get dressed and leave here with the remains of the diaries. I'm sure you'll be able to break out in a bit.

Please don't try it while I'm still here, though.

"I don't want to kill you, but I can assure you I am trained to know exactly where to shoot you in order to put you in hospital for quite some time."

Tilson moved into the bedroom once more, trying to avoid looking at the body of the real Helena Olsen. He felt frustrated that a family of innocents - however few in number - had been wiped out because of this mission. There should have been another way.

"In you go!" Kira gestured for him to enter the bathroom. Once he was in, she took the key from the other side of the door and closed it.

Then she locked it with a loud and deliberate click.

Tilson sat down on the Toilet and let his head collapse into his palms, shivering and sweating. At least now no one else had to die. It was then that it dawned on him that what he had assumed was just the effects of the cold were actually the signs of a hypoglycaemic attack.

***

Despite driving into what she suspected would be a dangerous situation, Ebony still marvelled at the stark beauty of the Norwegian wilderness. Tall pines stood like ancient sentinels on either side of the road, their branches heavy with snow. The air was crisp and pure, and the world seemed hushed. Even the sound of the Audi's engine was dampened by the blanket of white.

For his part, Kavanagh remained silent, his eyes scanning their surroundings, alert for any sign of danger. His earlier sarcasm might have rubbed her up the wrong way, but Ebony couldn't help but respect his professionalism. She fervently hoped he was handy with the gun he'd pointed at her when they first met, because she didn't think her Channel mace would do much good against the GRU if they stumbled across them in their search for Tilson.

As they climbed higher up the hillside, the trees began to thin and ahead was a large barn type building. Ebony pulled up a dozen metres from the farm building. Kavanagh looked at her.

"You think he's in there?"

"Could be," she replied, her tone making it obvious she thought his question was stupid. With some difficulty, she reversed the car around the nearest bend, making sure it was out of sight of the building.

"So, let's take a look, *MI6*!"

She switched off the engine, opened her door and climbed out. Pocketing the key. Kavanagh followed suit, coming to stand at the front of the Audi beside her.

"Keep an eye out for any signs of recent activity," he instructed her, his gaze flowing from one side of the road to the other. "Tyre tracks, footprints, anything that might indicate Tilson's presence."

Ebony nodded and started moving forwards scanning the road ahead.

"I'm not sure he's dumb enough to leave obvious traces," she said. "But we can look."

When they reached the barn, they could hear bleating from inside. "Sheep?" asked Ebony.

"Goats," Kavanagh corrected her. "The Norwegians farm them up here."

She nodded and opened one of the large doors. They both froze and Kavanagh produced the Glock 17 from the pocket of his coat.

Ahead of them, inside the warm and well-lit barn was a Skoda Yeti.

It looked out of place in the agricultural surroundings.

Kavanagh approached it and stared in through its windows. "Empty" he said. Only then did Ebony come forward, now looking beyond the vehicle for any other signs of life. She didn't have to go far. She found a makeshift fire and the carcass of what she assumed was one of the goats. While it could have been her colleague's survival situation they'd found, somehow it didn't feel right to her. Her intuition was screaming GRU at her.

She voiced this to Kavanagh who nodded and simply moved forward, searching the whole barn with his weapon drawn. He found nothing and circled back to Ebony once more.

"No one here."

"For now," she said. Perhaps it was her sometimes glass half empty approach or perhaps it was her intuition again, but the moment she said this, they heard voices outside. Russian ones.

Ebony and Kavanagh exchanged tense glances. It was clear that the barn was about to become reclaimed by the GRU – a seriously unwelcome development.

"They've found us," Kavanagh muttered under his breath, his eyes narrowing as he listened to the approaching voices. Ebony could see the wheels turning in his mind as he assessed their options.

"Should we hide?" Ebony whispered, her voice cracking a bit. The closest she'd ever been to a Russian threat before this was via the relative safety of a computer screen.

Kavanagh shook his head. "No, there's no time. We need to get out of here."

With that, Kavanagh motioned for Ebony to follow him, and they made their way to the back of the barn. As they reached the rear exit, they could see a group of four armed men in snow camouflage fatigues approaching the front of the building. Behind them were two other people – a man and woman dressed in civilian clothing. Ebony recognised the balding GRU agent. She let out a small gasp.

"Take it easy," Kavanagh said in hushed tones. "Come on. This way." He was pointing to a side door that led to the back of the barn.

Quickly and silently, they made their way back through the barn, out of door and into the cold, open air.

The snow-covered landscape stretched out before them, and Ebony felt suddenly vulnerable. The Audi was a good 50 metres away and she could hear the Russians entering the barn now, their voices becoming more echoey as they did so.

Kavanagh didn't hesitate. He started to lead the way, moving calmly through the snow. Ebony went to follow him, her heart pounding in her chest.

Without warning, one of the Spetsnaz special forces Marines – the 30-yar old brawler, Maksim Kuzmin – emerged from the same door, his assault rifle trained on Ebony. She looked into his scarred face, terrified. But Kavanagh didn't hesitate. In a split second he raised his Glock and fired twice, the sharp cracks of double tap echoing through the forest.

The Spetsnaz soldier staggered backward, like a drunk and then collapsed to the ground, blood pooling from his head.

Kavanagh grabbed Ebony's hand and dragged her away, running at such a rate she found hard to match.

Someone behind them let out a guttural cry and started shooting, the bullets flying past the retreating forms of Ebony and Kavanagh. They took cover behind a nearby tree, and Kavanagh exchanged fire with their determined pursues.

"Get the car!" he hissed urgently. "I'll keep them here."

To demonstrate his intents, he aimed another shot in the direction of the barn door. Ebony hesitated now but some hidden inner strength made her move one leg, then the other and soon she was sprinting back to the Audi.

The gunfight was fierce, the sound of gunfire and the scent of gunpowder filling the air. Making her ragged breaths catch in her throat. She plunged into a waist deep snow drift just as an arc of machine-gun fire raked the ground ahead of her. Ebony waded through the deep snow and crawled out onto the road, the Audi now within touching distance.

Her heart raced as adrenaline surged through her veins, pushing her to cover the final few feet to the car. Reaching the Audi, Ebony fumbled for her keys, her hands trembling with a mixture of fear and determination. She had to get the car started and back to Kavanagh. He was holding off the Russians singlehanded.

Finaly, the key slotted into the ignition and engine growled as it came to life. Ebony spared a quick glance towards Kavanagh. He was still behind cover, exchanging gunfire with the Spetsnaz soldiers. He was clearly a skilled field agent, but he was outnumbered, and the odds were stacked against him.

She put the car in gear and slammed her foot on the accelerator. The Audi roared to life, and she sped back towards the barn, tyres spinning in the snow as she approached the scene of the firefight.

Kavanagh saw her coming and quickly dashed from his cover towards the Audi, firing a few shots to keep the Russians at bay. Ebony spun the car and it turned, coming to a violent halt when it hit one of the pines sideways on. She was dazed but unhurt and before she could even register the impact, the passenger door was open and Kavanagh was diving into the car, slamming the door shut behind him.

"Drive!" he shouted, and Ebony didn't need any further encouragement. She floored the accelerator once more, and the Audi flew forward, leaving the Russians behind.

The snow-covered road stretched out before them, and Ebony could feel the tension in the car as they raced away from the barn. Kavanagh was using his phone, speaking rapidly to what she could only assume were the Norwegian authorities.

"We need to find Tilson and get out of here," Kavanagh said. "But we also need some help dealing with our violent friends back there."

CHAPTER 27

Ebony and Kavanagh continued their frantic escape through the snowy Norwegian wilderness, their Audi speeding down the winding mountain road. They knew the GRU agents would be on their tail and that they had to get back to civilisation fast.

Sure enough, as they rounded a bend, Ebony spotted the Skoda Yeti in her rearview mirror. She cursed under her breath. "Jed, they're still after us!"

The Audi's engine roared as Ebony pushed it to its limits, but the pursuing agents were closing in. The two people in the car – the man and woman – Lyuba and Vilkov were clearly determined to capture their quarry.

"The road's getting better," Kavanagh said. "We'll be OK in a minute."

"We fucking need to be!"

He glanced back and nodded grimly. "Hold tight," he replied as the Audi ploughed round another bend and Ebony had to slam on the brakes, bringing the Audi to a screeching halt in front of the unexpected sight of a Norwegian army roadblock of makeshift concrete slabs. Soldiers in winter camouflage uniforms and armed with rifles stood behind these, also blocking their path.

The car was just a few meters from the armed soldiers, who were approaching cautiously.

"Quick!" Kavanagh said, "Get out!" He opened his door and slowly raised his hands, showing that they posed no threat.

Ebony had done likewise, but then heard the Skoda behind them.

The Russians hadn't anticipated the sudden roadblock and the added presence of the Audi meant they could not stop in time. Their vehicle crashed into Ebony's rental with a sickening crunch, the force of the collision pushing the Audi forward and causing it to collide with the soldiers' roadblock. Ebony's heart raced as she dived out of the way, narrowly avoiding the oncoming impact.

The Skoda was now wedged between the Army blockade and the soldiers themselves, who were shouting and gesturing wildly. As Ebony struggled to regain her bearings, she saw the two Russians step out of their vehicle, their hands raised in surrender. She felt a huge surge of relief, knowing that they were no longer a threat.

As the dust settled, Ebony took a moment to catch her breath and assess the situation. The Russians were now surrounded by the soldiers, who had their weapons drawn and were shouting at them to get on the ground. Ebony couldn't quite grasp what had just happened. It all seemed so surreal.

Chaos erupted as the troops moved to apprehend the occupants of both vehicles. Lyuba and Vilkov, dazed from the crash, were quickly taken into custody, their weapons confiscated. The soldiers ordered them first onto the snow-covered ground, where they were handcuffed and detained, and thence to an ambulance where they were assessed for injuries.

Ebony and Kavanagh, though shaken from the collision, were relieved to be in the protective custody of the Norwegian military. They were taken to one of the concrete slabs and told to sit down.

The soldiers were rushing around, radios squawking, sirens in the distance. But then Ebony saw a police uniform among all the winter camouflage. She seemed to be a mixed-race Norwegian detective. And she was making a bee line for them.

"Kavanagh?" the policewoman exclaimed as she recognised the MI6 man.

Kavanagh gave her a nod of acknowledgement. "Hedda. It's good to see you."

"Who's this?" Hedda nodded towards Ebony.

"This Ebony Fadipe, she's working with me."

Ebony smiled in greeting. "How the hell do you two know each other?"

Hedda smiled back, but it didn't seem quite so genuine. "I was on an exchange programme through the Norwegian Embassy in London. Jed was my liaison."

She turned her attention back to Kavanagh. "So, tell me. What's going on?" she demanded.

Kavanagh quickly explained the situation. "One of our agents was sent here to retrieve the effects of a former British diplomat." "Herr Fox." Hedda said, nodding.

"Yes," he replied. "But it seems the Russians had other ideas."

"Mmm. We believe the woman who cleaned for him was killed by the female GU Intelligence Service agent." She pointed to an CV9030 COM armoured personnel carrier in which the Russians were now being placed. "She made a call implicating your asset – Mister Tilson?"

"Captain," Ebony said.

"I had no idea he was still on active service?" Hedda replied, with the return of the saccharine smile.

Ebony frowned.

"Her colleague also made an accusation of assault against..." the Norwegian detective hesitated. Ebony raised an eyebrow at her. "...your asset the same morning."

"We were looking for him, when we found them." Kavanagh jerked a thumb at the armoured car. "They chased us down this road." He shrugged. "The rest you know."

"You phoned in the request for a roadblock?" Kavanagh nodded.

"Then we owe you," she said, her gaze shifting to the captured GRU agents. "We've been monitoring their activities since they arrived in our country. At the moment, I have arrested them for illegal entry and suspected homicide."

"Not to mention bloody dangerous driving," Ebony said.

Kavanagh laughed. Hedda didn't seem to get the joke.

"So, where's Sam?" Ebony asked. She and Kavanagh looked at Hedda for answers.

She looked uncomfortable. "There is the missing daughter of Herr Fox's cleaner. The two may be linked. I didn't treat her disappearance as urgent compared to this."

Kavanagh nodded. "Of course."

"The police are looking for her," she said with a slight air of superiority. "I am not privy to their investigation as it falls outside my remit of national security."

"Don't you think finding her is a priority?" Ebony asked, offended by her snobbery.

"I am sure the local law enforcement officers will do so," Hedda smiled. "But I am going to need full statements from you both. And then we need to liaise with your Embassy..."

***

Tilson sat in the bathroom, his mind racing with the events that had just unfolded. He was finding it very hard to believe that Kira, the woman he had grown to trust, was actually a member of the FSB. But her words had made an impression.

Despite his unwavering loyalty to MI5, Kira's insistence on the importance of the diaries had left him questioning the status quo. What secrets lurked within those pages that could potentially alter the course of history? And had it been worth risking his life for? At least Kira didn't know he had a full copy of the diary on the iPhone. Then he recalled it was still in his clothing in the siting room. She could easily have searched his belongings and taken it.

He tried to remember what he'd seen as he snapped each of the pages in turn. The first volume he'd read pretty thoroughly, but everything else had been a bit of a blur. One name kept resurfacing and seemed to become the focal point of Fox's writings. Steven Drake – whom he referred to affectionately and then with increasing bitter vitriol – as "Quackers". The name meant nothing to Tilson. All he could see in his mind's eyes was a cartoon duck. More Donald that daffy.

He shook his head, but Tilson's mind was in turmoil, torn between competing thoughts and plagued by a splitting headache that only worsened with the sound of a nearby police siren. He was lost, unsure of who to trust or what to believe. And to make matters worse, he was aware that his blood sugar was plummeting, leaving him weak and vulnerable.

Drunk with the weakness such an event elicits, Tilson knew he had to act immediately. Clutching the basin beside the toilet for support, he leveraged himself up and onto his feet and half lumbered, half fell towards the door. Leaning against it hard, he started pounding on its wooden surface with all his remaining strength. At least the siren had stopped.

"Kira!" he shouted. "I'm... diabetic. I need sugar... Please!"

He closed his eyes, trying to maintain consciousness, shivering and sweating now.

"Please... be there..." he muttered. But no one answered. Kira was long gone.

Through the brain fug of the hypo, he thought he heard a crash, but he wasn't sure. He opened his eyes momentarily and saw there was a cabinet under the basin he'd used to stand up. He managed to take a step back to the toilet and ended up kneeling in front of the double doors of the low cupboard. Perhaps they had a cough sweet or even syrup. Those kinds of medicines were full of sugar. The real Helena might even have been the type to keep glucose energy tablets knocking around. He reached forward and snatched at the handles, but he missed, and he fell forwards, his head crashing into the panel.

"Help!" he shouted one last time and collapsed onto the floor, his breath shallow.

The door burst open and a blurry figure in blue stood there.

"*Faen i helvete*," A female Norwegian voice said. Tilson registered it as meaning "fucking hell". His mind relayed its agreement with the sentiment.

After a moment or two, he was being pulled upright and a sticky liquid was poured through his lips. He managed to swallow without choking, gulping it down, feeling the odd combination of carrot and caramel sweetness that told him it was a Cola of some sort. A Towel was placed behind his head, and he lifted his chin from its slack position to look up at his saviour. He grinned when he saw who it was.

"Hello... Tamsin!" he managed.

The woman looked down at him with a frown.

"You seem to be confused," she said. "My name is *Politioverbetjent* Frida Skardet. And you are under arrest."

***

The snow crunched beneath their boots as the three Spetsnaz troopers continued their steady march down the forested hillside. *Kapitan-leytenant* Nikolay Aliev led the way, his expression inscrutable. Despite the biting cold wind coming in from the north, his face was flushed red with a mixture of sorrow, anger, and resignation. It was clear that he was not in a good place.

As they descended further towards Aurlandsfjord, Aliev's mind wandered back to the events that had led them here. The loss of his comrade felt like a betrayal, and the mission that had been sold to him as a simple one had turned very sour. He felt a sense of hopelessness and guilt, but he refused to show it. His duty to his country and his men was all that kept him going.

With a heavy heart, he continued to lead his men towards their exfiltration. Despite the weight of events that had transpired in the last few hours on his shoulders, Aliev remained focused and determined.

He knew that while the mission had not been successful, he was determined to get the rest of his men home alive. And so, with each step, he pushed aside his own emotions and soldiered on.

Behind him were Dmitriy Nikitin, and the 24-year-old Artyom

Shevchenko seemed to be equally stoic and unreadable. The young Shevchenko looked as if he were in a state of shock, his youthful face etched with sadness and disbelief. Meanwhile, the older Dmitriy marched on, as determined to see his comrades safely back to their families as his commanding officer was. Between them, they were carrying the body of their fallen comrade, Maksim Kuzmin.

Aliev was angry. That emotion was prevalent. How the hell had there been another pair of British agents in the area without them having any intelligence on that fact? Only one enemy asset had been mentioned in the briefing. Although Aliev had sworn vengeance on the man who had shot Kuzmin once he found out who he was, he was also planning on something equally nasty for Vilkov – the GRU agent – who had so spectacularly underestimated the situation. He was certainly going to recommend to his superiors that Volkov and his female partner should not be extradited, if that possibility ever presented itself.

The officer was also aggrieved that the fresh-faced Shevchenko had been part of such an unprofessional infiltration. At least he now had firsthand experience of active service and had found out the hard way that nothing was ever straightforward in war, and all could very well end in bloodshed and death as it could glory and military decorations.

He gave the signal to stop when they reached the E16 road they had crossed only a few hours before. It was still not very busy despite the snow plough having cleared the road, and the small squad was moving again in a few minutes, remaining in complete silence like a funeral cortege.

At the beach, they placed Kuzmin's body near the water's edge and donned their dry suits and rebreathers. Aliev checked his watch. The *Severodvinsk* was scheduled to come to periscope depth and check for their signal from the shore at regular intervals every 12 minutes before the hour and stay vigilant for 10 minutes. The hands on his black PVD coated stainless steel MX10 NIGHT watch told him he was within that window: 11.54.

He nodded to *Starshina* Nikitin who had the XHP50 U3 tactical flashlight already in his hand. The NCO sent out a burst of morse code towards the last known position of the boat. Although no signal was returned, Aliev trusted that the submarine would be there. At least he felt he could depend on the sailors of the Russian Navy.

"Let's go," he said and pulled his mask down over his face. Then he attached the rebreather mouthpiece and entered the water. He waited in the shallows for his men to bring the dead body, now wrapped and weighted with stones along with the other scuba kit intended for Kuzmin, Lyuba and Vilkov.

With one final look at the looming Norwegian mountains, he followed his team, slipping under water barely leaving a ripple on the surface to signify they had ever been there.

CHAPTER 28

The full title of the British Embassy in Oslo is the chief diplomatic mission of the United Kingdom in Norway. It is strategically located on Thomas Heftyes gate, one of the most expensive streets in Norway. From the exterior, the embassy may seem like any other modern building, but behind the walls lies a rich history. The embassy's history dates back to 1906 when it was first established to strengthen diplomatic ties between the two countries.

Since then, the embassy has witnessed many significant events and played a crucial role in promoting peace and cooperation between the UK and Norway. The embassy's location on Thomas Heftyes gate also reflects the strong relationship between the two countries. The street is home to many other diplomatic missions, including the US and German embassies. This proximity allows for easy communication and collaboration between the nations, further strengthening their ties.

Moreover, the embassy's location in the heart of Oslo makes it easily accessible for citizens of both countries. This has enabled the embassy to serve as a hub for cultural exchange, trade, and tourism, fostering a deep understanding and friendship between the UK and Norway.

The embassy's architecture, although not visually appealing, serves a purpose. The modern dark brown cladding and wall to wall windows provide insulation and protection against harsh Norwegian weather. Additionally, the square shape is a symbol of stability and strength, representing the strong bond between the two nations. The embassy may not be the most beautiful building on the street, but its significance and contribution to the relationship between the UK and Norway cannot be underplayed.

It was only because of this solid relationship that Sam Tilson, Ebony Fadipe, and Jed Kavanagh had all charges dropped against them by the Norwegian State on the tacit understanding they were all repatriated as soon as convenient to His Majesty's Secret Intelligence and Security Services. It was advised they may not wish to return for some time. The only one this pained was Tilson as he loved the place, but he hoped he might come back one day.

For now, all of them were gathered in one of the consular meeting rooms on the first floor, overlooking the razor wire fencing and security cameras that delineated the border between UK sovereign soil and Norwegian state territory. The bombproof curtains had been drawn to ensure privacy and the harsh strip light above buzzed intermittently, making the meeting seem more like an interrogation.

The Head of station for MI6 will operate with a 'light' diplomatic facade, typically as a Counsellor for larger concerns such as Moscow or Washington, or a First Secretary for countries of less strategic importance. They are aided by a small team of officials - probably Second Secretaries - with additional support from file and document clerks, as well as communication and encryption officers.

The FCOD maintains a 'Diplomatic List' that allows for easy identification of their presence, although the number of Counsellor and First Secretary roles available is often limited. This means that the host intelligence and security agency is likely to recognize MI6 operatives. In certain situations, a senior operative may intentionally draw attention to themselves in order to shift the spotlight away from their colleagues.

They will then run agents, all of whom have been recruited, bribed, or blackmailed into spying for the UK. They seldom get their hands dirty and unlike field operatives can fall back on the luxury of diplomatic immunity. This prevents them from being prosecuted for breaking the law and allows them simply to leave or be expelled in those situations.

Oscar Chapman was just such a man. He was a desk jockey. Not a bad one, but Oslo was hardly Beijing, and he was only a decade away from retirement. He was an avuncular figure in an open-neck sky-blue shirt and dark jacket. His greying sandy hair elegantly coiffed and swept away from his forehead, reminded Tilson of a Mr. Whippy ice cream.

As Head of Station "O", Oslo, he was sitting at the head of a dull, grey table with eight chairs padded in some cheap burgundy material. In the two nearest to his right sat Tilson and Ebony. To his immediate left was Kavanagh. Chapman was positively thrilled to be chairing such an august meeting for it was something he quite literally never got to do. When he'd first met the three agents, he'd clapped his hands together and welcomed them warmly. He had been given the scantest briefing as to why they were all there and simply asked to chair the meeting and perform an initial debrief of the events of the past few days.

Tilson had been over his orders from Tony Gray and then from Anne. He omitted anything he thought Kavanagh and indeed Chapman didn't need to hear. For his part, Chapman then asked Ebony to fill in her role in the events, but Tilson interrupted him.

"I think we all know why Ms Fadipe came to Norway, right?" he addressed the question to Kavanagh, who raised his eyebrows and pulled an expression that said, fair point. "What I'd like to know is why Mister Kavanagh was here."

The MI6 agent smiled like a shark. "Call me 'Jed', please. We're all friends here."

There was a pregnant pause.

"Sorry," Tilson said. "Was that an answer to my question?"

Chapman held up his hands, palms facing the two men. "Gentlemen, please," he said. "As Jed says, we are all friends here; all on the same side."

Tilson kept his eyes on Kavanagh, he didn't trust him. "So?"

Kavanagh leant across the table, hands clasped before him. "I was sent for the same reason. Nothing sinister."

"Ebony says you told her that you were looking after me."

"Yes."

"Well, you didn't do a very good job," Tilson said. Ebony had to conceal a laugh. "But why did I need babysitting?"

"All I was told was that you were new to this and might need a hand."

"And so, they sent a soldier," Tilson stared into Kavanagh's brown eyes. "SAS? Can't be SBS. I'd know you."

He could see he'd annoyed the man sitting across from him. Tilson clicked his fingers.

"Right! You're SRR. Special Reconnaissance Regiment?"

Kavanagh smiled thinly. "Wondered if you'd get there in the end."

"How did SIS know about the MI5 op?" Ebony chimed in.

"We do talk to each other, Ebony," Kavanagh said. "And, with respect, foreign operations are usually our remit."

"That is true," Chapman offered.

Tilson's eyes bore into Kavanagh's, his frustration simmering just below the surface. "Maybe, but you still haven't told us everything, Kavanagh."

Kavanagh leaned forward, his manner stern. "Sam, you need to understand that there are things you're better off not knowing."

Ebony couldn't contain her irritation any longer. "That's not good enough, Jed. We risked our lives out there, and you expect us to just accept half-truths and secrets?"

Kavanagh sighed, his expression weary. "Look, I understand your frustration, but this is how intelligence work operates," he said. "There are layers of secrecy for a reason. You two should know that!"

Tilson clenched his fists. "I've been through quite a lot on this, and I won't be kept in the dark, understand? You owe me that."

Kavanagh's eyes narrowed, and for a moment, it seemed like a standoff. "I'm not the bad guy here," he said slowly and deliberately.

Another awkward silence.

"Fine," he said through gritted teeth. "We knew both the GRU and FSB were sending agents to ensure the diaries did not fall into British hands – or anyone else's for that matter. Somehow, they got wind of the fact you were coming, Sam. I don't know how."

Tilson wasn't sure he believed him but said nothing. Kavanagh continued.

"The GRU picked up your trail in Oslo. Your fake huntress – Helena or Kira or whatever – was FSB. We don't know where she slotted in. We do know she absconded with the diaries."

Chapman chimed in. "I thought you said they were destroyed?"

"Water damage," Tilson said. "I doubt they could have gleaned very much from them after they'd been in the fjord."

"Did you get a chance to read them?" Kavanagh seemed almost too casual in his questioning.

"I read one of them – the first one. There's wasn't a great deal in it. Fox seemed to be upset by his family situation. It wasn't exactly a smoking gun."

"And just to clarify, one of them was left in Helena Olsen's car?" Kavanagh asked.

Tilson nodded. "I think it was a later journal, so that may be of use to them."

"If they still have it," Ebony added. "The GRU agents might have been still carrying it when they were arrested."

"I'm guessing they gave it to the Spetsnaz team," Tilson said. "Or they just took it off the agents seeing how much they'd bungled the mission."

Ebony leaned back in her chair, absorbing the information. "So, the GRU and the FSB were both after the diaries? That explains a lot." She glanced at Tilson. "But that suggests they knew what was in them and didn't want us to find out what that was."

They all mulled this over for a moment.

"That does make sense," Kavanagh agreed.

"Well, if that is the case, then their mission was successful, wasn't it?" Tilson added, a note of bitterness conjured in his voice.

Kavanagh sighed. "I suppose we'll never know. But I am guessing whatever the contents were, it was important."

Chapman nodded. "I'll coordinate with the Norwegian authorities and see if we can't at least get transcripts of what the two GRU operatives have to say for themselves."

"Probably something about enjoying the tourist spots of Norway if their MO in Salisbury was anything to go by," Kavanagh said.

Tilson allowed himself a flicker of a smile at the other agent's reference to the ridiculous alibi the GRU agent sent to poison Sergei and Yulia Skripalhad had concocted. "And what about you, Jed? What will you do?"

Kavanagh hesitated for a moment before responding. "As far as MI6 is concerned, the diaries are lost. I imagine it will be very much the same as you, Sam. We'll focus on damage control."

Ebony pushed her chair back, thinking that was the end of it. But Kavanagh had one last opportunity to poke fun at the former Royal Marine.

"If only you hadn't been... *compromised* by the Russian femme fatale, eh?"

Tilson smiled at this. He had him there. "We live and learn."

"Well," said Chapman, blowing his cheeks out. "I would say that's that, wouldn't you?"

As the meeting concluded, the three agents left the consular room with a mix of relief and uncertainty. They had survived a dangerous mission, but the mysteries surrounding the diaries and the true motivations of the various intelligence agencies involved remained - for the most part - unresolved.

CHAPTER 29

It was fast approaching Christmas when the Inconclusive Covert Enquiries unit was all back together. The festive mood that usually filled their small offices on the fourth floor of Thames House was noticeably absent. The team was finally back together after Tilson's medical emergency and prescribed days of rest, but the incident had taken a toll on everyone. Ebony had returned to work before Tilson.

The team was still reeling from the shock of the depth of the mission in Flåm and the level of failure they had suffered. It had been a close call for Tilson as well as Ebony, and a stark reminder of the dangers of their job. They were all soldiering on, but Tilson's absence only made things worse. Even the Christmas decorations that adorned the office walls - put up by the ever-enthusiastic Camille - seemed to mock their sombre mood.

Almost immediately upon his arrival, Anne had called a meeting, and they were all gathered in the larger, outer office with the six desks, and the mountain of paper files that didn't seem to have changed at all in the time Tilson had been away.

Anne's commanding presence was accentuated by her choice of attire - a charcoal grey dress paired with a cardigan of mismatched, garish colours. As she stood in the centre of the office, surrounded by her team, she exuded a sense of authority and control. Her sharp, keen eyes peered out from under her bob as she fixed her gaze on Tilson. Despite her stern demeanour, there was a hint of genuine concern in her expression as she observed him closely.

She stood in the centre of the room like a Ringmaster surrounded by her disparate acts. Keen eyes shone out from under the fringe of her bob as she brought her gaze to bear on Tilson. She was regarding him with a mixture of stern curiosity and genuine concern.

As the ragtag team gathered around her, Tilson felt a real sense of belonging. These people had his back just as much as the hairy Nepalese and dour Scotsman he'd been with when this journey began back in Devon.

He felt comfortable there, despite the subdued atmosphere.

He knew that with Anne at the helm, they would be able to tackle any challenges that lay ahead. She was solid and he liked her. She was what some people might have described as "old school", but that made him like her even more.

He also knew he could lift their mood and was happy to be able to do so. He may have been a Royal Marine Commando, an SBS veteran and now an MI5 operative, but he was still a bit of a showman.

Anne wasted no time in starting the meeting.

"So, Sam," she began. "It seems like quite the harrowing experience you had over there in Norway."

Tilson was grateful for her acknowledgement. Ebony and Camille looked on with compassionate expressions, while Gareth Hazel nodded in understanding. They all seemed relieved to have him back, which was always nice. Tilson was leaning on one of the desks, only a few feet from Anne. Ebony was next to him at the adjacent desk and then Camille and Gareth Hazel completed the circle.

"I think Ebony had a hard time, too."

"Yes. I heard." She smiled affectionately at Ebony. "I saw the report from your debriefing at Station O, and Ms Fadipe has filled me in on a few other things."

Tilson smiled. "Of course she has."

"What I'd really like is to get a full understanding of the contents of the diaries," Anne said. Tilson saw Hazel nodding in agreement. "As far as you can recall them, of course."

Tilson took a deep breath. "I have a little secret," he said, digging into his jacket pocket. He produced the iPhone he'd taken from the other Sam in the bar.

"You had great coverage in Norway?" Ebony asked with a twinkle in her eye.

Anne had her head cocked on one side, trying to guess what he was about to reveal. "Go on."

Tilson hesitated for a moment, then unlocked the device and opened the photos app containing a series of high-quality photos of page after page of handwritten notes.

"Well, while the Russian FSB agent was asleep, I managed to take photos of the six diaries I had in my possession at that time."

Camille gasped. Ebony was on her feet. "What?" she said, drawing out the word. "Why didn't you tell me at the Embassy?"

Tilson's voice was low and intense. "Because I don't trust MI6. I don't trust anyone except you, Ebony and a few select colleagues in MI5." He opened his arms to take in the three other people in the room.

"This is my new home," he said, echoing Anne's words to him on his first day.

"You thought MI6 might try to take the images from you?"

"I wouldn't put it past them," Tilson replied. "I know I haven't been in this game long enough to know up from down, but I do know that information is power, and people will do whatever it takes to get it."

"Well done," Anne said.

"You could've fucking well told me!" Ebony collapsed back into her chair, feigning as much hurt as she could muster.

Tilson exchanged a knowing glance with her. "You played your part perfectly," he said. "Whatever you think of him, Kavanagh's a good agent. He might have smelt a rat if I'd told you. He'd already travelled with you, spoken with you. Knew your 'tells', for want of a better word.

"He'd only just met me. And I can be quite a good liar."

"Too bloody right you can," Camille said. "You are a real asset to this team, you know that?"

"Sam, this is remarkable," Anne added. "Truly."

"Hand it over then, Royal, and I'll get to downloading the images," Ebony said. "Then we can transcribe them and cross reference with all our files here. Bound to get something interesting."

"I think that may well be an understatement, Ebony." Anne said as Tilson handed his partner in crime the phone.

"Once we've analysed Fox's diaries thoroughly, I am willing to bet the information within could lead to significant breakthroughs in our intelligence efforts."

As they brought their discussion about the diaries and their implications to a conclusion, Tilson couldn't shake the feeling that their mission was far from over. But he'd have to be patient to find out what if anything they revealed.

By the time the weak winter sun was disappearing from the sky outside the north-facing windows of the ICE offices, Ebony had finished transcribing the diaries and was running searches through all the pages, cross-referencing them with the database she already had of indexed past files.

Tilson wandered from his desk to peer over her shoulder.

"How's it going?"

"Good," Ebony replied, a pen sticking out of her mouth as she concentrated on the screen. Then she removed it and pointed at a list of phrases that was slowly appearing on the screen. The technical whizz was using a proprietary AI that Anne had okayed for use in conjunction with MI5's Nexus operating system.

"It's slowly crunching a lot of data," she said. "But so far, you were right about Fox's mental state and his guilt around his family. It seems that has prompted him to confess his belief that a very high-ranking member of the security community in the UK was a Russian mole."

Tilson snorted. "Not the bloody Fifth man?" He was referring to the infamous Cambridge spying ring from the 1960s that had undermined British Intelligence for years and led to so many witch hunts even the services involved had lost count.

"We-ell..." Ebony said. "Possibly. All pointing to Sir Stephen Drake."

She sighed. "It's all so *yesterday*!"

"Isn't 'yesterday' what we do here?"

Ebony considered this then looked up at him with a cheeky grin.

"True."

"Sir Stephen Drake?" Anne had appeared behind them.

"Yes. That does seem to be the case." Ebony had suddenly become all businesslike, like a naughty child caught talking during class.

"Drake?" Anne almost laughed. "Are you telling me that all this was about 'Quackers'?"

Tilson remembered the name now, from what he'd read and the scrambled memories from his collapse on Helena Olsen's bathroom floor. "Wasn't he a super spy in the 80s?"

"I'm not sure I'd describe him like that," the older woman said. "He was very influential and very good at this job. Everyone loved him, hence the stupidly sentimental name!"

"He worked with Fox on the Joint Intelligence Committee, too," Ebony added. "Before Fox left and Drake stayed on in the Cabinet Office."

"Yes," Anne confirmed. "Although he was junior to Drake, Fox seemed to follow him around."

"Thus, if anyone might know if there was something fishy going on, it'd be Fox," Tilson said.

Anne considered this. "Yes, I suppose... But such an accusation would be a catastrophe for us."

"That'd explain why the Russians were so keen to stop us from getting the diaries," Ebony said.

"He was a one-off," Anne said, shaking her head. "He was the first man to become head of MI5 and later MI6. It's inconceivable he could have been working for the Communists."

She gazed into space for a moment. "Anyway, he was instrumental in unmasking the Cambridge spy ring. He was a Whitehall 'mandarin'. A man who held senior positions as advisor to several British Cabinets. He was knighted for his services, for Christ's sake!"

Tilson felt this would take a while to sink in. Maybe she was right, and Drake had nothing to do with the Russians. It was something they were going to have to investigate in the coming months. A lot of laborious cross referencing and double-checking.

"Is there anything more 'today'?" Anne asked with a wry smile.

"It's strange," the younger woman said. "Towards the end he seems to abandon his claims about Drake and focus on something else."

"Another bee in his bonnet?" Tilson asked.

"Yeah. But this is way more cryptic," Ebony was sucking her pen again. "He keeps mentioning the phrase 'finder, keeper, loser, weeper'."

"Isn't it 'finders, keepers; losers, weepers' – all in the plural?" Anne asked.

Tilson nodded. "That's what I've always said."

"Me, too," Ebony replied. "But that's not how Fox used the term."

They fell quiet, trying to think what it might mean.

"Finder, keeper, loser, weeper," Tilson repeated quietly. "FKLW?"

"Not sure that means anything," Ebony said with a sarcastic smile. "Don't worry, I'll keep digging!"

Anne patted her on the shoulder. "Good work," she said and started walking away. She seemed troubled. Tilson followed her into her office and closed the door behind him. Anne took a seat at her desk, a little wearily.

"What can I do for you, Sam?" she asked.

"I trust you, of course," Tilson began awkwardly. "But I need assurances. I need to know that this information will be used for the right reasons. Whatever the outcome. After all, if the Russians were willing to risk an armed Spetsnaz squad on foreign soil, the Drake thing could be true."

Anne met his gaze, her expression resolute. "You have my word, Sam. We'll handle this with the utmost discretion and integrity."

Tilson nodded. He was going to have to take her word for it. He'd taken a significant risk by keeping the diaries a secret, but he hoped that his boss would ensure they were used for the benefit of national security, not a cover-up.

"Honestly, Sam? I believe that this is far from over," she said, suddenly serious. But then twinkle returned to her eyes. "And we're going to need your skills now more than ever as our 'active service' wing!"

Tilson nodded again. She was a wily bird for sure. "But no need for heroics right this minute," Anne added, returning her attention to her own paperwork. "So, back to work! The files assigned to you have built up a bit since you've been gone.

When he returned to the main office, all eyes were on him. Quizzical but trusting. He took in each one of his friends in turn, nodding or grinning to them before sitting at his desk opposite Ebony. She looked up and gave him a wink before returning to the search.

While he was uncertain as to what the images held in terms of true intelligence, he knew that it would almost definitely point to a web of intrigue and deception that extended way beyond the snowy Norwegian wilderness. This game had only just begun, and the next move they played in the shadowy world of counter-espionage would be even more crucial.

CHAPTER 30

The tube journey home that evening proved uneventful and Tilson made it to the entrance of his apartment building on Jupp Road unscathed by youths or low blood sugar. He opened the communal door and went in, climbing the two flights of stairs. He fished out his keys and quickly opened up, letting himself in before closing the front door behind him with his foot.

The moment he'd done so, the hairs on the back of his neck stood on end. There was someone else there. In the flat. With him. He could sense it. But if whoever it was thought he didn't know, Tilson would have the advantage.

He tried to act casually, and went into the bathroom, leaving the door open. He waited about ten seconds and then flushed the toilet before turning on the taps in the basin, all the time facing the door. He was expecting whoever had broken in to either use the fact he was simulating taking a slash to either leave or come for him. Neither happened.

Tilson left the sanctuary of the bathroom and switched on the light. This was stupid. He stopped, halfway down the narrow hall.

"Look," he said, feeling slightly foolish that he was in effect addressing thin air. "Whoever you are? I've had a long day, and I will beat the shit out of you if you try to attack me, so why don't we talk?" There was a second of silence.

"Reckon I'd put up a half decent fight," a male voice said.

Tilson knew who it was even before he walked into his living room and switched on the overhead light. Sitting in his favourite chair was Kavanagh.

"Fuck me," said Tilson half laughing. "You know you're a total cliché, sitting in the dark like that!"

"I had to make sure you were alone," the MI6 man said enigmatically.

Tilson nodded. "Drink?"

"Sure. Got any whisky?"

"Got a McCallan here." Tilson opened a cupboard and extracted two glasses and then took the bottle from a shelf above the sink. He returned to his sofa and sat, unscrewing the bottle.

"How did you get in?"

"Balcony," Kavanagh said, casting a look at the double door to his right. "Easier to pick than your deadlock on the front door."

"Right. No damage I hope?"

Kavanagh snorted. "Course not. I'm a pro."

Tilson had to say he was warming to this guy. They were both military people now employed to do a much shadier and more complicated job. He grinned. "I appreciate it."

He poured the whisky and passed Kavanagh one of the glasses. Then he raised his own.

"What are we drinking to?"

Kavanagh sat almost unmoving for a moment as he thought, his hand frozen in mid-air, grasping the glass.

"How about inter-service co-operation?"

Tilson raised an eyebrow. "Are you talking about now, or in Norway?"

"Now."

They clinked glasses and sat back sipping the harsh, warming liquid.

"Nice," Kavanagh said. "I appreciate you not palming me off with the Bells."

He was referring to the bottle of blended Scotch Tilson kept for cocktails. "Took the opportunity to go through my cupboards?"

The other man shrugged as if it would have been rude not to.

"Find any skeletons?"

Kavanagh chucked. "Not yet." He placed his glass down and leant forward, suddenly in earnest. "Sam, can I ask you something? About Norway."

"You can."

"The diaries. What actually happened to them?"

"Believe it or not, I told you the truth in Oslo," Tilson said. "One was left in the bloody car and the others were screwed when they went in the water."

"Yeah. I believe you," Kavanagh said. But then he locked eyes with Tilson. "But did you manage to read them all? Or maybe make a copy?" The question was so unexpected that Tilson could feel he'd reacted.

He also knew his fellow agent had spotted it.

"What's the big deal if I did?"

The MI6 man sighed and rubbed his face with the palms of his hands. This response had clearly stressed him out.

"OK. What I'm going to tell you must never go any further, *capisci*? Not Ebony, not Anne and not Tony bloody Gray."

Tilson held his gaze. "You have my word, Jed."

"That's good enough for me." He smiled slightly to try and ease the tension in the room before clearing his throat. It sounded like he had a tale to tell.

"Stephen Drake. The bloke our old friend Malcolm Fox had a suspicion was a Russian mole? He wasn't."

"Definitely not?"

"Definitely not. In fact, the complete polar opposite. He was a triple agent. He had been recruited by the Soviets back in the 50s at Oxford, but they didn't know he was already working for MI5. The decision was made to use this to our advantage.

"Now, usually, this wouldn't be such a big deal. But Quackers was a special man. He rose through the ranks and the more he did so, the more valuable he became. Not only to us but to Mother Russia as well.

"Did it ever occur to you why we haven't been beset by double agents and moles since the whole Trinity spy ring? Because of good old Sir Stephen. He was walking a fucking dangerous tightrope, feeding the Soviets what secrets it was agreed we could afford to share in exchange for finding out what they really wanted to know about and – most importantly – why."

Tilson was amazed by this. "So, any double agents recruited by Russia after that… He'd have known about them?"

"Exactly." Kavanagh paused. "And that still holds true to this day."

He let that sink in. "Yeah. We still have some agents feeding bullshit to the FSB, although now for money rather than ideology. But it's still crucial their identities are kept secret.

"If Putin and his gang ever found out not only would our key flow of intelligence dry up overnight, but they'd probably send the GRU dogs out and about with the Novichok on a revenge killing spree."

"Why didn't anyone just tell me?"

"I'm not sure anyone in MI5 knows!" Kavanagh said. "Hardly anyone in MI6 knows either. It's that sensitive."

"You know," Tilson said. "And, no offence, but you're a field agent, not the Chief of SIS."

"I made it my business to find out," Kavanagh said ominously. "Like you, I don't like being played." There was a pause.

"In a way I wish I hadn't, but there we go." He drained his glass and smacked his lips. "Now, your job is to convince those you may have shown the diaries to that Drake is a dead end. No point in looking at it in any depth. Fox was nuts, paranoid, that kind of thing."

Tilson nodded earnestly. "I'll try." Now it was his turn to drain the whisky glass. Kavanagh stood.

"Before you go, Jed.," Tilson said. "One thing."

"Shoot."

"Does the phrase 'finder, keeper loser, weeper' mean anything to you with regards to Fox, or more likely Drake?"

Kavanagh cocked his head to one side, and he screwed up his eyes.

"Don't... think...so."

"Right."

"Isn't it 'finders, keepers' anyway?" he asked.

"That's what I thought," Tilson said.

As the door closed behind Kavanagh's departing form, Tilson sat down once more and stared at his balcony door. Cheeky sod. He laughed. Kavanagh had helped unravel one mystery and perhaps there might be scope for the two to work together in the future. They seemed to be cut from more or less the same cloth, even if Kavanagh was a blunter, heavier instrument than Tilson.

For his part, the MI5 man still felt bad that it had cost the life of two innocent Norwegian bystanders. But that was the game he was in now.

No straightforward rules of engagement. Not for the Russians. They did whatever the bloody hell they wanted. And that's why he was determined to keep fighting. No doubt there would be other secrets from the past to shed light on, especially if they might have an impact on the present.

The whole strange use of the 'finders, keepers' phrase though was going to drive him mad, though. But he wouldn't have to work on it alone. The ICE maidens – and Gareth – would be there to help him.

For now, however, there was nothing he could do. He needed something to distract him.

He may not have been able to save the lives of Ingeborg and Helena Olsen, but he could at least make up for one thing. It was minor and stupid, but it was one thing over which he had control. It would take a little bit of research, but he was in no rush. Tilson had gleaned a few facts from the iPhone that Ebony had hacked.

An address in Texas and the woman's full name.

EPILOGUE

Samantha Adam returned to her home in Bovina, Texas just two days before Christmas. She'd been writing postcards from the Cruise Ship to all her friends and couldn't wait to share her adventures and her customary slide show – converted from digital images especially for the purpose – with them all in her two-storey brick hacienda on 4th Street. Of course, she'd had to fall back on her actual digital camera as her phone seemed to have been broken by that clumsy boating enthusiast she'd met in Flåm.

In fact, that was one of the stories she intended to tell. She might even embellish the tale a little, make it seem like he was coming onto her. She smiled at this as the cab dropped her off outside her home.

The large Mexican driver with a bald head slowly left the indent of the driver's seat and made his way around to the trunk. As Sam got out, he grunted as he lifted the first of her heavy bags onto the sidewalk.

After paying him and giving a minimal tip, Sam carried the two bags to her front door one at a time. Then she moved over to her mailbox, sitting beside the house on a post at chest height. It was stuffed to the brim with circulars and flyers. She tutted and opened the little door with an equally small key.

Clutching them to her ample bosom, Sam made her way back to the front door and – having opened the outer, metal grille – she unlocked it, and manoeuvred her cases into the hall. Finally, she dumped the pile of letters and bills onto the wagon wheel coffee table and collapsed into her La-Z-Boy recliner chair.

After a minute's composure she sat up and started going through her mail. She'd been abroad four times in the two years since her beloved husband, Roy, had passed so she was used to the piles of junk mail she got. What she wasn't accustomed to was finding a UPS delivery note saying they had tried to deliver a package. She hadn't ordered anything.

The little card told her that she could collect the parcel at her local United States Postal Service office on 2nd Street. She knew it. It was a tiny little building with a parking lot for just three cars out front.

Intrigued, Sam walked into her garage and clicked the button on her remote to open its up and over door. She then had to climb up into the huge, wine red 2021 Chevrolet Tahoe 4WD RST before setting off on the 3-minute drive.

When she got there it was a simple matter to retrieve the parcel, giving the number on the UPS card and showing her passport, which she still had in her purse from the flight. The skinny old woman behind the counter passed the package to her.

"An early Christmas present, dear?" she asked, her voice cracked with age.

"I have no idea," Sam replied and stared at the packet.

"You gonna open it?"

Sam shrugged. "I guess so."

She ripped open the package along the line segregated for the purpose and felt inside. There was a bubble wrap interior that was protecting what turned out to be an identical iPhone to the one that had been broken. She frowned.

"New cell?" the woman asked enthusiastically. Sam could tell she got her thrills by living vicariously through others' parcels and packets.

"I don't think so."

There was a note inside the bubble wrap. She removed and unfolded it.

"What's it say?" The old woman was becoming more intrusive, but it was short, penned in hand, so she read it aloud.

"'Hi Sam. I think I managed to take your phone by mistake when we bumped into each other at the Flåm Marina restaurant. I wanted to get it back to you in case it had precious memories or all your friends' contact details on it. Plus, you wouldn't want to have to start Candy Crush all over again! If you still have my broken phone, please put it in the trash. I have a new one now. Best Wishes, The Other Sam! Kiss, kiss'." "That's nice," the old woman said.

Sam frowned. "But I didn't give him my address." She started to walk from the Post Office, her mind doing cartwheels as to how he'd tracked her down. And then she turned back to the old woman who was still watching her in mortified horror.

"And how in the Sam Hill did he know I played Candy Crush?"

FIN

Take a sneak peek at the next book in the Cold Secrets Series and follow the further adventures of Sam Tilson over-leaf...

READ ON!

Sam Tilson and the ICE Team will return

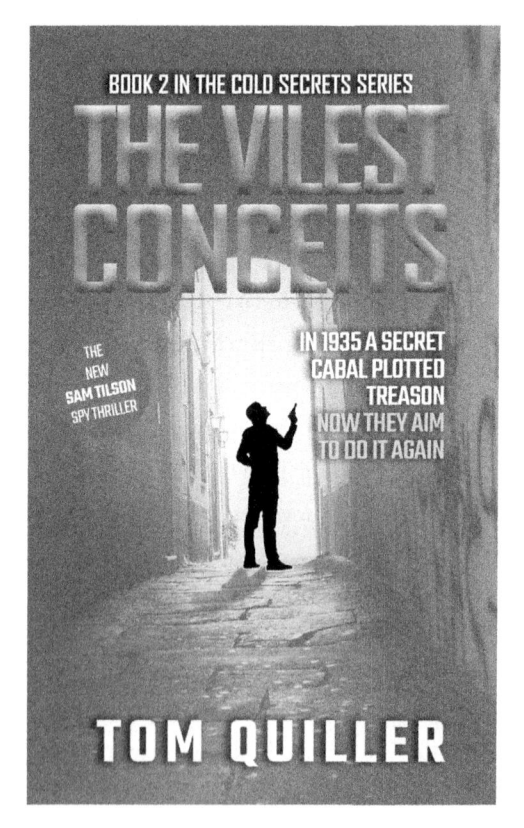

ORDER NOW

And read on...

PROLOGUE

Although the crowd was large and enthusiastic, one man within the throng was neither. He was a short, stocky man in a well-worn brown suit. Under his equally battered trilby of matching colour was a balding head of dark blonde hair. But most noticeable about him, as he pushed his way between flag-waving enthusiasts, was his pronounced limp. He had what was once called a 'club foot'.

The condition—called talipes equinovarus or TEV these days—is caused by a shortened Achilles tendon and is twice as common in boys. His real name was Jerome Bannigan, and he had never quite come to terms with what he saw as an affliction. That said, whenever he had to talk to people about it, he always fell back on something he'd heard about the poet Lord Byron. He too had a club foot but nonetheless was quite the ladies' man and accomplished batsman, playing cricket with a stand-in who would run up and down the crease for him. It was a comfort that the contact he was meeting didn't care about that.

It was the morning of July 16; sunny and warm. The crowds lining Constitution Hill were three to four deep. Everyone was waiting patiently for a glimpse of the King. Sometime soon he would appear on horseback and ride down the Mall from Buckingham Palace to take the salute at the Sovereign's Birthday Parade, better known as Trooping the Colour.

However, Bannigan was intent on another sighting—that of his handler—the man he knew as Michael De Havilland. As he left the press of people and moved behind them into Green Park, he glimpsed him sitting on a bench with a newspaper resting in his lap. De Havilland was a tall man with poise and elegance. He was dressed in a fashionable but understated grey suit, all neatly pressed, and a matching hat positioned at just the right angle of propriety. He exuded the bearing and confidence of an ex-public school and ex-army man.

As the chimes of Big Ben sounded midday, Bannigan tried to increase his speed as he shuffled up to him. De Havilland looked up, and a gloved hand slid up to his face and stroked his black moustache twice. "'Mister McMahon'," he said in clipped Received Pronunciation. "How nice to see you on this glorious afternoon. Do please sit."

Silently, Bannigan took a seat, grateful to be off his feet. McMahon was part of the cover he'd been given. If anything went wrong, he was to tell the authorities nothing of his assignment; only that his name was George Andrew McMahon, a 35-year-old journalist with an anti-Royal bent and a list of grudges against the Prime Minister and his Cabinet.

"Have you read the news?" De Havilland asked casually. He tapped his copy of The Daily Telegraph.

"Not today," Bannigan admitted.

"Then please do avail yourself of mine," his contact said. "There is something weighty within that may be of interest to you."

He met Bannigan's puzzled gaze and lifted an eyebrow, as if trying to tell him something. Then the Irishman realised that the mission was going ahead, and that he was being supplied with the tools to carry it out.

"My wife, is she—" Bannigan began, but De Havilland leant in closer to the shorter man.

"Just take the fucking paper, Mac."

Bannigan flushed; no one spoke to him like that. He may be short and crippled, but his fists were still the size of hams, and he could pummel those who might try to bully him in the pubs of Derry or Glasgow.

De Havilland held his gaze. "Naturally, you're jolly concerned for your wife," he said, tapping the copy of The Telegraph folded on his knees once more.

This time, Bannigan looked down and saw some words handwritten in pencil along the margin of the back page: May I Love You. It was a pre-arranged coded message. His wife would be protected as long as he carried out his mission. Nodding that he understood, Bannigan lifted the newspaper from the Englishman's lap with two hands. It was indeed weighty. Heavy, in fact. Once he'd transferred it to his own lap, he surreptitiously lifted a corner of the paper to peek at what was inside.

It was a silvery-coloured gun.

He didn't notice a young woman navigating the crowd, who had been forced to stop by the sheer number of people. As she tried without success to push on, she looked over at the pair as they sat on the bench, talking intently. She carried on staring for a matter of half a minute before she was swept forward as the masses swarmed forward again.

De Havilland was on his feet. "Good luck, Mister McMahon."

Bannigan watched him go, fading into the crowd of couples strolling through the park, all smiles and gaiety. Groups of less well-dressed individuals, some clutching bottles of ale and all waving union flags of varying sizes, finally obscured the mysterious Michael De Havilland from view.

Knowing he did not now have much time, Bannigan rose to his feet with difficulty and began hobbling away from the park and down Constitution Hill. Trying to smile at the revellers waiting for their monarch, the Irishman managed to push his way to the front of the multitude. There he stood, nervous now, his palms sweating, casting anxious looks back the way he'd come towards the railings of Green Park as if he'd see De Havilland there, egging him on. He did not.

Again, he failed to spot that the very same woman who had earlier noticed him in the park was standing just to his right and noticed his slightly out-of-place behaviour.

At around 12:25 pm, the sound of distant cheering told the crowd that the King had left Hyde Park and was only a few minutes away. Bannigan removed the gun from the folds of the newspaper and held it loosely in his left hand, hidden from the surrounding people.

The weapon was a six-chamber, .38 nickel-plated revolver made by the Chicago Arms Company, and its design made it relatively easy to unload with one hand. All one had to do was unclip the barrel with the locking mechanism, upend it with the barrel facing upwards, and the chambered rounds would tumble onto the floor.

Bannigan was sweating. The sun was beating down, and the heat was exceptional for a British summer's day, but it wasn't for that reason. The anxiety was unbearable. Was he being an idiot? Why was he doing this? Were they telling the truth about looking after his darling Rosie? And him? He had assurances that his life would be protected.

He started tapping the folded copy of The Telegraph against his thigh—a nervous tick he had picked up as an adult and one that spoke of his mental state.

At precisely 12:30 pm, the military band of the Coldstream Guards leading the parade emerged from Wellington Arch as rippling applause and cheers broke out at the top of Constitution Hill. Following close behind was the King on horseback in full-dress scarlet tunic and bearskin as Colonel-in-Chief of the Regiment.

Like almost all in the crowd, the eagle-eyed young lady—Alice Lawrence—who had spotted Bannigan behaving suspiciously, was now waiting patiently for a glimpse of the King and the various regiments of the Household Division as they processed down the Mall on their return to Buckingham Palace.

But the movement of Bannigan's paper so close to Alice drew her attention to the strange man once more. So when the King's horse passed her, she was not concentrating on the monarch but instead watching the man in the brown suit with increasing worry.

Sure enough, at that moment, he dropped the copy of The Telegraph to reveal he was holding a shiny, silvery pistol. As she watched in horror, the man raised the gun and pointed it directly at the King.

Without thinking, she dived at the man, only a few feet away from her, instinctively grabbing his arm to try to divert the shot, crying out as she did so. Alerted by the cry, a Special Constable—who was facing away from the scuffle to salute the King—now turned and, seeing the gun, smashed his fist into the assailant's lower arm.

With the intervention of both Alice and the Police Officer, Bannigan was never able to discharge his nickel-plated revolver, and it flew from his hand and into the roadway where it landed just between the legs of the King's horse. It reared up in surprise at the projectile, but King Edward VIII managed to steady the animal and continue almost without a second look.

By now, several men from the crowd had come forward enthusiastically to pinion the would-be assassin and help deliver him securely into the hands of uniformed officers and a Chief Inspector who came pelting over from nearby.

Bannigan was put into the back of a Wolsey Wasp saloon, marked with a light over the windscreen illuminated with the word "PO-LICE". Two uniformed men accompanied the Irishman and Chief Inspector John Sands of Scotland Yard on the journey to Hyde Park Police Station.

During the car journey, Bannigan tried to protest his innocence, telling Sands that he had no intention of harming the King, "only did it as a protest", and that it was all the fault of the then Home Secretary, Sir John Simon. At the station, he gave his name—as per the plan—as George McMahon, and Sands cautioned him under that alias.

A body search performed on him by one of the uniformed constables yielded an envelope containing a picture postcard of the King, along with two rounds of ammunition for his revolver, and the copy of The Daily Telegraph he had dropped moments before he took aim at the King. On examination, the Police found the words "May I Love You" pencilled on the back page, but "McMahon" would not say what it meant. And he never did.

McMahon was charged at Bow Street, where the magistrate, Sir Rollo Campbell, remanded him in custody for eight days. Although McMahon made no further statements that day and only cursory inquiries by the police had been made, the King was told that evening that Scotland Yard had put the case to bed.

McMahon was painted as a frustrated Irish journalist who had convinced himself that the Secretary of State for Home Affairs had conspired to prevent him from publishing a journal called the Human Gazette. He had also written many letters of complaint to Scotland Yard, having a "grievance" against the Police.

It was only later that Special Branch established that McMahon's real name was Jerome Bannigan—a married Irishman living with his wife who worked at a dress shop in Westbourne Terrace. He was also purported to have Nazi sympathies, a claim seemingly confirmed by several members of the public who reported seeing him sell the fascist newspaper The Black Shirt in the Paddington area.

When McMahon finally appeared at the Old Bailey in September, he gave a detailed account of what he maintained was behind the incident. Too many, it sounded like a flight of fantasy or the ravings of someone with mental illness of some sort. He claimed to have been working for MI5, passing on information he had gleaned from workers at the Italian Embassy, then under the thrall of Mussolini.

The Times reported the widely held belief that McMahon's sensational tale was an embellished afterthought, dreamt up to aid in his defence.

However, Bannigan's solicitor did manage to establish from Chief Inspector Sands' investigations that, as McMahon, he had indeed been in communication with MI5 and had a handler known only as "Major K C". At the Old Bailey trial, despite being subpoenaed to appear, this Major K C failed to do so, and nothing was ever done to follow up on this.

Instead of High Treason or attempted murder, McMahon was instead charged with "intent to alarm" and sentenced by the judge to 12 months of hard labour. By the time he came out of prison in 1937, King Edward VIII had abdicated. Bannigan never spoke of the incident again and died in 1970, only three years before the King he had apparently meant to kill.

CHAPTER 1

Despite the lack of interest from the media, both at the time and since, this matter caught the eagle-eyed attention of MI5 Information Officer Ebony Fadipe. She is employed in the Inconclusive Covert Enquiries unit—ICE for short. It was the remit of this tiny department to sift through historical files, most still only held on paper. Part of Ebony's job was to digitise them and tag them with metadata for searchability and indexing. This allowed comparisons with newer electronic files to identify previously unnoticed similarities or discrepancies.

The office of the Inconclusive Covert Enquiries unit, known as ICE, occupied the north-west corner of the slightly sterile, light grey building of MI5 Headquarters. This iconic structure, commonly referred to as Thames House, stands prominently on the north bank of the River Thames in London. Positioned on the fourth floor at the back of the building, the department was something of a forgotten backwater. Certainly, the fast-track university graduates in anti-terror or counter-espionage thought of it as akin to the restricted section of the library in Harry Potter. The older staff viewed ICE as a place where old agents and even older files went to die. This was not the case. Each member of the team was an expert in their field, occupying one of two adjoining rooms—one larger with eight desks and one smaller with just one.

The outer office, despite its number of desks, only had five full-time workers, each with a particular skill that contributed to their overarching mission. They were tasked with trawling former investigations, dusty manila folders, past events, old records, and the personnel files of long-departed operatives for any hint of either misconduct or a threat that might re-emerge. Their remit covered both the UK's interior Security Service of MI5, the Secret Intelligence Service or MI6, and the covert communications hub at GCHQ in Cheltenham.

Leading the hunt through the past was the resolute and hard-nosed Anne Barnard. She was as wide as she was tall, with a blunt bob of greying mouse-brown hair, a stub of a nose, and piercing eyes that sparkled with a mix of high intelligence and world-weary experience.

She was usually secreted away in the side office, her own domain beyond the main room, with the door always open, probably because—as Tilson knew all too well—she was always on the move; always bustling.

Right in front of that door sat the impossible-to-age blonde bombshell that was Camille DeSouza, the department's jack-of-all-trades. She had worked in every department and knew almost everything and everyone in the building. She was also what Anne described as "one of the best document experts in the Service". She oozed sex appeal and what Tilson affectionately thought of as "naughtiness". She was an Essex girl, and while that exterior led some to underestimate her, she was as shrewd and smart as an alley cat.

Sitting two empty desks away from her, under one of the leaded windows that let the sunshine of an early spring day in London stream through, was the 42-year-old Gareth Hazel. Formerly a financial analyst in the City, Hazel had sandy hair, a long face, and an equally long nose, giving him a hangdog expression that suited his often-awkward demeanour. The fact he was wearing a baggy three-piece suit in a Prince of Wales check while everyone else was dressed far more casually also spoke to his eccentricity. Softly spoken and slightly shy, he was without a doubt a maths genius.

Ebony occupied the desk across from his. No window seat for her. This seemed to suit her, however, due to the trio of screens set up around her as if she was a coder for a triple-A game or addicted to flight simulators. She was neither.

The latest team member at the desk across from hers was Sam Tilson, formerly of His Majesty's Royal Marine Commandos and the Special Boat Service, or SBS. He had been medically discharged from the elite squadron due to a diagnosis of Type 1 diabetes shortly after a training mission.

That had landed him in the fustiest, dustiest corner of MI5 as the unit's "active service" operative. This meant he was the one person who was suited to and trained for field work and thus more or less the only one who could ever leave the office to pursue ICE investigations or go up against potentially dangerous situations.

He had just finished reading the account of Bannigan's rather bizarre attempt on the life of the King back in 1936. He wasn't entirely sure why Ebony had given it to him to read, no matter how interesting it was. He'd certainly never heard of the failed assassination attempt. Tilson ran a hand through his dark brown hair and leant back, pushing his chair far enough away from the desk that he could see the person sitting opposite him.

Ebony Fadipe was a beautiful young woman. She could easily have been a model but seemed oblivious of the fact. Instead, she was always focused on her work, which meant bringing her wits—which were even sharper than her looks—to bear on strange coincidences or spotting patterns. She had formerly been at GCHQ, and when she'd managed to piss off her boss there, had sought a secondment to MI5 and ended up at ICE.

"What do you think?" she asked, spotting him looking at her.

"I remember you showed this to me ages ago," he replied. "Before Norway."

He was referring to his first assignment for ICE, now several months in the past.

"Good memory, Royal," she said, using her nickname for him. "So?"

Tilson hesitated. He really didn't want to look stupid, but he had no idea what the relevance of this file was to him. "It's a page-turner," he ventured.

Ebony smiled, an amused if brief smile. "You don't remember the other bit?"

Tilson wracked his memory. Nothing was forthcoming. "Nope."

She leant forward, hands together as if in prayer, looking at him through the crack between two of her screens. "That name," she said. "Bannigan's handler 'Michael De Havilland'. It cropped up in a contemporary file when I cross-referenced the assassination file with our database."

Tilson frowned now. "If he was a handler in 1936, he must be dead by now."

"You'd think."

"So, what contemporary file is this? His obituary?"

Ebony smiled. "Not quite," she said. "It was filed very recently. It's in connection with The Prince and Princess of Wales' trip to Italy."

"Connected how?"

"So, there was a group of liaisons between Kensington Palace and the Italian Government. One is listed by MI6 as a liaison between the Italians and Buckingham Palace. And that's our Mister Michael De Havilland."

"And the trick being, there should be no liaison between Buck House and the Italian Government, right? Because it's Kate and Wills. Why would the Palace be involved?"

"Exactly," Ebony said. "Now, I checked this against an earlier visit by the then Prince Charles and Duchess of Cornwall only a few years ago, and the liaison there was solely with Kensington Palace."

"What do we have on De Havilland then?"

Ebony sighed. "That's the thing," she said, leaning back in her chair. "There is no record of him working for MI6 or the Palace – any of the palaces."

"Are we assuming that this De Havilland and the one in 1936 are not the same person? Are they family?"

Ebony picked up a biro from the desk and started fiddling with it, rolling it around her fingers.

"And that's the second thing," Ebony said. "No record of a Michael De Havilland working for MI5 then either. In fact, according to personnel records, there's *never* been a Michael De Havilland employed by MI5, MI6, or any other of our agencies."

"It's a cover? A legend?"

"Doesn't seem to be that even," she said now, tapping the biro on her teeth. "There are just those two instances of the name. Almost 100 years apart, both associated with events—extraordinary and more mundane—linked to the Royal Family."

Tilson frowned. "You say only two, but have all the records had metadata added to them?"

Ebony nodded. "Nice one," she said. "But not much help until we go through the older files."

There was silence as they both pondered the situation. After a minute or two, a chirpy voice piped up from the back of the office.

"There you go," It was Camille DaSouza. "Personal File on your George McMahon. PF 42090. He was a person of interest to MI5 back in 1933. According to this, he wrote a letter to the Home Secretary in 1935 about acting as an agent for the Italian military attaché here in London. That letter has been redacted. But then John Ottaway, the man heading MI5's enquiries and investigations section B4, got McMahon in for interview."

"How did you find that?" Ebony asked, nose slightly out of joint.

"Oh, nothing complex like what you do, sweetheart," Camille replied, smiling. "I'm just old school. Been around a bit, so I keep a copy of the old filing system. They were a bit more haphazard when it came to filling out forms back then. Some things they missed out, others they went into more detail. I guess when it got updated, some of the info was just left out as 'not important'."

"That's worse than covering it up!" Tilson said.

"Sloppy, yeah," Camille said. "But files are my thing, babe." She winked.

"So, what do you have for us, oh queen of the files?" Tilson asked.

"It seems McMahon worked for MI5 from then as an informant, under his handler, whose name has also been redacted. But as you said, Ebbs, there was a court subpoena that slipped through, naming that handler as Major KC."

"And I've searched through the personnel files dating back to the 30s, and there's no employee of MI5 with the initials KC. And while there are a few Majors on the payroll, none of them have names anywhere near those letters. The rank must have been made up, a fabrication. And if that name is anywhere—or whoever the alias is applied to—it's been redacted, I'd guess."

"Redacted?" Ebony said suddenly, leaning forward in her seat. "That's not possible. We're MI5; nothing is redacted to us!"

***

READ ON NOW! AVAILABLE ON AMAZON AS AN E-BOOK OR PART OF KINDLE UNLIMITED.

ABOUT THE AUTHOR

Tom Quiller

Tom Quiller is a *nom de plume*. He has been many things in his lifetime. From a soldier to a private investigator. From journalist to fiction writer. He is passionate about all things do to with the military and espionage.

Printed in Great Britain
by Amazon